Long Ride,
Unforgiving Land

Perry E. McCutcheon

Copyright

Long Ride,
Unforgiving Land

Chapter One

It was raining when Tom woke up. He could hear it on the tin roof and lay awake for a few minutes, dreading having to get up. He put on his clothes and boots and went to do the morning chores. Sloshing through the mud to the barn, he fed the mules and cow and collected a few eggs from the chicken coop for breakfast. On his way back to the house, he stepped in a hole and fell forward on his face. He rolled over on his back and began cursing. He cursed the rain and the mud but most of all, he cursed his life. He lay there with the raining mixing with his tears for a couple of minutes. He raised his arms to the sky making his hands into fists. At first he was not sure if he was going to curse God or prey to him. Finally he relaxed his hands and said, "God, please help me. I have tried my best to be a good husband and father but I have failed. I have failed my family and I can't stand it any longer. Something has to change."

He picked up the eggs that were not broken and went back to the quiet dark house. He pulled off his boots and clothes on the front porch, washed his face, hands, and arms in the wash basin, dried himself off and entered the house. His wife and children were still asleep. Tom put on dry clothes, lit the fire in the cook stove, made a pot of coffee, and poured himself a cup. As he sipped the hot coffee he felt a sense of relief. He knew what he had to do.

Tom had been feeling confined, restless, and hopeless. He had long ago outgrown his little seven acres of land, but he had tried his best to be a good husband and provider for his family's needs. Even after his wife, Mattie had stopped being a wife, he tried. They were happy for the first few years of their marriage. They had a son, Matthew, who was now eleven, two daughters that had died as babies from poverty diseases, and they had another daughter Lizzie, who is five. The overwhelming poverty and hard work had worn Mattie out. When she lost the two little girls she had no more to give. Even the birth of Lizzie did nothing to improve her state of mind. The worry of also losing her just added to her misery. Tom would at times encourage Mattie and sometimes scold her when he thought she was not taking care of the children. But nothing he did seemed to have any affect. She sank deeper and deeper into her own mind. And Tom depended more and more on Matt to help with Lizzie. He worked day and night just trying to make the little farm feed them. Some days when he had worked all day and came home expecting a hot bath and a cooked meal, he had neither. At some point Tom had also given up. He started drinking more and spending more time away from the farm. He was ready for a change. Anything that would get him away from his little hill farm he would jump at. When he heard there would be a war between the North and South, his restlessness turned to anticipation. He heard at the Crossroads that a local militia leader named Captain Lewis Shy with the Perry Guards was recruiting men to join the Confederate Army and he could not wait. In September 1861 he signed up for the Confederate Army. One morning he packed a small leather bag with a few clothes, got his old gun with the powder horn and shot bag and loaded it all on one of his mules and rode off into the morning mist without saying a word to anyone.

Lizzie was the first to wake up and she crawled up into the loft and woke up Matt. She was hungry but did not want to disturb her mother. There was some cornbread left over from the night before, so Matt fixed Lizzie and himself some honey and cornbread and they ate. When they finished eating, Lizzie went out to play as usual and Matt started doing chores. When he was feeding the hogs and the mules, he noticed that one of the mules was gone. That was unusual, normally his father would have taken both mules to work but he thought no more about it. He finished the chores and went back to the house. He noticed that his father's gun was missing and felt a little mad that his father had not taken him hunting. Now he didn't know what to do, so he just sat there with Lizzie buzzing around him until his mother woke up. She finally stirred around nine and started doing some stuff in the kitchen.

"Mom do you know where pa went?" She didn't answer for a few minutes. He said it louder: "Mom, do you know where pa went?"

She wiped her hands on her apron and said, "He said he would be gone a couple of days, and we should take care of the animals."

"Where did he say he was going?"

"He did not say and I don't give a damn where he went."

Matt was sensitive to his mother's moods and tried very hard not to make things worse for her. He just turned and walked outside and called for Lizzie, scooped her up, and hugged her. He didn't want Lizzie to worry.

She kissed him on the cheek and said, "I love you Matt."

"I love you more."

They had become close, with Matt taking care of her since she was a baby. He was everything to her and gave her the attention she needed and not given by either her father or mother.

Around three in the afternoon, his mom came to the door and called them in for some lunch. Matt went in with Lizzie on his shoulder. For the first time in a long time, their mom had a full meal cooked and the table set. As they sat down to eat, their mother seemed unusually strange. She had put on one of her old dresses and she looked young and beautiful.

"You look pretty Mom." Matt said.

"Yeah, Mom you look pretty." Lizzie echoed.

"Thank you kids, now sit down and eat before it gets cold." That's all she said for the rest of the day.

Even without Tom being there, the little family could survive. The corn had already been harvested and taken to the mill at the crossroads so they had meal for bread. Big Tom and Matt had butchered a hog within the last month so they had meat in the smokehouse. Mattie had come out of her stupor long enough to preserve what she could from the garden. The potatoes had been harvested and placed under the cabin and covered with straw for storage though the winter. Big Tom had at least made sure they would not starve for a while. He had no idea how long he would be gone, but he thought he would be able to check in on his family from time to time.

They expected him to ride in each day. But one month passed, then another, then another without hearing anything from their father and husband. Each missed him in their own way and at times their worry turned to desperation. Everyday became the same with the daily chores for Matt, with Lizzie helping when she could, but always following Matt around. Mattie cooked when she felt like it, otherwise Matt would make due. He got where he could cook almost anything. Pretty soon Matt took on all of the chores and cooking and cleaning. They were lucky the winter was mild. It only snowed a couple of times but melted quickly. Mostly it rained, which made doing the chores a real mess. In January, the cow went dry so they had no more milk or butter. They didn't have food for the last hog, so Matt just turned it out to fend for itself.

Mattie spent her time wandering around the woods looking for Big Tom or in bed. She had totally lost her mind, and the long dreary winter had not helped.

They lived at the end of a long rough trail in a little house that Tom's father had built when he settled the land. Their nearest neighbor was five miles, as the crow flies, across the hills. The neighbors had their own lives to live without worrying about someone else, so no one came to their little house.

When Big Tom had not returned after six months, Matt, who had turned twelve in January, knew he had to do something. "Mom, I am going to ride to the crossroads tomorrow to see if they have heard anything about where pa has gone."

"I don't give a damn where you go or where the hell your worthless father has gone. That son-of-a-bitch left me here in this God forsaken place with you sniveling little brats."

Lizzie was scared by her mother's outburst and climbed into Matt's lap and hugged him tight. She whispered, "What's wrong with Momma?"

"She is just sad because pa hasn't come home yet."

He held Lizzie close to him and gently rocked her. "I am going to get up real early tomorrow and ride into the crossroads to check on daddy. I want you to stay here and take care of momma. Okay? I will be back before dark, I promise."

When Lizzie went to sleep, Matt laid her in her little bed in the corner. He stoked the fire in the fireplace and went to bed. He lay there and planned what to do the next day, even thinking about what would happen if he did not find his father.

Matt got up the next morning long before daylight. He wrapped some cornbread and ham up in a napkin and put it in his pocket. Then he made a plate of food for Lizzie because he knew she would be hungry and their mom would not get up.

As quietly as he could, he left the house and caught the mule and put a bridle on her. He didn't have a saddle, so he just threw a burlap bag over her back. They had burned all the kerosene except for some left in the old lantern, so he put a dozen eggs in a basket and tied it, along with their kerosene can, to the burlap bag.

Crossroads was a small settlement with a country store with a post office, a blacksmith shop, a grist mill, and a couple of houses. Five roads crossed thus, the name. It was about ten miles from Matt's house over a rough rocky trail.

Matt had been to Crossroads a few times with his father, but not in over a year and the place had changed. Lots of people and wagons and horses everywhere. They had built a ferry across the Tennessee River there, and it had changed everything. He recognized the store, and rode up, tied his mule, and went inside. There were about ten people in the store, and a couple of them wore gray uniforms. He remembered the owner's wife, Mrs. Dora Singer, whom he had met the last time he was there and he went up to her. She was busy with a customer so he waited his turn. When she was no longer busy, he spoke to her, "Ma'am, I am Matt McCall from up the holler. You might remember me, I came in here last year with my pappy, Tom McCall."

Before Matt could go on, one of the men in uniform spoke to him. "Boy, did you say your pa was Big Tom McCall?"

"Yes sir, he left us and never came home and we don't know what happened to him."

"Well, I have bad news for you. Your pa was captured by a group of Tennessee Federal Union troops and is in prison."

"Sir, what does that mean? Why would they put my pappy in prison? What did he do?"

The uniformed man talking to Matt took him by the shoulder and led him outside. "Son, my name is Major Shy. I am the commander of Company G, Twentieth Tennessee Infantry. Your pa joined my company back in September, and while he and a platoon of soldiers were checking out conditions in Linden just before Christmas, he was captured by a company of Tennessee Federal Union troops. They are Tennessee boys fighting for the north."

"Sir, I still don't understand. Was my pappy in the army?"

"Yes, he joined my company in September. Is that about the same time he left home?" Matt nodded, tears just now starting to stream down his cheeks. It was finally seeping into his mind that his father was in prison and would not be coming home anytime soon. How could he tell his mother and little Lizzie?

Major Shy put his hand on Matt's shoulder and said, "Where do you live?" Matt nodded towards his home. "About ten miles up that a way."

"Who is there with you?"

"My mom and little sister, Lizzie."

"Do you have kinfolk that can help take care of you all?"

"No sir, just me. My mom is sick and I don't know what I am to tell her."

"Did you come here to shop? Do you need anything from the store?"

"Yes sir, we need kerosene for our lamps. I brought eggs to trade."

"How did you get down here? Did you walk?"

"No sir, I rode my mule tied up over there."

"Go get your mule and I will be right back. I will ride back to your home with you."

In a couple of minutes, the major returned with another soldier who introduced himself to Matt as Lieutenant Dodge. Lieutenant Dodge was carrying a kerosene can that he held out for Matt to take.

They rode quietly for a few miles until the lieutenant said, "Son, you should be very proud of your pa. He was an outstanding soldier and he could whip his weight in wild cats."

The major laughed and said, "And he could whip his weight in Yankees also."

The rest of the way, the two officers talked about Big Tom as though they had known him for years and told Matt what a great soldier he was. Matt felt very proud and sad that he had to hear this from two strangers. He was worried about what his mother would do when she heard the news.

When Lizzie heard Matt returning she ran outside to meet him but stopped when she saw the two men with him. She looked closely at each one, hoping one would be her pa, but she was disappointed.

Before the men could get down, Mattie came running outside. She had waited so long to hear from Tom and every day she prayed he would return to them. She had long since became desperate, and when she heard more than one horse she hoped and expected it would be Tom. When she saw the two soldiers and slowly realized that Tom had not returned, she tried to scream but could not make a sound. She fell to her knees and held her head in her hands. She raised her face up and scratched down both sides from her eyes to her neck. Major Shy slipped down from the horse and moving quickly he picked her up and held her hands so she could not hurt herself. He took her back into the house and laid her on the bed. Matt and Lizzie started to follow, but the lieutenant stopped them and asked them to show him around the farm.

Mattie jumped up from the bed and looked at the major with her red pleading eyes and said, "Who the hell are you and what are you doing here?"

"I am here to talk to you about your husband. He joined the army of the Confederacy in my company. He was captured by the Union Troops and is in prison up north in Ohio. We will try to trade union prisoners for his release, but we don't know how long it will take. In the meantime, we will make sure you get paid his money so you can live."

Barely able to breath she growled through gritted teeth, "I don't want your Goddamn money, I want my husband. That bastard didn't even tell me he was joining the army. He didn't even tell us. He didn't even say goodbye to me and the kids. That son-of-a-bitch didn't even say goodbye."

Mattie fainted from lack of breathing normally and almost fell to the floor before the major caught her. He put her in her bed and covered her up.

The major came out of the house just as Matt and the lieutenant arrived back at the front door. "Son, your mother is in a bad way. Are there any kinfolk who can come here to take care of you?"

"No sir, I don't know of anyone who can come here. I don't know anyone."

"You mean you don't know anyone here in the hills, or anyone at all?"

"I don't know anyone."

"Lieutenant, we have to make it back to the crossroads before the main group gets there tonight so we have to get going. Boy, we have to leave, but I will send someone by here in a couple of days to help you out. Do you think you can hold out a little longer?"

"I been holding out here since pa left, so I suppose I can hold out a little longer."

The major had to look at Matt again to make sure he was only a twelve-year-old boy. He sounded like an adult.

They mounted and, as they rode away, both soldiers turned their heads and saluted Matt.

Now they all knew where their pa and husband was, but they were in the same situation, only this time without hope.

Matt picked up Lizzie and carried her inside. He would skip the chores tonight. He was too tired. He picked up the kerosene can from the porch where the lieutenant had left it and filled the lamps. The lamps gave them much brighter light than the candles they had been using, making the little house less scary. He stoked up the fire in the fireplace and rebuilt the one in the cook stove. He fried some salt bacon and cooked some eggs in the grease and he set the table for three. His mother woke up while he and Lizzie were eating and joined them. She seemed a little better. She quietly ate the bacon and eggs and leftover cornbread. When she finished eating, she went outside and used the outhouse and came back and went directly to bed without saying a word. Mattie's outward calm hid a maelstrom of emotions and if she ever exploded, she might never recover. Lizzie took Matt's hand and he led her outside to use the outhouse and when they came back in and he tucked her into bed. He cleaned up the kitchen and then fell into bed going to asleep almost immediately.

Chapter Two

Mattie had lain awake all night, and at three, she eased out of bed and quietly packed a small bag with clothes and some food. It was raining heavily, so she put on a long wool coat and an old rain coat that belonged to her husband. Making sure she did not wake up the kids, she wrote a short note to the person who Major Shy would send out to help them. The note read: Please take my children to their grandmother at the Jacob Bing's Mercantile Store on Main Street in Linden, Tennessee. Mother, please take care of my children until I return ---I have to find Tom, or I will die.

Mattie had moments of clarity, a time when she felt almost normal, and she could make rational decisions. But mostly, she saw the world thought a haze of distorted thoughts and bad memories. She wanted to be alright. She tried hard to be alright. But something had snapped in her mind and would not let her go back to sanity. She hated Tom for taking her away from her parents. She hated her children for living when the other ones had died. She envied Tom's ability to carry on with life. She hated it when he wanted to make love to her. Yet, she had to go find him and bring him back. Somehow she saw him as the key to her finding her sanity again.

She rode slowly to the crossroads, letting the mule pick its way. The rain didn't let up and she was soaked through when she got to the store. As soon as Mrs. Singer saw how wet she was, she led her into the back room and made her change clothes. "Mattie, what in the world are you doing here? I saw Matt yesterday leaving here with a couple of soldiers, didn't he come home?"

"Yes, he made it home. But I have to go find Tom. The soldiers told me he was a prisoner in Ohio and I have to go try get him out. I have to go or I will go crazy."

Of all the years Mattie had lived there, she had seen her only a few times, but they had become friends. In the last few years, Mattie stopped coming to the crossroads altogether. It had been over two years since she had seen her, and almost didn't recognize her.

"Mattie, you have Matt and Lizzie to worry about. What are they going to do without you and Tom?"

Mattie looked at the woman with a crazy look that sent a chill down her spine and then Mrs. Singer understood. She had known many hill women who had gone insane with the mundane existence they led. For a woman to survive in these hills, she would need a combination of good humor and faith and be totally devoted to her family. Mattie had none of those strengths.

She hugged Mattie and said, "Mattie, you do what you have to do. Can I do anything for you?"

"I'm going to need some money. I have a good milk cow, a big pig, and the mule outside. I will sell them to you for fifty dollars."

"Honey, fifty dollars ain't near enough money for you to do what you want to do? I will pay you seventy-five dollars. But if you want them back when you return you can get them back."

"Thank you Dora, you are a kind woman."

"You will need more. Can't your folks help you?"

"No. Have you seen that soldier, the major, here today?"

"Yeah, he is still here."

"He said he had some money for Tom's back pay. I will talk to him."

"I will get my boy to find him for you. You just stay here by the stove and dry out."

In a couple of minutes, the boy came in, followed by Major Shy.

"Come back here major."

Major Shy was surprised when he saw Mattie. "Mrs. McCall, you didn't have to come all the way out here. I was sending a man to your farm tomorrow to give you some money and see what help you needed."

Mrs. Singer motioned for the major to follow her out of the room. "Major, she is determined to go to Ohio and find her husband." Then whispering said, "She is crazy with grief and worry and will do this or die trying, and there is no way to talk her out of it."

"Even if she finds her husband, they will not let him go free."

"I know that and you know that, but we could never make her understand that. She has left her little children at home by themselves, so you need to send someone out there right away."

"She just left them there alone?"

The major had a feeling he needed to do something to assist one of his men's family but he was a little over his head. He had lived a privileged life and could not imagine the hardships some of his men experienced on a daily basis. He liked Tom and respected him as a fighter and he would try his best to help his family.

The major went back into the bedroom, followed by Mrs. Singer.

"Mrs. McCall, here is sixty dollars of back pay for your husband. This should help you get to Ohio and find a place to stay, while you are trying to get your husband out of prison."

Breaking down, Mattie said, "God bless you, sir."

Mrs. Singer hugged Mattie and let her cry.

In a couple of minutes, Major Shy said, "I will send two soldiers to your farm today to take care of the kids"

"I left a note for your men. They should take the children to my mother's house. It is the Jacob Bing's Mercantile Store on Main Street in Linden. Even though my father and mother disowned me when I married Tom, I am sure they will take good care of the children."

"Okay, we will make sure they get to your mother's house."

Major Shy left the store and talked to one of his sergeants. He gave him specific instructions on what they were supposed to do with the children. Telling him to assign two of his best men to handle the job, ensuring both were married with kids, and trustworthy.

When the major entered the store, he said, "Mrs. McCall, the last time we heard anything, your husband was being held in a Union prison called Camp Case located at Columbus Ohio. Do you think you could get there?"

Mattie didn't answer for a minute then she said, "I suppose I could get a train in Nashville going up that way."

Mrs. Singer added, "Mattie, since the war has been going on, we have to get more and more goods shipped to us. I have a man who goes to Lawrenceburg a couple of times a week. There is a railroad spur there that connects to the Nashville Railroad. He will go tomorrow and you can ride with him. At least that's a start."

The major nodded, giving her a compassionate look. "I've written down the name of the place where Tom is being held. I have also noted his number, which you will need to identify him. I will give you a letter of passage that might help you when you encounter our soldiers and the Union soldiers. Just show this letter when you are questioned and tell the truth."

Mrs. Singer put her arm around Mattie and steered her towards the store. "Let's get you cleaned up and get you some new traveling clothes."

Mattie seemed to notice herself and the way she was dressed for the first time in years. "I'm a mess and I use to be so young with pretty dresses and my hair gold and long and curly. What has happened to me?" Then she broke down, sobbing.

Sergeant Daniels had chosen Private Smith to ride out to the McCall farm to pick up the kids. Lt. Dodge had drawn them a rough map showing the way to the little house and given more instructions on how to handle the children and where they were to be taken. The last thing Lt. Dodge said was, "Treat these children like you would your own. If anything happens to them, the major will have your hides."

"Don't worry lieutenant, Big Tom was a friend of mine. I'll make sure these kids get to their grandmother."

Chapter Three

Matt was usually up and out doing chores before the rooster woke him up. But this morning he waited for the rooster to crow, and even then he did not want to get up. He rolled out of bed and pulled his shirt over his head and put his overalls on and then his shoes. He made his way outside quietly and used the outhouse. He did not have much to do. He started pitching hay for the cow and when he started throwing some out for the mule, he noticed the mule was gone. He immediately dropped his pitchfork and ran to the house. He let the door shut quietly and went to his mother's bed. His heart dropped when he saw she was not there. He sat down on his mother's bed and put his head in his hands and cried. He was too young to take care of Lizzie by himself and was mad at his mother and father for leaving him alone. In a minute, he got up and wiped his tears and nose on his sleeve. The expression on his face and his body language changed. He had made up his mind that it was up to him to take care of Lizzie and the farm, and he would do his best. And even though he was only twelve, he felt much older and felt the weight of the responsibility. Being quiet, he prepared breakfast for himself and Lizzie. By the time he had finished preparing the eggs and bacon, Lizzie had stirred from her bed and used the outhouse and sat down at the table. Matt had also made some coffee, which was his father's job in the morning. But since he was the man of the house now, he felt he deserved a cup of coffee, even if he had to put a lot of sorghum in it to make it drinkable.

Matt let Lizzie finish her breakfast before he said, "Mom has gone. She took the mule and left during the night. Probably gone to the crossroads to talk to the soldiers."

Lizzie did not say anything. She just shrugged her shoulders.

Matt touched her hair and said sweetly, "Don't worry, I will take care of you and the farm."

Matt cleaned up the table putting leftovers in the cook stove. By now, the inside of the cabin was fully lit and Lizzie found the note on the little dresser beside her mother's bed. She picked it up and looked at it as to read it, but of course she couldn't read. She handed the note to Matt and he looked at it, trying to make out words. But he could not understand it either.

"The soldiers are supposed to come back to help Mom, so this note is probably for them."

They were sitting on the porch when they heard the horses coming up the path. Their shod hoofs clanging off the stones meant you could hear anyone coming almost a mile away. When the two riders came into view, Matt and Lizzie said at the same time, "Mom's not with them."

Matt hugged Lizzie and said, "Don't worry. They are here to help us."

Sergeant Daniels was a big man, around six foot, two hundred pounds with a short salt and pepper beard. He swung down from his horse and said, "You must be Matt and Lizzie."

He held his hand out to Matt who shook his big hand. Then he picked Lizzie up over his head and hugged her to him. "Hear you folks been having some troubles. Well, we are here to help you out.

That feller over there is Private Smith. He has a little girl about your age."

Talking to Matt he said, "I have a boy bout your age Matt and he is a good boy too."

Private Smith got down from his horse and shook hands with Matt and Lizzie and said in his best duck voice, "How do you do boys and girls."

It made Lizzie smile and that was what he was looking for. But Matt did not smile, and that also was what he was looking for. Matt had all the responsibility and he was feeling the weight, so he would have to take some of it onto himself.

"Did your mother leave a note or something?" Before he got it all out, Lizzie was back on the front porch with the note. Sergeant Daniels read the note and put it in his pocket.

"Private, let's get our stuff packed and get out of here. We have a long ride ahead of us."

The private went into the house followed by Matt and Lizzie. When they came out, Lizzie and Matt each had a small bag of clothes.

"Sergeant, I packed all the food I could find for the trip. If we need more, guess they will have to eat the stuff we eat."

Sergeant Daniels smiled then spit, "Lord let's hope not. Only soldiers should have to eat the stuff we eat."

Her interest aroused, Lizzie asked, "What do you'll eat?"

Private Smith smiled. "Mostly we eat horse meat and Johnnie cakes."

With a straight face, Lizzie said, "Least it ain't mule."

Both the soldiers laughed, surprised at Lizzie's comeback and very pleased.

Private Smith smiling, said, "She will be ok. Now we have to do something to get Matt cheered up."

When the lieutenant told them about what they were assigned to do, they were pleased. They both had children and would not want their own to undergo such turmoil. In addition, they liked Tom and they knew he would have done it for them, had the tables been turned.

"Matt, Lizzie, Private Smith and I are going to take you for a long ride. Your Mom ask us to take you to your grandma's house in Linden. Do you know your grandmother?"

"No sir, we never even knew we had one."

Fixing her face into an inquisitive squint, Lizzie asked, "Matt, do we have a grandmother?"

"I guess we do since Mom is sending us there."

Lizzie ask, "How long is it to Linden?"

"It will take us about six or seven hours to get there if the roads are not flooded."

Sergeant Daniels and Private Smith made the children as comfortable on their horses as possible, letting them set on their little bags of clothes. They made sure the kids had all the coats they could put on so they would not be cold. It was about midday when they started out and it would be after dark before they arrived in Linden. That is, if they did not run into any problems, such as washed out bridges, or raiding Union Soldiers.

As they rode down the path away from the farm, Matt could not help the feeling deep down inside that this might be the last time he ever saw his little bit of paradise, tucked into a hollow in the hills of middle Tennessee.

Chapter Four

The next morning when Mattie came out of the bedroom into the store, Major Shy almost did not recognize her. She looked ten years younger and was very pretty. She was dressed for the road in clothes provided by Mrs. Singer and for the first time in a long time, she felt beautiful. When she saw him looking at her, she felt a little shy and turned around so he could see all of her. Then she grinned just a little. He thought, "She just might get Big Tom out of prison after all."

"Yesterday I sent two of my best men to escort your children to their grandmother's house in Linden. They should have gotten there around eight last night. My soldiers have not returned yet, but I am sure everything went ok. So don't worry about Matt and Lizzie.

Not trusting her emotion, she did not say anything. She hugged Dora and Major Shy and waived her hand and boarded the big freight wagon.

Mrs. Singer said, "Lord, I hope she don't run into any trouble.

Major Shy said, "Don't worry, even though there is a war going on, people are able to move around the country without being harassed most of the time. Even if the trains is raided, it is rare for civilians to get hurt. So Mattie has a good chance of reaching the prison camp in Columbus Ohio. Anyway, she is on her way."

Chapter Five

It was way past dark before the soldiers delivered Matt and Lizzie to their grandparents. At first it took a very long explanation before Jacob and Minerva Bing would even talk to the two Rebel soldiers who said they had a delivery for them, and it was two children. Finally the grandmother said she would take them in and sort it out later. She saw the kids were worn out and already fast asleep on the floor of the big store. She motioned for the soldiers to bring the kids with their little bags along with her. She led them into a small room with a bed. She motioned to lay them down. As she turned to leave the room she motioned for the soldiers to follow. When they got downstairs to the store again, she offered them some coffee and some food. As they ate, they told Mr. and Mrs. Bing all that they knew about the McCall family. Mrs. Bing broke down crying when they told her about Mattie almost losing her mind. She could not help but feel guilty because they had disowned their daughter. She glared at her husband every few minutes, blaming him for everything. When the soldiers had finished eating they said their goodbyes and left.

A little tired and a lot disappointed in the way the Bings had greeted them, Pvt. Smith said, "People like that just make me mad. I'll bet it's the old man's fault. At least the old lady blames him."

"Yeah Grady, they do not know how much they lose by treating people that way. Them kids are just sweet as can be. And that Matt, he is only twelve years old and already a man."

"Where we going to stay tonight?"

"I know this rebel family that will let us bunk for a night. We just have to be out of Linden before daylight. No use taking any chances some Union bastard will see us."

The first few years after Mattie had ran off and married Tom, Mrs. Bing had begged Jacob to go visit them and welcome them back into the family. But, her husband was a stubborn man and his pride would not let him humble himself to a dirt farmer. His resentment had increased over the years, and when George Sawyer came to him with a plan to get rid of Tom and blame it on the war, he reluctantly agreed to help. But he regretted it almost as soon as he had agreed. He didn't have the stomach for murder and tried to minimize his part in any plan. Of course, he never mentioned the plans he concocted with George Sawyer to his wife, knowing she would never approve. He knew well that if Tom found out about it, he would kill everyone involved, even if one of the parties was his father-in-law. Their plan had almost worked, but Tom wasn't killed. He was only taken prisoner, which made things worse for his daughter. And now she was off someplace looking for Tom and they had the children here to take care of.

"Hon, do you think Lizzie favors Mattie?"

"I don't know yet. Hard to tell with her being so dirty."

"Well, I will get them cleaned up in the morning and get them some new clothes. Poor little babies. They look so scared and lonely. We have to take good care of them. They are our grandkids. And it is all our fault. We should have been in their lives all this time."

"Yeah, I am sorry. We have to take care of them."

Chapter Six

Tennessee was the last of the Southern States to secede from the Union, primarily because there were so many Union sympathizers in East Tennessee. The people in West Tennessee wanted to secede and the folks in East Tennessee wanted to align with the North so it fell to people of Middle Tennessee to cast the deciding votes. And in June 1861, they voted for secession. However, the northern loyalist in the east never gave up. They established units that fought on the side of the North called Tennessee Federals. It was a divided state. Only Virginia hosted more battles than Tennessee during the Civil War. The hostilities washed over Tennessee like a high tide washes over an almost submerged sand island. Loyalties were switched on a whim or could be bought for enough gold. The two sides fought for control of the rivers and railroads passing through Tennessee. There were bands of raiders on both sides that roamed the countryside attacking opposing units and generally killing and terrorizing people. It was one of these Tennessee Federal units that attacked the train carrying Mattie, about twenty miles south of Nashville. They took over the engine and stopped the train. Twenty men swarmed the train from end to end, looking for anything they could use to further their cause. The leader was a Major Smithson, who prior to the war, was a local politician of dubious reputation. He was five feet small, and had the insecurity of a small man. He always felt he had to make up for his smallness by being loud and aggressive and by putting people in their place. He used to say that no one was better at putting people in their place than he. When war was declared, he had enough money that he could establish a command. A practice common in the south and the north. Behind his back, his peers referred to him as the little Napoleon. And he justified their mocking by having a uniform just like the one Napoleon is wearing in the famous painting by Jacques-Louis David.

When he along with two of his men entered the car where Mattie was sitting, he was yelling at the top of his little voice. Here was this little man, dressed like Napoleon, yelling at the top of his lungs, using a voice with a pitch so high it was barely legible. The combination of this little man's hysteria and appearance struck these hard men as being funny and some could not help laughing. His yelling and the fact that he was scared and nervous made his voice even funnier. The more instructions he gave, the more laughter broke out in the car. Even the two men that came in with him were looking at each other and smiling. To make it worse, he was holding two large Navy Dragoon pistols, which made him seem even smaller than he was.

The major was so incensed by the laughter that he could hardly contain himself. He motioned towards one of the men who was by now only smiling and said, "Stand up."

When the man stood up he must have been all of six foot three and the laughter started all over again. There was a big boom and the big man slumped forward and fell onto the isle floor. He motioned for another man to stand up and when he refused, the little major shot him where he sat. By this time Mattie was in hysterics and screaming. She tried to run out of the car but he fired at her, hitting her in the back. She crumpled to the floor of the car with her dress turning red from the blood. When the men recovered from their shock of seeing the little major shoot a woman, they pulled their pistols and killed the major and the two soldiers. At that point the car became a fort and the battle raged. Anyone who opened the door at either end of the car was shot. As it turned out, most of the men on the train had weapons and knew how to use them. Little firefights broke out throughout the train, and the raiders seeing their comrades dying beside them, finally had enough and someone gave the order to withdraw.

The train crew collected themselves and continued onto Nashville. Including the two men and Mattie there was a total of eight passengers killed. Including the major and his two men there was a total of ten militia men killed who were still on the train. There were probably more who were left in the darkness alongside the track.

When the train arrived in Nashville it caused a lot of excitement. The Confederate commander was notified, and he took over the investigation. When the doctor was checking on Mattie, he found a letter addressed to her mother and gave it to the commander. The letter told the whole story about Tom, Mattie, and the children. All the newspapers were there getting the stories from all the passengers. All the stories were interesting and exciting, but the one about Mattie was the most tragic. After all, it was her death that set in motion what happen in the end.

The story was told in virtually all the newspapers in the South and a lot in the North. The story of how this funny little major dressed in a Napoleon uniform, had entered the car yelling in his little funny voice, brandishing his big pistols, which made everyone laugh, which led to him first shooting two tall men. How when the beautiful young woman just could not stand the horror any longer, had gotten up to run, and how the little major had shot her in the back. How her courage had emboldened the hardened men on the train, to rise up and kill their captors. How after fifteen of their comrades had been killed they, ran like the cowardly dogs they were. Then it goes on to identify Mattie as a wife of a Confederate soldier, named Private Tom McCall, being held in a POW camp in Ohio. It also tells about her two children, who are staying with their grandmother in Linden.

The cartoonist had a field day with Major Smithson in his Little Napoleon uniform with those two big pistols.

The story garnered so much attention and empathy for Mattie, her two little children, and her husband, there was a groundswell of support to get Tom released. At some point even President Lincoln was said to have intervened on the part of Private Tom McCall. Regardless of when, where, or who, the mechanism had been set into motion for Private Big Tom McCall to be released from the prison camp, and returned to his children.

Chapter Seven

Lizzie was the first to wake up, and she immediately woke up her big brother. She was dancing around like she needed to go pee badly. Since neither had been in the house before, they did not know where to go. So Matt ran down stair holding her hand to find their grandmother. Seeing her, he blurts out, "Lizzie's gotta pee bad."

Her grandmother got her by the hand and led her through a small door in the back of the store. When she got back with Lizzie, she pointed to the door and said "You can go there."

When Matt returned his grandmother said, "Ok children we have to get you two cleaned up and get you dressed. Follow me."

They followed her back through the small door through to another small room where there was a big tub. "Get undressed and give me your clothes."

The grandmother heated some water and poured it into the cold water which was already in the tub. She helped them clean themselves, and wash their hair, and dried them off. She had new clothes for them to put on, and when they looked in the mirror, they hardly recognized each other. They had never had nice clothes before, and now they felt giddy. Even Matt smiled at himself.

When they came out of the back room, their grandfather was standing there. He nodded at his wife and said, "They'll do." And he smiled.

"Kids, I am your Grandma and this is your Grandpa. We are happy you are here and we will take care of you until your Mother and Father come for you, Okay?"

They were a little shy and shook their head.

"Are you hungry?"

They again shook their head.

"Ok, follow me."

She led them upstairs into the big kitchen. It smelled of bacon, and it made them realize just how hungry they were. They had eaten some cornbread and ham on the way, but that was a long time ago. They ate like they did at home prompting their grandmother to say, "We will have to work on your table manners."

"Yes ma'am." And they went on eating.

"After breakfast you can go outside and play. But don't get in the street, or you will get ran over by a buggy or wagon. There is lots of traffic since the war started. You can cross the street to the courthouse, but be careful. Understand? Stay out of the street."

The store was across the street from the courthouse, which had a large grassy area with benches. On one side of the store was a hotel, on the other side was the post office. The sidewalk was wide, and a good place for the children to play, or just watch the world go by. But they did not know how to play in town. They had never been to town before, and were lost. They just sat on the step and watched the people go by. They had never seen so many people, with all kinds of things with wheels.

The store was busy with people going and coming all day long. Finally bored with watching people, they went back inside the store.

"Is there anything I can help you with, Grandpa?"

Surprised at being called Grandpa, he could not answer right away. But then, "Thank you Matt, I believe there is something you can do. Follow me."

His grandpa led him and Lizzie into the back of the store, where there were a lot of boxes and packages unopened. "Do you have a pocket knife?"

"No sir."

He walked away and came back in a minute with something, and handed it to Matt. Matt looked at it and smiled. "Is this for me? Is it mine to keep?"

"It is yours to keep forever."

"Thank you very much. I never had a knife before."

"Use it to cut the strings on these boxes and open them, and take everything out of them and bring it up front, so we can put it on display."

From then on, Matt and even Lizzie made themselves useful in the store. Lizzie, being younger, adjusted more easily than Matt. She was used to Matt taking care of her, and nothing much had changed for her, except of course the nice clean place to live and the clothes. But Matt was used to working around the farm, and taking care of the animals, and cooking for his mother and Lizzie. Now, he had hardly anything to occupy his time. Plus, he was worried about his mother and father. He wanted to know what was happening to them and where they were. He still had Lizzie to take care, so he would do the best he could, and wait.

Five days had passed since Matt and Lizzie had come to live with their grandparents, when the local constable and a Confederate Captain came to the store. The soldier had a newspaper and showed it to Mr. Bing. As he read it his face turned white, and he dropped the newspaper on the floor.

Mrs. Bing picked up the paper and began reading. She cupped the paper to her face and started crying. "It can't be true. It has to be a mistake."

"I am very sorry to bring you this terrible news, but it is true. We check before we brought the newspaper. "

Matt and Lizzie came to see what was going on and Mrs. Bing pulled them to her and cried even more.

"Are these her children?"

"Yes."

"The body is on its way here now. Should arrive today or early tomorrow."

"What's going on Grandpa?"

"Son, your mother has died."

"What does that mean? She is dead? How? I just saw her a few days ago." Matt turned away and wiped tears from his eyes and hugged Lizzie. He did not believe it at first, he was in shock and did not know how to react. He felt he should cry, but he couldn't for some reason. He had mixed emotions about his mother. He was angry at her for being so cold and ignoring him and Lizzie and for not being a kind mother. He would have to make sure Lizzie was protected.

As the constable and officer left the officer said, "We will be in touch with you soon."

Matt led Lizzie outside and they sat down on the step. "Did that man say our mom was dead?"

"Yeah, she's died."

"Does that mean she won't be coming back to get us?"

"She won't be coming back for us."

"Just you and me now Matthew." Matt hugged her close and cried.

Mattie's body arrived later that day and the funeral was the next afternoon. Many people had read the papers and knew the story by now and they all come to the funeral. Everyone wanted to see the famous woman and her children. But seeing the children grieving for their mother was so sad that many left unable to endure it. At the funeral after seeing his mother in the coffin, Matt finally broke down and cried. He remembered only the times when his mother was happy and smiling. All the bad times faded with her death.

Mrs. Bing had cried many nights after Mattie ran off and married. She thought she had cried her last tear for her, but when she saw Mattie in the coffin, she could not be consoled. Her only daughter had died before they could reconcile their differences and she would never be the same again. She cried for days. She poured her love into the children, doting on them even more than before. Mr. Bing was more reserved, but inside his heart had broken. He blamed himself for everything and vowed he would do better.

Newspapers picked up the story about the funeral of Mattie and how sad the children were to lose their mother, and the cry to let their father go spread even louder and further.

The Bings had to keep a close eye on Matt and Lizzie after the funeral to keep people away from them. Everyone wanted to see them and talk to them and ask them questions about their mother and father. So the kids stayed inside most of the time.

Chapter Eight

Private Tom McCall was led to the Commandant's office where he was ask to sit and wait. After about fifteen minutes he was led into Colonel Moody's office. "Please have a seat Private McCall. I have very bad news for you. It seems your wife has been killed."

Tom turned white and tears filled his eyes. He made a gesture with his hands as if to ask how.

The Colonel continued, "It seems that it is quite a story and has made your family famous, even you Private. It is in all the newspapers and I am surprised I had not read about it."

Tom looked at the officer quiet confused.

"I am sure you will hear the full story sooner or later, but the reason I am here today is to inform you that you are being traded for prisoners and let go. Your paperwork is being processed while we are speaking. You will be escorted all the way to your lines, and then on to your home."

Tom could not say anything. He just sat there dumbfounded. When he was told to report to the Commandant's office he was expecting to be punished for something. He was constantly sick from lack of food and clean water. He had to fight fellow prisoners for his rations and recently almost killed a boy from Kentucky who tried to take his bed. So he figured one of the guards had reported him. But when the Commandant told him he would be going home, he did not believe him. He did not trust him and expected to be taken out to be punished at any minute.

Going on, the Colonel said, "I know it sounds too good to be true, but you are on your way home."

There was a knock on the door and a young soldier came into the room with a few newspapers in his hand. He handed them to Colonel Moody without saying a word.

"I ask my clerk to get me some recent papers with the story in them."

He handed one to Tom who took it and started reading. He read it slowly and then looked at the colonel.

"Yeah, hard to believe. I would have probably laughed at that funny little man also." Then he smiled.

There was another knock at the door and a young captain and two privates entered the room. "Sir, we have the paperwork and the passes and we are ready to go."

The colonel held out his hand and said, "Well Private, I am truly sorry for your loss, and I wish you luck. You are free to go. Just make sure you do what these men tell you to do."

Tom saluted and turned to follow the three soldiers out. He was surprised when they let him through the prison gates.

Tom was taken to a nearby hotel where he was placed in a room and ordered to get a bath and put on the clothes provided. While he was bathing, he had time to think about what he had just heard. Besides questions about how his wife was killed, he needed to know what had happened to his children. He had been shot and not given adequate care for his leg, then imprisoned with little food and lots of abuse. It was a new prison that had not reached it full capacity, but it was terrible. The officers and guards were not the best soldiers and had something to prove. They seemed to be especially hard on him, he felt because of his size. Whether they were just cruel people or they were just mad at the world, they took it out on the prisoners. Tom had lost over fifty pounds in the few months he was there. He became a leader through his association with other prisoners. Whereas before, he was quiet and reserved, he now felt obliged to speak up whenever he felt the urge. He had a different perspective on the war and promised that when he got out of prison, he would be a different person.

Once Tom was finished with his bath and fully dressed, he went down stairs to where the three men were waiting for him. He was taken to the local train station to begin their journey south.

It was four month from the day the constable and officer came to the Bing's store to tell them about their daughter's death, and the day Big Tom McCall and his escort Lieutenant Dodge road into Linden to get his children.

When Tom reached the Confederate lines he was treated like a real celebrity. Everyone he met had heard the heart breaking story about his wife and were eager to help him. In addition to fitting him with a proper uniform with sergeant stripes, he was presented with a very fine horse that had been picked up in a recent raid. The horse just happened to be fitted with a matching pair of Colt Army Model 1860. He had been paid his back salary with a bonus. A Top Sergeant presented him with a brand new Yankee long gun with all the fixings. When Lieutenant Dodge met him at a designated location he told Tom that he was well dressed, well-armed, and well shod. But Lt Dodge also noticed the changes in Tom. Before he was captured he was a big tall man, now he was a tall skinny man with a pronounced limp. His leg still had not healed properly and might require more attention from the surgeons. And that is the way he rode into Linden.

The children had gotten into a routine. Breakfast, then play outside, then help in the store, and in the afternoon after lunch playing some more. That is how they just happened to be sitting on the step of the store when their father rode up. He saw them, and had to look real close to recognize them all dressed up. They had not taken note of him, thinking he was just another man on horseback until he stopped right in front of them and swung his leg off. Matt jumped up and ran to him and leaped into his arms. Lizzie followed and jumped as high as she could. There they stood all three of them holding each other on the sidewalk crying.

"Mommy is dead, Daddy."

"Yes, Lizzie I know. Are you ok? Both of you have grown so much. Matt you are so big. Soon you will be as big as me. And you Little Lizzie. I am going to have to stop calling you little Lizzie and start calling you pretty Lizzie."

Mrs. Bing came out to see about the kids and saw that their father had arrived. She stood back and let the kids enjoy the reunion with their father. Finally she said, "Welcome home Tom." And she hugged him. Tom was surprised and didn't know how to react.

"It's ok now Tom, we are a family. Sorry for all the bad times in the past. But having the children with us made us realize what a mistake we had made. Especially Jacob."

Lt Dodge had stepped down and the children noticed him and ran to him. Lizzie said, "Thank you for bringing my pa home." And they hugged him.

Mrs. Bing said, "Come in we just had lunch and it is still on the table. You have to be hungry."

They followed her in and sat at the table to eat.

Mr. Bing came up and held out his hand to Tom. "I did wrong by Mattie and you and the children and I would ask you to forgive me."

Tom took his hand. "I am so sorry about Mattie."

After he ate, Tom led the kids outside and took a seat on the step.

"When we going home Pa?"

"Yeah, when we going home Pa?" Lizzie echoed.

"I will stay here tonight but tomorrow, I have to report back to the Army for a while. Would you mind staying with your grandma for just a little longer?"

Lizzie said, "I don't mind, I like it here. I have pretty clothes to wear every day."

Matt didn't say anything.

"How about you Matt? Would you mind staying here a while longer?"

"Well, I don't mind so much, but I want to be with you and ain't nobody taking care of our farm."

"I understand, but it will only be for a little while. I have some unfinished business. I will be in the area and check on you when I can. I will also check on the farm and make sure everything there is ok."

Tom and Lt Dodge checked into the hotel next door and once cleaned up they went to the Bings for supper. After they finished eating and the children were in bed, Tom said, "Would you'll mind taking care of the children for a while longer? I have some business with the Army that I have to finish. I will still be in the area and check on them from time to time and when I am able, I will come get them. I can't tell you how much I appreciate you taking care of them. I hate to think of what might had happened if you had not taken them in."

"It weren't no trouble. These kids are family and we love them very much. We will care for them as long as you wish."

Mr. Bing ask, "Where will you be going?"

"I don't quite know. Something bothers be about the night I was captured by the Tennessee Federals. I just got the feeling we might have been set up. With Major Shy's permission I aim to do some investigating and if I find out someone betrayed us, he will pay with his life. "

All the time Tom was speaking he was looking directly at Mr. Bing. Feeling the glare, all Mr. Bing could do was chew on his pipe stem.

As Tom and Lt Dodge got up to leave Tom said, "We will meet the children for breakfast and then we will be leaving for a while."

As they walked outside Lt Dodge said, "Tom, sounds like you have some idea as to who betrayed you. Do you know who it was?"

"No, not yet but I intend to find out. "

The next morning they got their mounts and tied them to rail in front of the store. When Tom was riding he had holsters on each side of his saddle for his colts, but when he was not riding, he tucked them inside his wide belt. Even with his limp he was a formidable opponent to anyone who crossed him.

While they were eating breakfast Tom ask, "Sir, when I was up north I saw a gun called a Henry repeater. Have you heard of such a gun?"

"Yes I have. In fact, I ordered ten of them from a salesman who came through here last year, but have not been able to sell even one. They are very expensive and the cartridges are also expensive."

"How much are they?"

"I can sell you one for $45.00 and throw in a box of ammunition."

Holding up his brand new Yankee long rifle Tom said, "How much will you give me in trade for this one?"

Mr. Bing took the new gun and looked it over. "Since you are family, I will give you fifteen dollars trade and throw in another box of ammunition."

"It's a deal."

Tom paid Mr. Bing thirty dollars and got his Henry with two boxes of ammunition and a cleaning kit. Before he left the store, he loaded it and paid for two more boxes of ammunition. He had work to do and now he was equipped to handle anything that came his way.

Lt Dodge had watched with interest the trading for the Henry and as they were talking he had picked up the gun and took a closer look at it. And after Tom and Mr. Bing had finished their business he said, "Will you give me the same deal? Without the rifle trade of course." "Sure, and I will even throw in an extra box of ammunition. How about that. Haven't sold any in over a year and now I sell two."

Lt Dodge seemed very pleased with his new rifle when they walked outside with it glinting in the sun. He loaded it and stuck it in his saddle holster. He mounted and waited for Tom to say his goodbyes and they rode off at a quick pace. They had been in town too long without attracting attention.

The children stood on the sidewalk in front of the store and watched their father ride out of sight. Lizzie turned to go inside but Matt stood there for a bit longer feeling lonely and uneasy. What if something happened to his pa, what would they do?

That evening around sundown a gentleman rode up and tied his horse to the rail in front of the store. Mr. Bing walked outside as soon as he saw him ride up. "What are you doing here?"

"I just came to check on your visitor. Someone told me that your son-in-law had come home. Is there going to be any problems."

"Everything is ok, he is just interested in getting his kids and his life back on the farm."

"But he was dressed in uniform. Where was he going when he left today?"

"He has to check in with his unit so he can get discharged legally. You worry too much."

"You had better worry more. If someone finds out you were the one who betrayed him, he will kill you whether you are his kids grandpa or not."

"Well he better not find out. Just make sure Bill is not around to talk."

"Are you saying that I should kill Bill?"

"I am not saying that, I am saying that you should make sure he leaves these parts and stays gone."

Matt walked outside to where the two men were talking and said, "Grandma said come to supper."

"Okay, I will be right in."

Matt had come close and got a good look at the man talking to his grandpa, and did not like him. It was just a feeling but Matt noted it.

When Mr. Bing walked inside, his wife asked, "Who was that you were talking to?"

"Nobody hon, just a business acquaintance."

Mrs. Bing kind of looked at her husband funny and he nodded towards Matt and she understood that he did not want to discuss it in front of the children. There was not much that Matt missed and he had seen the interchange between his grandparents. They were hiding something and it had to do with the man talking to his grandpa.

Chapter Nine

The next day when Lt Dodge and Sgt McCall rode into Major Shy's camp, there was an impromptu celebration. All the men that knew him, and most of the others, rushed forward to shake the hand of the most famous man in the unit. Major Shy led the cheers, "Hip hip, hurrah! Hip hip, hurrah! Hip hip, hurrah!"

Big Tom was visibly embarrassed by all the attention but there was nothing he could do. When the hoopla died down Major Shy motioned for Sgt McCall and Lt Dodge to follow him to his tent.

"Well Sgt McCall, how are you? Looks like you picked up some stripes, some hardware, and a very fine horse on your way back to us."

Tom smiled, "Yes sir. The best thing I have picked up I got from my father-in-law in Linden."

Tom held up the Henry rifle for the major to look at. The Major took it and looking at Tom said, "I have heard about this gun, but I have not seen one. Does it work the way it is advertised?"

"Better, sir. It will win this war and change all future wars."

Major Shy looked at Tom trying to understand where the outburst came from. Tom was usually quiet and spoke only when spoken to. "I see you have one also, Lt Dodge."

"Yes sir, I also bought it in Linden."

"Sir, my father-in-law purchased ten of these guns a year ago and has been unable to sell them. They are very expensive especially for local farmers. Plus, no one around here has a need for them. But if our unit had ten of these guns, we could fight against a much larger force and win handily. We have to figure out a way to get those guns, even if we have to steal them. But, I believe if we had the money in gold, we could get the guns at thirty five dollars apiece and get all the ammunition he has."

"We will talk further about the guns when our meeting is over."

"Have a seat gentlemen and lay it all out for me. You first Tom and then Lt Dodge will pick it up from where he met you."

"Where do you want me to start?"

"Start with the trip to pick up the horses and what went wrong."

"We rode out of camp at dusk and traveled along the back roads and trails. It was raining hard most of the way. We were to meet our contact just to the just south of Linden, where the Buffalo River washes up against the bluffs. There is a narrow pass there between the river and bluffs which is very secluded. We dismounted about a mile from the meeting place and walked as quietly as possible. The rain had let up a little and it was hard not to make some noise. I sent Private Bishop ahead on foot to scout and when he didn't return in a few minutes I was concerned. I told everyone else to go back along the trail about a mile and wait for me. And if they heard any firing, to hightail it out of here. As they turned to go back, I slowly made my way without my horse along the trail staying close to the bluff out of the light. When I got within twenty yards of where we were to meet, a large group of riders descended upon me. I raised my gun but was shot in the leg before I could get a shot off. The one that shot me and another man stopped and hog tied me and threw me on a horse. About ten other riders rode off towards where my men had gone. Were any of my men killed or captured?"

"No, when they heard the shot they rode out of there. The only ones captures were you and Private Bishop. Private Bishop was later found with his throat cut."

"Major Shy, I have a bad feeling about what happened. I think I was set up. Someone betrayed us."

"I agree with you. Do you have any ideas about who it might have been?"

"I have some ideas but I will talk to you about it later."

"Go on with your story. Where were you taken after you were captured?"

"I was taken to a Tennessee Federals camp just on the other side of Hohenwald and held there for about five days. There was a doctor there who treated the gunshot wound. My leg was torn to bits. The bullet just nicked the bone enough to get bone splinters in the flesh, and that is the reason it has taken so long to heal. The unit that captured me was the Sixth Tennessee Federal Cavalry, under Captain Webb. They had about forty to fifty man unit all total. There were about fifteen in the unit that picked me up. I was interrogated for about twelve hours and when they saw I was not going to talk, or that I was too dumb to know anything, they sent me to Knoxville. I don't remember much of the trip. I was in and out of consciousness and cannot tell you the exact route, but the roads were good so it must have been the main roads. I woke myself up yelling in a hospital with a doctor picking bone fragments out of my leg. I guess he did not have anything to give me for the pain or maybe he was just saving it for the Federals. I do remember there were other prisoners there and in a few days, we were all packed into a wagon and taken to the railroad station and put on a train. We had no idea where we were going or where we were when we arrived. When we arrived at the prison, we were given a briefing by the Commandant about rules and regulations and the bad things that could happen if we tried to escape. The rest you know. But there is one thing. Major from what I have seen, there is no way we can ever win this damn war. You cannot believe the stuff they have up north. They have military encampments everywhere and they have enough men and equipment to take over the world. On my way south I saw field after field of heavy guns. They have large herds of horses and more mules than you can count. It's all stockpiled along the railroads and rivers ready to head south."

"Have you told anyone else about what you saw?"

"Yes sir. Every place I stopped along the way I had to debrief and I told them all the same. Only, I went into more detail pointing out on maps the locations of things I saw. Sir, with all due respect, it is my belief that the only way for us to have any impact on this war is to fight as a hit and run unit. If we are ever forced to join a major battle, all of us will be slaughtered."

"I agree with you and have been thinking in the same way. Tennessee is setting right in the middle between the north and south and the fighting will wash through Tennessee for the duration of the war. And we have to be ready. The Tennessee Federals have been running roughshod all over middle and east Tennessee and that has to stop. We will talk more about this later when we get our staff together."

"Okay, Lt Dodge you can start with when you met Sgt McCall."

"The armies of the south and north have set up a VIP prisoner exchange program at Lynchburg, and that is where I met Sgt McCall. I was unable to see or talk to him until he was debriefed by the Confederate General Staff which took about five days. They also checked out his leg to make sure he was able to travel. Everyone knew his name and his story and every general and private wanted to see him. That is how he wound up with the Sgt stripes, new uniform, horse, and weapons. Once he was turned over to me, we made our way down through Virginia to Tennessee and on to Linden to see his children."

"No trouble from the Tennessee Federals?"

"No sir. I figure they were instructed not to harass us."

"I suspect that you are right. Anyway, we are happy you are home."

"Orderly, get in touch with the top sergeant and call a staff meeting. Then bring us some food in for all of us."

Picking up Lt Dodge's Henry rifle he said, "Now about these guns. You say that your father in law has eight left with some ammunition. Do you know how much ammunition?"

"No sir."

"That might be a problem but we have different ways of getting ammunition."

"I just wonder how many other country stored have these Henrys, which they can't sell."

The staff begin to arrive and took seats around the field table. The unit included Captains Day and Wright, Top Sergeant Teague, Staff Sergeants Daniels, Bell, and Creasy. And Lt Dodge and Tom, now a Staff Sergeant. As they arrived they again shook hands with Sgt McCall.

The children had told him about Sgt Daniels and Private Smith and when he saw Sgt Daniels he took his hand and then hugged him. "Thank you for taking care of my children. If you ever need anything, just ask."

Sgt Daniels just shook his head not trusting his voice to answer Tom.

With everyone seated and the food served, Major Shy began by saying, "Gentlemen we are so grateful that we have Tom back. Not only has he found his freedom but he has found his voice. Captain Day and Captain Wright and I have been discussing our future plans. What things we can do to fight this war? And just so happens that Tom having seen all the resources the North has at their disposal was thinking the way we were. We have to turn ourselves into a fast moving hit and run force. We do not want to get caught up in a carnage of another Shiloh. The Tennessee Federals have been the cause of all our troubles up to now. They have been riding around Tennessee like they own it and that has to stop. And I don't just mean to bloody their noses, but strike a blow which will be felt in Virginia to help the Generals fight this war. Tom and Lt Dodge were able to pick up a couple of the new Henry repeating rifles and we know where we can get eight more. But we need more than eight. We need a hundred and lots of ammunition."

He picked up one and passed it to Captain Day and Lt Dodge passed his to Captain Wright and they in turn passed them around to the men in the room.

"Gentlemen these guns hold sixteen rounds and can be fired rapidly and reloaded just as fast. They can kill a man at three hundred yards. This gun will make us a formidable unit the likes of which have never been. Again, we need more of them. Since Tom found these in a mercantile store in Linden, I wonder just how many more country or mercantile stores have these guns. I want you to talk to your people, and send them to each store within the area, or wherever they think they might find this gun, and buy them and all the ammunition you can. We will pay gold and therefore they will sell them at a discount. I do not have to tell you to be discreet. Make sure the person you chose to go inquire about this gun is trustworthy and smart enough to know how to ask for them. If they run into someone who don't want to sell or have any suspicion of the seller, they need to contact me right away. Is that understood? I do not want anyone to know we have these guns. Get your people on this right away and we will meet again in three days."

"Attention. Dismissed. Lt Dodge and Tom stay with me."

"When do you want to go get the guns from your father in law?"

"I am ready whenever you get the money."

Major Shy opened a big field trunk and opened a small box. "How much do you want to take with you?"

"At thirty five dollars each it would be two hundred and eighty dollars just for the guns and then depending on how much ammunition he has…."

He interrupted Tom and said, "I will give you four hundred just in case. That should be more than enough."

"You may leave whenever you want and take anyone along you think necessary.'

"Yes, sir." Tom saluted and turned to leave.

On his way out, he saw the orderly and said, "Please find Private Smith and have him report to me at the corral. Thank you."

"Yes sir."

In a few minutes Private Smith ran up to Tom and said, "You send for me sir?"

"Grady, thank you very much for taking care of my children. If you ever need anything, just let me know."

"It was no problem Sir. They are great kids."

"Anyway, thank you again."

As he left Private Smith, he found Lt Dodge and told him about his plans to return to Linden just in case anything went wrong.

Chapter Ten

Tom timed his trip so he would arrive at the store in Linden a little after sundown. He used a small buckboard wagon which was light enough to be pulled by one horse, but able to carry whatever he purchased and move fast if the need arose.

Mr. Bing was surprised when he opened the door and found Tom there in civilian clothes. "What are you doing here so late?"

"Just came to see if the kids were ok. They seemed sad when I left before."

"Kids, look who is here."

The kids jump into his arms and he picked them both up. "You guys are getting so big especially you Matt. How old are you now? I plain forgot."

Lizzie answered the question, "Why Pa, Matt is twelve and I am five."

"Is that right?"

"Come on in to supper, Tom."

When they were finished eating, Tom tucked the kids in and went into the living room and sat down opposite Mr. Bing. "Mr. Bing, I want to buy the rest of those Henry rifles. Since my Army career has been cut short because of an injury, I am going into business for myself. I met a man who after seeing my Henry, ask me where I got it and I told him I had bought it up north. He wanted to buy it and I told him no. Well he offered me forty dollars for it but, I still would not sell it. He told me that he would give me forty dollars for all the henrys I could bring him. So I figured if I could buy them from you for thirty five dollars and sell them for forty, I could make some money to get back farming. I lost my mules and cow and hogs."

Mr. Bing had lit his pipe while Tom had been talking and was chewing on the stem. "How are you going to pay for the rifles? Where would you get that much money?"

"Well, that is the thing, this gentleman said he would pay me in advance since we had a mutual friend. We both know Mr. Stevenson who is the Mayor of Clifton."

"You have been busy since you were here. Do you have the money with you?"

"Yes, and I am ready to pick up the guns tonight. This whole thing has to be held very quiet. I suspect the gentlemen has some sympathies towards the Tennessee Federals but I am not sure. Is that a problem with you?"

Mr. Bing cleared his throat nervously and said, "I really don't hold any particular sympathies in this war, so I am not concerned as to where these guns might wind up. I am a business man and sell to the customer whichever side he may be on."

That was about the response he was expecting from his father-in-law but Tom felt sure where his sympathies were placed. "Well anyway, please keep this whole thing quiet and if you can get some more guns we can sell them for more money the next time."

"Shall we go downstairs and get to business?"

They both finished their coffee and moved down to the store.

"How many do you have left? I think you said eight. Is that right?"

"Yes, there are eight more."

"How much ammunition do you have?"

"I am not sure, I will look."

Mr. Bing disappeared into a back store room and came out with a case of ammunition.

"I have four cases this size. Four hundred to a case."

"Great I will take all of it. I have four hundred dollars in gold."

"You have that much in gold?"

"Yes, and there is more where that came from. Do you think you can get more of these rifles and ammunition?"

"Well, I am not sure with the war going on. It will probably be impossible to get any kind of gun for that matter."

Tom paid Mr. Bing and they loaded up the buckboard.

"Tell the kids I will be back real soon and hopefully we can get back to farming."

Mr. Bing held out his hand for Tom to shake and said, "Hopefully we can do some more business soon."

Tom rode all night back to his unit taking it slow on the back roads. He was very careful, making sure no one saw him with the rifles and ammunition.

He pulled the buckboard up to Major Shy's tent and reported, "Sir, Sgt McCall reporting."

"Come on in Tom. What do you need?"

"Sir, I have eight brand new still in the box Henry rifles and 1600 rounds of .44 rim fire cartridges."

"You got'em? Alright. Orderly, ask Captains Day and Wright to report to me immediately."

"Gentlemen, we have the first eight Henry rifles and ammunition for them. You know your men and you know who among them who are the best riflemen. These guns should be issued to them, but they are to be kept a secret so caution your men to not talk or brag about our unit having them."

"Sir, I need to talk to you more about the night I was captured."

"Alright, come in and sit down."

"The first I heard of the meeting with the horse trader was the morning of the day we rode to the meeting. Can you tell me how it came about?"

"Captain Wright, who is from Linden, was told by his neighbor about a horse trader that bought horses in Kentucky and sold them in Tennessee. And Captain Wright told me. As you know we are always looking for mounts and mules, so I ask our men to be on the lookout for anyone who had horses or mules for sale."

"Can I talk to Captain Wright?"

"Sure. Orderly run and get Captain Wright."

In a minute Captain Wright came into the tent. "You wish to see me sir?"

"Yes, Ben. Sgt McCall and I are discussing the events that led to the day he was captured. Tell him about your meeting with your neighbor."

"Mr. Leonard, who is my next door neighbor heard me mention that I wanted to buy some horses. He said he knew a horse trader who passed through Linden a couple time a month. He said he would be glad to meet him and tell him about me needing horses. So about a week later, I saw him at the post office and he told me the man was in town staying at the hotel on Main Street. When we finished our business in the post office, we walked to the hotel and met Mr. Joe Swafford, the horse trader. He had four horses with him, and we walked to the back of the hotel where he had them stabled. They looked like good animals and we made a deal. You remember when I brought in those four horses Major?"

"Sure I remember. Good horses and a good price."

"Well from that day I told him that we would be able to take twenty more horses and twelve mules, if he could get them and they were all as good as the ones he had just sold me. I told him that since we were taking so many, that we would like to keep it as quiet as possible. He agreed and we set a date for delivery but not a place. When the date of the meeting was getting close I was contacted by a man named Bill Henderson or Anderson I am not sure now. It was the first time I had ever met him. He told me where we were to meet and even suggested that Tom McCall might know the location well."

"Wait, are you saying that Mr. Anderson or Henderson, whatever his name was, actually mentioned Sgt McCall's name?"

"Yes sir. That is the reason I chose Sgt McCall to go on the trip."

"Just as I suspected. I was set up."

"Looks like your hunch was correct."

Captain Wright said, "You think you were set up to be captured?"

"I had thought of it and now with this information it seems I was right. Some son-of-a-bitch is going to pay."

"We need to find this Bill and maybe have a talk with him and Mr. Swafford. But, I don't want anyone to get word of our investigation so let's keep it quiet. Captain Wright, please don't say anything to your neighbor. Not that he is suspected of anything but just in case he might happen to mention it to someone else. I don't want anyone knowing about this until it is finished."

"I agree. This is bigger than just you getting set up, it is about someone knowing our business. We have to start being more careful. We have to move our operation more often and have more than two locations where we can operate out of."

"Sgt McCall, do what you have to do to find out what happened. Just keep me up to date."

"Yes sir."

Chapter Eleven

Knowing the children hadn't received any formal education, Mrs. Bing began teaching Matt and Lizzie how to read almost as soon as they moved in with her, and now she felt they were ready to start to school. She knew that Lizzie would do just fine. She was smart like her mother. She expected it would be more difficult for Matt, since he was older. Also, since he was from the country, he would have problems with the town boys. They would try to bully him, but find that Matt had taken after his father in both size and temperament.

Mrs. Bing was right, Lizzie took to school like a duck to water. Her concerns about Matt were also well founded. A couple of the biggest town boys had tried to bully him, but Matt had quickly put them in their place. After that, he only occasionally had to make his point. Come to find out, Matt was also smart, and quickly picked up the reading and arithmetic, but as most boys, had problems with his writing. He practiced every night determined to get it right. He had a drive inside him to do better. He was going to be a big man like his father, well over six foot and all the hard work on the farm had made him lean and hard. Each time Tom came to see them, he would comment on how pretty Lizzie had become and how much Matt had grown. Matt idolized his father and wanted to be just like him and could not wait until they were back on their little farm. He did not like staying with his grandparents. He felt their coldness towards him and his sister just under the surface. And he did not trust his grandpa. There was something about him that did not set with Matt. He always seemed to be hiding a part of himself. He was too careful when he spoke around certain people. He did not have any friends nor did his grandmother. And he seemed always afraid of something. Occasionally he would get quiet for days and be on the verge of scolding Matt for something he deserved to be scolded for, but always thought better of it. It was like he did not want to get on the bad side of Big Tom.

After a while Matt knew that he could do almost anything and not get called on it. But he was almost grown and knew right from wrong and chose the higher ground. He felt that as long as he and Lizzie needed a place to stay he had to respect his grandparents and as long as they did not mistreat Lizzie, he would do right.

Chapter Twelve

Major Shy received a dispatch from headquarters and called a staff meeting, "Gentlemen, Colonel Frierson wants us to do some raiding along the river above and below Linden. Gunboats on the river have been harassing our units and their raiding parties have been burning stores of ammo and supplies. He seems to think they are going to make a push before winter to take land and prepare for a large spring push into the south. Before we start our raids, we first have to move our headquarters. We have had a couple of desertions in the past week and if they talk to someone who cares, we could have be vulnerable sitting here. Any questions or comments?"

But before anyone could ask a question, Major Shy continued, "Captain Wright, how are we coming on acquiring those Henry rifles?"

"Sir, we have been able to buy six more with two cases of ammunition to date. But we have not been to all the places that sell firearms. One store in Hohenwald had seven but would not sell them to Private Lepping. I sent Sgt Bell in civilian clothes and the store proprietor refused him also. He told Sgt Bell that another store owner had ask to buy them and all the ammunition he had and already paid him half with gold to hold them for him. He would not tell him where the other store owner was located."

Tom spoke up, "Sir, I might know who that store owner is. Last time I talked to Mr. Bing, I told him if he found any more rifles, I would buy them and pay him forty dollars each." "Your father-in-law?"

"Yes, sir. I will check on it right away and if it is not him, I will ride to Hohenwald and get the guns one way or the other. War time is no time to be standing on protocol. That bastard is just trying to make money."

"All right Sgt McCall, I will trust you to get the guns either way. Now, back to the move. We have to get it done quickly and efficiently and we need a place where we can set out the winter. Sgt Daniels's father makes about the best corn whiskey in Tennessee and the reason is the water which comes out of a big cavern. We rode up there recently and it would be a great place for our headquarters. Completely defendable with a small force and totally isolated. Gentlemen get your troops together and get it loaded up and ready to leave by sundown tomorrow."

Over the next two days Major Shy's camp had moved lock stock and barrel to their new location. The only thing left behind was the tracks and horseshit where the horses were kept. The new location was a natural fortification, so far back into the hollow that if you did not know where you were going you would never find it. Everyone who lived in the area were loyal southerners, and would warn them if any outsiders approached. Major Shy was a generous man making sure that he had jobs for all that came in to camp. He made sure that when he brought food and stores to his camp, that the people in the hills shared it. He developed a very loyal following.

Each major unit in the army had messengers to deliver orders for combat operations. Like any war, there were ebbs and flow. Much of the time was spent in camp waiting for orders to go somewhere and do something. Sometimes the orders were specific as to the date, time, and place. But occasionally the instructions are more general like: Raid Federal Units on the Tennessee River above and below Linden. And that is what they did.

Major Shy had split his command in two operational units with Captain Wright in charge of the unit to raid north of Linden and Captain Day's unit was to raid south of Linden. But if the scouts found a force too large for one unit, then the two units would go on the raid together. Nothing was done without prior planning. The scouts were very important to any successful operation and Big Tom McCall was the best scout in Major Shy's command. Each unit had their own Staff Sergeant and designated scout so Sgt McCall worked freelance for Major Shy. He went where the major sent him and the major relied heavily upon his advice. He often told his officers that Tom was a natural soldier. And he wished to assign him a commission when the opportunity came.

When they were in their new camp prior to any operation he sent Sgt McCall on a scouting trip from Pope Road in the north to Cero Gordo to the south. The major wanted to know exactly what was on the eastern side of the Tennessee River that they had access to raid. Strengths of units, any fortifications, where they had put in ferries and the degree with which the roads were traveled. He also wanted to know where they had built ports and storage facilities.

On his swing north he stopped by Linden one evening after dark and knocked on Mr. Bing's back door. The children had already had their supper but were not in bed.

"Pa, me and Matt can read now."

"Is that right, both of you have learned to read?"

"It's true Pa, show him Matt." Matt picked up his reader and started to read slowly at first and then with more confidence.

"Boy you can read. I am so proud of both of you. Your grandma and grandpa have done well by you."

Tom stayed and talked to the children for another thirty minutes and then tucked them in.

"I can never thank you enough for what you have done for the children. They can read and write. I don't know how I can ever repay you."

"That's ok Tom, they are our kids too."

He walked down stairs and Mr. Bing followed him. "Tom, I got seven more of those Henrys for you and six cases of ammunition. Got them from a man over to the east. I haven't been able to find anymore. And I sent a letter to the factory and they have a waiting list of over two years. They are building them just for the Army. I pity these southern boys when the Union soldiers gets these rifles."

"Yeah, that will be a bad day for the South."

"Let me guess, you got them from a store owner in Hohenwald, right?"

"That is right, how did you know?"

"Information gets around. I will pick up the guns on my way back. I am headed up north for a couple of days. Just make sure you don't give them to anyone else."

As he turned to leave he said, "By the way Mr. Bing, do you know a horse traded by the name of Joe Swafford. I heard he comes through here periodically with horses for sale."

Tom could not see Mr. Bings face in the shadow, but felt the hesitation in the voice when he said, "Don't think I ever heard the name. But there are a few horse traders who come through here. Could be one of them. Why, do you need horses?"

"No, but I lost my mules and I am going to need to buy some soon."

Completely recovered, Mr. Bing said, "I will ask around to see if anyone has any for sale. Hard to find any stock with the war going on. But you already know that."

"That's okay, hell, I might just have to steal them." And he laughed.

Tom shook hands with Mr. Bing and rode away up Main Street.

Mr. Bing breathed a sigh of relief. He was now happy that his instincts were correct; first of all to hold the guns for Tom and second, to tell him the truth about where he got them. Now he was even more worried about Tom finding out that he knew who set him up. He would have to check to make sure Bill was not around for Tom to find.

Tom was sure now that his father in law knew more than he was telling, and he would have to decide what if anything he would say or do. The Bings were taking good care of the children and it seemed less and less important that he should take revenge. He would decide when the time came.

Chapter Thirteen

Tom rode northwest towards the Tennessee River when he began his scouting trip. He was an imposing figure. He wore civilian clothes with a western style hat. Two big pistols tucked into his wide leather belt. A big steady horse with a Union officer saddle and harness. His Henry was under his right leg ready for action. He avoided the main roads and rode quietly along little traveled trails that he knew well. He had been raised in these hills and knew the people with their strengths and weaknesses. He knew how to talk to people regardless of their positions or stature in their communities. He could make the professor feel dumb and the idiot feel smart. He could play the victim or bully whichever role was called for. He was the right man for this job.

He was to scout the entire river starting at Pope Road and the land on the east side of the Tennessee River out to the ten mile limit. He rode virtually every mile along the route and talked to every person he felt could give him information without compromising his mission. He did not expect trouble but was ready for it. On his third day he stopped into a small country store under the pretense of getting something for his pain in his leg. He often used the wounded leg to break the ice or as an excuse for stopping to talk to people. As he rode up, he noticed two men setting on the porch, he dismounted and exaggerating his limp entered the store.

Before he was able to talk to the clerk a voice from behind him said, "Ain't you that feller whose wife was killed on the train?"

The other man who had entered with the first one said, "Yeah, you are that feller that got his wife killed. Ain't you?"

Tom turned and looked at the men individually sizing them up just in case they were not friendly. 'Yeah, my name is Tom McCall."

"See Skeeter, I told you it was him. Mister that was a low down thing to do shooting your little lady. Did the government pay you any money for shooting your wife?"

The one called Skeeter said, "I heard they gave you a thousand dollars for them killing your wife."

"Skeeter, it wasn't one thousand it was two thousand they gave him."

"Gentlemen, I am afraid what you have heard is a big lie. Them Yankees didn't give me a dime for killing my wife. But they did let me out of prison."

Tom turned to the man behind the counter and said loud where everyone could hear him, "Sir, do you have anything for severe pain. My leg is all infected and hurting like hell."

"I got some laudanum which folks say is the best for pain."

"How much is that? I only have a little over two dollars. "I'm on my way back to my farm."

"It's a quarter."

Tom paid the clerk and started to leave. The two men were still inside the store and had not taken their eyes off him. Tom touched the tip of his hat to them and left the store. As he mounted up he noticed the two men had come outside and watched him leave.

He rode down the road about three hundred yards, then he suddenly turned off the road and stopped behind some thick brush and waited. If he was right, the two men would be tailing him and he would wait for them. They had messed it up so he could not talk to the clerk about what union activity there was around here, so maybe they could tell him.

He waited what seemed like fifteen minutes when he heard riders coming fast. He waited to make sure of who was following him and when he was sure it was the two from the store, he rode out and stopped in front of them. Surprised, they reigned in their horses so hard they reared up almost dropping their rides.

Tom said, "You boys looking for me?"

Tom had both colts drawn and level at them, they did not move. Tom slid off his horse and motioned for the riders to dismount. They dismounted and he relieved them of their pistols and the one called Skeeter had a knife that he took. The one called Skeeter was well over six foot and huge. His partner was about five eight with a slight limp. Tom figured he was in charge.

"Lead your horses and follow me."

Tom led them about twenty yards off the road. "Tie your horses in case I need them to put your bodies on after we talk."

"Why you stopping us on the road, we weren't bothering nobody."

"Yeah, we didn't do nothing. You can't just pull down on somebody."

"Gentlemen in the store back there you seemed overly interested in some money you thought the government give to me, and I just have to make sure you did not intend to search my dead body for that money. Maybe to reassure me, you can start by telling what your names are and what business you are in."

"That ain't none of your business. We weren't bothering you. But now you done made us mad. If you know what's good for you you'll let us go. We know people."

"Shut up Skeeter."

"You boys aren't from around here are you? What side of the war are you on and don't lie to me. I have ways to tell which side you are on. I noticed your boots. See you can tell a lot about a man's boots."

"What's wrong with our boots? These are brand new."

"Shut up Skeeter. You dumb bastard."

"Stop telling me to shut up and you the dumb one. I told you we should have just shot him in the store, but you wanted to wait. He told us to ambush him on the road but you wanted to wait, hoping he would lead us to his money. Now look at us. So you are the dumb bastard."

The small one reached in his boot and took out a small pistol and shot Skeeter and then started to point it at Tom. Tom did not hesitate. He fired his big colt and when the smoke cleared the little man was sprawled on his back covered in blood. Tom cursed under his breath. "Damn, I wanted to talk to them. I should have checked their boots for guns."

He knew the little one was dead, but the other one might still be alive. Hard to kill a big man with a small gun.

Bending over him he said, "Skeeter, are you alive?"

Skeeter rolled over on his back and raised up. It surprised Tom that he sat up, but made him glad. He wanted to talk to him and find out who sent them to kill him.

"Is Bill dead?"

"Yeah, you partner is dead. How do you feel?"

"It hurts like hell. It burns like fire."

"Lie still and I will see if I can help you." The man had been shot in the gut and would die a slow painful death with or without seeing a doctor, but Tom lied, "I Know a doctor close by that can help you, but I will take you there only if you tell me what I want to know."

"I don't know nothing."

"Well, you can lie here and die and you will never see your family again, and your mother will never know what happened to you."

"If I talk will you take me to a doctor and let my mother know I am ok?"

Tom lied again, "I will get you a doctor and ride to let your mother know you are ok."

"It was all Bill's idea. Someone in Linden ask him to get rid of you. They told him it was either Bill or you. Seems like Bill was in on some kind of horse trading deal that turned into an ambush with you winding up in the prison."

"Who was it in Linden hired Bill?"

"I don't know. I swear I don't know. Bill just hired me to help him. He was afraid they would kill him if he didn't kill you."

"What is Bill's last name?"

"His name is Bill Anderson."

"So now we know Bill's last name."

Tom believed Skeeter and anyway he thought he knew who had hired them to kill him. Tom learned early in the war that his job was to kill the enemy before they killed him or one of your friends. At first it made him feel ill when he killed a man. But in a large and furious battle one had to kill many men or they would kill you. At some point, he had killed so many that it no longer bothered him. There was no right or wrong on the battle field. You killed and lived for your fellow soldier. Tom was like the majority of the soldiers. He didn't even know what states' rights was nor did he give a damn. And he never owned a slave or knew anyone who did and he had no opinion either for or against the practice. He joined the fight because he was bored at home and tired of his dirt-farming existence. Now, the fight was personal, and he would not stop until the person who he felt was responsible for his troubles was dead.

In this case, he knew Skeeter would die a painful death and no one could save him. He took Skeeter's knife and slipped it under the ribs directly into the big man's heart. Skeeter died instantly. He then fired a shot from Skeeter's pistol and dropped it beside him. The other pistol he dropped beside Bill. Tom made the scene look like the two men had killed each other. Tom searched the big man finding the usual things; tobacco, pocket knife, some change. He also found a twenty dollar gold piece and that was unusual. As he took another one out of Bills pocket, he clinked them together in his hand and said out loud, "Payment for a job not done."

He untied the dead men's horses leaving them to wander around wherever, and then mounted up and rode on south. He finished his sweep of the north of Linden and rode to camp to report to Major Shy. He also needed to pick up the rifles from Mr. Bing. He wondered if Mr. Bing would be surprised to see him. On second thought, he would send someone else to get the guns and see how Mr. Bing reacted. Sgt Daniels knew Mr. Bing, so he would ask him to go.

Tom gave his report to Major Shy and the rest of the staff. It was thorough and concise covering every road, river crossing, every building, and back trail north of Linden. The report included the name and location of everyone he talked to, with the information they provided about troop movements and who was friendly and who was on the other side.

Many of the staff grew up in Middle Tennessee and when they heard information about the areas they knew, they would speak up and affirm the information, or say they knew the person Tom had mentioned in his report.

Major Shy finally said, "A blind man could use this report to attack any target in the area. When will you be ready to leave to scout the south?"

"I will be ready tomorrow sir."

"Good. Take off when you are ready."

"Sir I have found those seven Henrys and if you don't mind I would like to ask Sgt Daniels to pick them up. I will give him the details. It will be forty dollars each plus the ammunition."

"Give him the details and tell him to stop by when he is ready to go."

Tom found Sgt Daniels after the staff meeting. "James, I have to ask a favor of you. While I am scouting down south of Linden, will go into Linden and get some guns from my father in law. You remember where it is at right?"

"Sure, no problem."

"Another thing James, tell him the reason I didn't come was that you had not seen or heard from me in over a week. I don't want him to know where I am or in what kind of health I am in. I will explain it to you in more details later."

"No problem Tom, I understand."

They shook hands and Tom mounted and rode off.

Chapter Fourteen

Tom rode to his farm, since it was on his way, intending to check on the place and spend the night. The road in was rough so he rode slowly letting his horse pick his footing. He had just came within sight of the little house when he noticed he had picked up a small branch on his stirrup, and as he leaned over to pull it out, he heard a gunshot and he rolled off his horse and lay still. He waited until the shooter had walked up to him and poked him with his gun when he moved. He pulled the gun and kicked at the same time sending the man flying back over an old stump, and he lay there moaning. Tom stood over him with his Colt drawn.

"Wild Bill McCall, what in the hell are trying to kill me for? Hell, all you had to do is ask and I would deeded this place to you. You didn't have to try to kill me."

"Damn, boy I didn't even know you – you lost a lot of weight. Didn't they feed you in that damn prison?"

Tom held out his hand and the man took it and Tom pulled him up. They hugged and walked to the little house.

"What the hell are you doing here Bill?"

"Well, things were heating up over where I live. You might say I got myself into a little bit of trouble. You see, like a lot of people now days, I can't hardly decide which side I want to be on in this here war. So, you might say, I am neutral. I just try to do the right thing as I see it. But some people just can't leave a person along with his own beliefs. And I am the kind of person who insists that I be left along which led to my last little bit of trouble."

"So how in the hell have you been cousin?"

"Well if I could just get this damn leg fixed I would be ok."

"What the hell is wrong with your leg?"

"Caught a bullet that nicked the bone. Can't get it to heal."

"There is a doctor in Hohenwald by the name of Dr. Boyce who is the absolute best. He fixed me up a couple times when I got shot."

"Are you hungry? I cooked some beans and squirrel and even baked some cornbread. I thought I would find someone living here, but no one has used the trail in. So I just made myself at home. You left a lot of food stores here. Guess you had to leave in a hurry."

"Didn't you hear about my wife getting killed?"

"Yea, I heard that but I figured you would move back here with the kids."

"Well, I had some stuff to do before moving back. So you are welcome to stay as long as you want."

"Thanks cousin. I knew I could count on you."

The next morning Tom cooked up some breakfast and said bye to Bill. He told Bill not to tell anyone that he had met him. Bill agreed without asking any questions. Wild Bill McCall was Tom's first cousin. He was about five years older than Tom and Tom had always looked up to Bill who was always a reckless boy and man. Bill was quick tempered and quick to shoot. A good man to have on your side in a fight. The fact that he stole from both sides of the war did not surprise Tom but seeing Bill still alive and well and in his house did surprise him. He thought aloud, "Maybe Bill had heard the rumors about the money I supposedly got from the government, and was looking for it. Can't trust anyone when money is involved."

He looked over his shoulder as he rode out of sight of his house and Bill was still on the porch.

He had a week of hard riding ahead of him and his leg was hurting him more each day. He did not want to take too much laudanum because it dulled his senses. He needed to be sharp at all times. The told himself he would go to the doctor when his scouting was done.

He covered every inch of his territory and on the morning of the sixth day he briefed Major Shy and his staff. While he was down south, Major Shy had sent Captain Wright's command to the north and he had kicked the hell out any Union units he could find. Burned twenty two barges and four tug boats as well as three large weapons/ammunition storage facilities. They had captured numerous Tennessee Federals and had taken them to the prison down south in Alabama. The rest of the Tennessee Federals would think twice before entering the land of the 20th Tennessee Mounted Infantry. With every other man using a Henry, they were no match for Major Shy firepower. When the Brigade Commander heard that Major Shy had been able to acquire Henry, he called him to Headquarters to brief him. After that, the word went out for all the Tennessee units to look high and low to get those guns.

The rest of the summer and into the fall Tom's unit kept the pressure on in their little part of the war. He was so busy fighting and running that he had no time to go to the doctor. But it soon became clear that he had to get something done.

He stopped by to see the children three or four times and the first time he knocked on the door, Mr. Bing seemed very surprised to see him. He nervously chewed on his pipe stem the whole time Tom was there. He would not look Tom in the eye. He still was not sure if Tom knew about him, and if he did then why didn't Tom confront him so he could deny his involvement. After Bill Anderson disappeared, he had hoped it would die down and Tom would not find out. The children had grown so much that Matt was becoming a young man. He was nearly six foot tall towering over his classmates even those older than him. And he could more than handle himself in a fight which he had on few occasions.

Chapter Fifteen

Major Shy called him into his tent. "Tom, I know you have been putting off seeing a surgeon until our many campaigns were over. Well, we are going to hunker down for the winter, so the time has come for you to get that leg checked out."

"Yes, sir. In fact there is a very fine surgeon in Hohenwald that I heard about. I will ride over there and get it fixed if that is alright with you."

"Good, take off as soon as possible. Do you want me to assign someone to accompany you?"

"No sir, I have someone who will go with me."

"Ok, see you when you get back."

Tom rode to his farm and was very careful to approach on foot making sure he did not get shot. He moved off the road about a mile from his house and climbed a steep hill, following the hollow down to his house. Smoke was coming from the chimney, so he knew someone was there. He quietly walked up on the back porch and opened the door. Will Bill was lying on the bed. "Are you sick?"

As quick as a man can move, Wild Bill McCall rolled across the floor and his hands were full of cocked pistols.

"Whoa, don't shoot, it's me."

"Dang boy, you damn near scared me to death, and you come very close to getting kilt."

Bill shoved his pistols into his belt and held out his hand. "How have you been cousin?"

"Not so good. This damn leg is still killing me. In fact that is the reason I am here. I wonder if you might accompany me to that doctor in Hohenwald, and watch my back while I go under the knife?"

"I would be glad to accompany you and watch your back. Be glad to get out of this cabin. Course I am broke not having stolen anything lately."

Tom reached in his pocket and took out the two twenty dollar gold pieces and pitched them to Bill. "Will this be enough to get you by for a while? And before you ask, the answer is no. The government, neither ours nor theirs, did not give me any money for the killing of my wife. I took these two coins from a couple of bad men I killed a while back."

"Well I had heard the rumor that you had some money, but I didn't believe it. I knew you would have taken the money and your kids and gotten out of this country."

"After the war, I aim to head out west with my children. I am going to get enough money out of this war so I can buy a place out west and start a farm or ranch as they call it out there. Do you want to go?"

"Sounds good to me. If I can stay ahead of the law that long."

At supper they talked about when they were young boys roaming the hills hunting and the creeks fishing. They were the best of friends even though Bill was older. Bill started feeling that old loyalty coming back to him and hoped that he and Tom would become friends again. His going along with Tom and covering his back would bring them closer than they had been in fifteen years. Bill had married when he was young but his wife and only child died of influenza three years after he married. He never married again. He roamed around the country making a living however he could. He never got into any real trouble until after the war started. Then when people started pressuring everyone to take sides, he resented being pushed, and had pushed back a couple of times. He had made some enemies in the east and was careful not to go back that way. Even going to Hohenwald with his cousin might put him in danger, if the right people found out where he was. But he hadn't gotten the nickname of Will Bill for no good reason. He was a rough man with quick hands and he was as big as Tom before Tom got sent to prison.

Prior to the war, Hohenwald was a just wide spot in the road. But, now it was a crossroads of the two armies in Tennessee. The people of Hohenwald did not know from day to day whether to play Dixie or the Battle Hymn of the Republic. When Tom and Bill rode into Hohenwald it happened to be under Confederate control. But they did not relax their vigil. They rode in after dark directly to Dr. Boyce's house and knocked on the door. A young black woman came to the door and led them back into the doctor's waiting room. In a minute a small man came into the room and said, "Wild Bill McCall, have you been shot again?"

Bill laughed and said, "No sir, Doctor. This time my cousin has the problem. He got shot almost a year ago and it hasn't healed very well."

"Ok, then come on back gentlemen."

"Take off your pants. What is your name besides cousin?"

"Name is Tom McCall. I appreciate you seeing me."

"It's ok, I see a lot of folks lately."

After examining his leg, Dr. Boyce said, "Son, that leg is in very bad shape and to be very honest, I don't know if we will be able to save it. The fact that you have lived with it all this time is a miracle."

"Sir, I would appreciate it if you could try to save it. I have two children that I have to take care of and I have a war to fight. So please do everything you can to save it."

"I will open it up tomorrow morning and see what I can do. I can't make any promises, but I will try. You and Bill can stay here tonight in the back room and I will wake you up early to get started."

"Thank you doctor."

"Bill, I know your reputation of being a wild and rough man, but I have known you all my life and know there is a soft and nurturing side also. I want to ask you to take care of my children if anything happens to me. I know it is a lot to ask, but I don't have anyone I can turn to. I do not trust their grandfather. I suspect he was the one who set me up to get killed or to go to prison. I will take care of him in my own due time but I need a place for the children to stay for the time being. I am telling you because I don't want you to trust him. Somehow and someway he was involved getting sent to prison."

"Tom, I will be happy to take care of the children so you don't have to worry. But I have faith in the doctor that he will fix you up as good as new."

The doctor gave Tom an extra dose of Laudanum to help him sleep that night and for the first time in a long time, Tom slept. He awoke rested and ready for anything.

A middle aged nurse came in and got him ready for the surgery and before eight, Tom was under the knife. Bill waited outside, sometimes pacing and sometimes cursing and sometimes sleeping. But he never left the building, always on guard with his pistols loosely tucked in his belt.

"Mr. McCall, you are a very lucky man. I was able to easily find the infected areas. They are bloody pus pockets where the splinters of the bone were not removed. I was able to clean out five before I had to sew you back up. You were losing a lot of blood and I could not chance staying in any longer. We will get the rest later."

Still groggy from the ether, Tom shook his head, or at least he thought he shook his head. He wasn't sure so he managed to say, "Thank you doctor."

"Nurse, put him in the recovery room and ask his friend to come in."

"Your cousin is very lucky. I was able to find and take out five bone fragments. There are more that need to come out but I could not keep him out any longer. He would have bled to death."

"So you will need to go back in for more fragments?"

"That's right. He should be strong enough for me to go back in in a couple of months with lots of rest and good food."

"Well, I will make sure he gets what he needs. Can I see him?"

"Yeah, you can go back and stay with him while he is waking up. He will not be able to travel for a week at least. Do you have a place to stay locally? Also, I will want to see him in three days or before if he starts bleeding."

"We will be in the local boarding house. I will bring him in."

"How you felling, cuz?"

"Like I been run over by a team of horses. Could you holler for that nurse and tell her to bring me some Laudanum."

Bill was true to his word and took good care of Tom. He made sure he made it back to the doctor in three days and once the week was up, they started home. Tom was still in very much pain and was running a high fever on their way home so they could not travel very far each day.

During the war, so many people were on the move that many people opened up their homes for people to stay. Of course, they expected to be paid for the bed and board. But it was worth it. It was downright dangerous traveling and staying out in the open, especially with a sick man. Not that Wild Bill McCall gave a damn about danger, but he had to consider Tom, so he looked for a place to stay inside.

"Be dark soon Tom, we better find a place to hold up for tonight. You ain't looking so good. I have a friend who lives about five miles from here, maybe they will let us stay the night in their barn."

"That is fine with me. My dang leg is starting to hurt something awful."

In a couple of miles, they turned off the main road and rode up a rutted dirt trail.

"Just a mile or so up this trail and we will be there."

As they made a turn in the road, they saw a bright light in the sky.

Tom said, "Looks like something is burning." And he spurred his horse into a gallop.

As they got close they could tell that a barn was on fire. They did not think to be cautious but rode up to the barn. They pulled up quickly when they saw a boy fixed to the barn door. Bill slid off his horse and ran to the young man. Tom slid down and limped up to where Bill was trying to figure out a way to get the young man down. He was looking around for something to cut the wire. The young man who looked to be around fifteen, had been bound to the barn door with barbed wire. It was then that Tom pulled his guns and started looking around for someone who had done this to the boy. Bill found some plyers and cut the wire and eased the body down to the ground. He then moved to the house cautiously opening the door and moving inside. Tom waited outside making sure no one would ambushed them. When Bill came outside, his face told it all. He pointed towards the house and said, "Sarah and Jane inside there, dead."

Tom went inside and saw a woman in her thirties and a young girl, maybe thirteen, in separate beds. They had been brutally murdered.

"They had another young boy. We have to find him."

As they were looking for the young boy, they heard a couple of horses coming and men talking loud. They moved their horses behind some trees and waited.

In a couple of minutes two Tennessee Federals rode up. One of the soldiers said, "I can't believe you left your damn rifle here. You are lucky the lieutenant didn't just shoot you instead of letting you come back to retrieve it."

"Well, hell I didn't leave it here on purpose. If you remember correctly, we was busy. While the lieutenant and the rest were busy fixing that boy to the barn, we were busy in the house."

"What happened to the baby?"

"I left him in the chicken coop."

"Ok, get your damn rifle and let's catch up with the rest."

"They will wait for us at the bridge."

As soon as the soldier came out of the house with his retrieved rifle Tom shot him in the gut and then walked up to him and shot him in the head. At the same time the other soldier, who had not dismounted, was shot by Bill.

"Do you know what bridge they would be talking about?"

"Yeah, I think so."

"Let's take care of the soldiers and then come back here to bury these folks."

They put on the soldiers coats and hats and rode their horses towards the meeting place. They didn't know how many soldiers they would find so they were very careful.

As they approached the bridge someone said, "That you boys? Did you get your rifle?"

Tom said in a muffled voice, "Got it. Just where I left it."

"Well hurry up, we need to get out of here."

As good as they could tell, there were about six of them. And Bill whispered, "Six."

They were all mounted and ready to ride. Tom and Bill rode up closer and opened fire killing four right away. Two of the soldiers had been able to ride off into the woods and it took Bill and Tom another five minutes to find them. Tom shot and killed the one he found, but Bill rode down the one he was chasing. He hit him with his gun knocking him out of his saddle. Once he was on the ground he yelled for Tom.

Tom rode up and dismounted. When he saw it was a lieutenant, he said, "Great, you got their leader. Is he still alive?"

"Yeah, I made sure of that. He has a lot to answer to."

They put the lieutenant on his horse and led him back to the farm. When they got to the farm the first place Bill checked was the chicken house. He found the body of a young boy of about five years old. The boy had been killed by a blow to his head. Probably a butt of a rifle. Bill picked up the little body and brought him outside and laid him at the feet of the lieutenant. He grabbed the lieutenant by the throat and would have chocked him to death if not for Tom.

Bill broke down and began to sob.

Tom picked up the lieutenant and dragged him into the house where the bodies of the woman and young girl were. He sat him down at the dining table and found some paper and pencil.

"Write a complete report of what went on at this farm today. Don't leave out one little detail or I will cut off one of your hands."

The lieutenant was writing his statement when Bill came into the house. The lieutenant got up and moved away, afraid of Bill. But Bill just sat down at the table. Tom moved the lieutenant back to table and sat him back down.

Bill said, "Tell me one thing. Why did you do this? Don't lie."

The lieutenant knew by Bill's voice that he was right on the edge and just as soon kill him as not. He said, "Calvin Jones was initially a part of our unit until he changed sides. Once he changed sides and went into the Confederate Army, we had to make an example of him."

"Why did he change sides?"

"He never believed in our cause and only joined because of his cousin. But after he saw how we operated, he got cold feet and ran away."

"Yeah, I see how you operate."

"Ok, write it down and don't leave out anything. Make sure you name the people in charge of your unit and who gives the orders."

Once the report was finished to the satisfaction to Bill and Tom. They made the lieutenant sign it. Then they pushed him outside and made him dig four graves and bury the dead.

When they left the farm, the lieutenant was hanging from the hay loft pulley. He had written a detailed report on what had transpired at the little farm with all the gory details. The report named names and operating tactics of the Tennessee Federals and their allies.

On their way back to Tom's farm they stopped by the Crossroads Post office and sent the report to the Chattanooga Daily Rebel newspaper. When the report hit the newspapers it was a sensation. The Union tried to disown the units involved, but they could not. It sent the rats into their hiding places and many of the prominent players were found dead under mysterious circumstances.

No one ever knew where the report came from or who released it to the newspapers. Calvin Jones became a Confederate hero, was commissioned a 2nd Lieutenant, and survived the war. So devastated by his loss, he never returned to his little farm. After the war, he wound up in Pulaski Tennessee and was one of the original founders of the Ku Klux Klan.

They rode silently back to Tom's farm. The only time the incident at the farm was mentioned between them was when Bill said, "I am far from being a saint. I have killed men. But what can make a man so crazy and mean that he would nail a young boy to a burning barn, rape women and little girls, and kill babies?"

Of course Tom had no answer and didn't say anything. He had never seen Bill in such a sorrowful mood and was worried about him.

Once they arrived at Tom's farm, they settled in but kept vigil. Any supplies they needed they were able to get at the crossroads. When Tom was feeling well enough he told Bill he had to report to Major Shy and see what was going on. Bill tried to talk him out of it, but Tom was a good soldier and the next morning he rode off.

Chapter Sixteen

It was November and the trees were turning to all colors and losing their leaves, making traveling through the woods a problem. Not only could you be heard but you could be easily seen. Tom was very careful on his way to the headquarters. Lots of people would like to find their winter compound. And they would pay good money for the location.

Late in the first day, he had the feeling he was being followed. He was a woodsman, so he knew ways to find out if someone was tailing him. He kicked his horse to speed up a little and when he came to the next big tree with a low hanging branch he could reach. He kicked his horse a little faster, so he would go a piece before he stopped. He swung up on a limb, and quickly moved towards the tree trunk and hid on the other side of the tree. In a few minutes Tom saw three riders coming up the trail. They were riding slowly and were not talking at all. Normal travelers will talk as they ride along. Riding is boring and people talk to entertain themselves. So Tom knew they were being careful. As they rode under his tree, he dropped down behind them and yelled, "Stop your horses and turn around with your hands empty."

They were startled and one of them started to ride off. Tom shot him and he fell but stood right up holding his arm. The other two turned around with their hands up high.

"Get down slowly and back up to me."

The two men complied without hesitation. They already knew this man was no one to rile up. Tom stripped them of their hand guns and this time he check their boots and found a small piston tucked in the smaller ones right boot. The wounded man had moved over with the others.

"Where you boys going to?"

"We on our way home. We tired of this here war."

"Why are you following me?"

"Sir, we didn't know we was following you."

"Really? Do I look like I was born yesterday? I tell you right now, my leg is starting to hurt me something awful from climbing that damn tree, and I ain't in the mood to listen to your lying. So one of you need to start talking, otherwise I will just leave your damn bodies here on the trail."

The men could see that Tom's leg was bleeding through the bandages and his pants and knew he was not kidding about his leg, and probably was not in the mood to be lied to. The man who had been shot spoke first.

"Sir, we are looking for the headquarters of Major Shy command."

"Shut up Reese."

"You shut up. I don't want to die here on this damn trail. I have two children in Knoxville waiting for me."

The man that had not spoken lunged for the one they called Reese. "You son-of-a –bitch."

Tom hit him behind the ear with his piston and he fell.

"I am tired of killing men from Tennessee. I am tired of killing the children of Tennessee mothers. I am tired of killing. But if you don't give me the information I need right now, I am going to kill you. Do you understand?"

The one Tom shot from his horse spoke, "Sir, we are scouts for the Tennessee Federals. We were sent to follow you to Major Shy winter camp."

"How did you know to follow me? Who told you that I was in Major Shy's unit?"

"We were given our instructions from Captain Steel. Honest to God, we don't know anymore. Our Captain told us to watch your house and follow you when you left. And that is what we did. He even give Pierce a note and map to your house."

Tom believed what he was hearing.

Tom had a real problem. He knew he should kill these three soldiers but he was tired of killing. What would these men do if he let them go? "If I let you go what will you do?"

Reese said, "I will go home to my kids."

Pointing at the one he shot he ask, "How about you, what would you do?" I really don't have any choice, I have to go back to my unit."

"Do you think when the Yankees win this war they will give a damn about you helping them. All southerns will be treated the same."

"He is right. They won't give a damn about us. Hell they don't give a damn about us now. We get all the shitty jobs. They don't give a damn if we all die."

"Let me tell you something, right now I am about as mad as you will ever see me. My leg is killing me and I am tired and hungry. You are lucky that I have not already killed you where you stand. So each of you better tell me what I need to hear."

"You Reese, if I turned you lose, what would you do and where would you go?"

"Sir, I would get on my horse and go home by the most direct route not talking to anyone."

"Good, you may leave. Get your horse and go fast. Do not look back. And don't ever let me see you again."

Reese reached for his saddle horn and swinging up on his horse rode back the way they came at a fast gallop.

Looking at the man whom he had shot he said, "What is your name?"

"William Holt."

"Mr. Holt, if I turn you lose what will you do and where will you go?"

"You son of a bitch, you think you can scare …" Before he could finish, the top of his head exploded.

Looking at the last man he ask, "What is your name?"

"Pierce Jones."

"Mr. Jones, if I let you go what will you do and where will you go?"

"Sir, I will mount my horse and ride as fast as I can…" Before he finished, he lunged for Tom's gun, but Tom was ready for him and caught him in the chest. He fell at Tom's feet. "Stupid sons of a bitches. For what?"

He tied them to their horse and drug them off the trail where they would not be easily found. He looked through their pockets and found a hand written note with a crude map to his house. And on the bottom of the note was the initials G.S. "Damn, I wonder who the hell this G.S. is. I will have to find out."

He took their guns and ammunition and horses to take to his camp.

He caught his horse and rode on. From now, he would double back frequently and would shoot whoever followed him without conversation.

He arrived at the camp without further incident. He reported to Major Shy who upon seeing Tom said, "Damn Tom you look like you are about to pass out. You need to see the doctor right away. Orderly, call Doctor Philips and ask him to come to my tent."

While Tom was giving Major Shy a full and detailed report about the people who were following him, the doctor came in. Upon seeing Tom's leg, he ask Tom to move to the cot and immediately cut the pants leg and went to work. Tom was shivering from the infection and grimaced as the doctor worked. He dressed the leg and rewrapped it. "Sgt McCall, you have to take better care of this leg." "Yes sir."

Major Shy said, "Sgt McCall, it seems you were right about someone having a personal vendetta against you. Who do you think it is or do you have any idea?"

"I thought at first it was my father-in-law, but know I don't know. I need to find out who this G.S. is. Has to be someone in Linden."

"This is no longer just your problem. This could have been catastrophic if those men had been able to follow you here. We have to get to the bottom of this as soon as possible."

"I agree. In a few days I will ride to Linden to find out what my father in law knows about this whole thing."

"Now that you are here, there is no hurry. They can't find you now but if you leave, then they might follow you back. So just remain here for the rest of the winter then we all will go to Linden. We have been ordered to reinforce Colonel Frierson in Linden in the spring with two thirds of our unit. We will sort out the details later. It will give you time for your leg to heal."

Chapter Seventeen

Matt and Lizzie continued going to school and waited for their father to come for a visit. There were more and more soldiers in town and a lot of the activity was centered on the courthouse right across the street. And of course the store was busier now than ever.

Matt loved helping in the store, especially when they got a new shipment of farm implements or guns in to inventory and put on display. He loved guns and whenever possible, he would take them out of the display and play with them. Practicing fast drawing and twirling the guns on his fingers. He was getting fast on the draw and would show Lizzie. He was growing so fast that they could not keep him in pants. Mrs. Bing would have to get him a new pair almost every month. And they were still inseparable. Matt took care of her every need. Helping her with her school work and any chores her grandmother might assign to her. Matt was also very smart and observant. No one came and went without him knowing about it. And he took special notice of those who came at night. He often listened to the conversations without anyone knowing. One man in particular visited the store after hours about every week. He and his grandpa would talk quietly on the front porch. Matt only understood a little of what they were talking about. It seems that the gentleman's name was George and he had borrowed some money from his grandfather when he first moved to this area. But had since paid it back with interest. He also knew that the man had made a lot of money off the war from his mill of some kind.

As any boy his age, he was interested in the soldiers when they were in town, and often talked to them about their guns or horses. The soldiers liked Matt and were happy to talk to him. They played checkers and occasionally shot dice or gamble with cards. So Matt also learned some men games. But mostly he waited for his father's visits, longing for the day when they could return to their little farm.

Spring came quickly and Major Shy had his orders to report to Linden with his command. Tom was not to stay in Linden but was given permission to go there and find out if possible what was behind the personal attacks on him. When they rode into Linden in bright daylight it was the first time he had been there during the day since early in the war. He immediately went to the store and since the kids were in school he talked to Mr. Bing and confronted him straight up about whether he was involved in the attacks on him. At first Mr. Bing denied any involvement or even knowledge of the incidents.

"Listen Mr. Bing, I know you know more than you are letting on. You do not have to be afraid of me. I would never harm you or Mrs. Bing. You are the grandparents of my children and you have taken care of them all this time. So, if you know anything please let me know."

It was then that Mr. Bing started talking. He told Tom the entire story about how George Sawyer's son was going to marry Mattie and how he had killed himself after she married Tom. And how Mr. Sawyer had taken it so badly and vowed to get his revenge and had come to Mr. Bing to ask his assistance. At first Mr. Bing had supplied him with information and put him in touch with the horse trader and Bill Anderson. But then later he stopped helping him and tried to get Mr. Sawyer to call it off. Mr. Bing said Mr. Sawyer had promised him that he would called it off after Tom returned from prison. But he had not. The last thing he told him was that Mr. Sawyer had been a spy for the north and was helping them with information. He ran an ironworks and kept the north appraised of all the orders from the south and where the shipments were going. That Mr. Sawyer had gotten rich, and was getting ready to go out west someplace.

Curious, Tom asked, "Why did he wait so long to take his revenge?"

"He was afraid to come after you directly. But when the war started, he saw a way to kill you and make it seem like you were killed by the Union soldiers."

"That all sounds crazy. I do not believe that he would wait this long to try to kill me, if he blamed me for his son's death."

"He was busy building up his business and then when he had enough money, he started hiring people to kill you. He said you had deprived him of his only son and heir."

"Maybe when I talk to him, he will tell me why he waited so long."

Tom waited until the children came home from school. They ran to him with Lizzie climbing in his arms, and Matt being so tall that he just hugged him. They sat on the porch drinking tea and talking. It had been a while since they had been together and Tom was very interested in what they had been doing. Tom spent that night at the house and they talked late into the night. For some reason, Tom didn't want to leave, but he had to go.

"I will be back soon and after the war we will go out west and find us a ranch. How does that sound?"

"Does that mean we won't keep our farm?"

"Son, we just can't make a living farming that little piece of land. We will get us a lot of land and cows and horses."

When Tom was ready to leave he shook Matt's hand and scooped up Lizzie into his arms and kissed her and held her tight.

Matt thought he saw a tear in his pa's eye.

Chapter Eighteen

Tom found the major and told him about Mr. Sawyer and the major gave him permission to take care of it in his own way.

Tom rode to Mr. Sawyer's house but the only person there was an old black man.

"Master Sawyer is out of town and won't be back for about a week."

"Did he say where he was going?"

"No sir, didn't happen to say where he be going."

"Does he often leave for a long time?"

"Yes, sir."

"Is his wife here?"

"No sir, his wife left quite a while back."

"Thank you sir."

Tom had worked himself up to confront Mr. Sawyer and he was very upset when he was unable to do so. "God damn it. He has already gone. He knows something."

Tom rode out of town to the Iron Works and ask the man at the gate if he knew where Mr. Sawyer had gone. "Don't know where he went. Didn't even say anything to the manager, just left."

Tom rode back to Linden and reported to Major Shy. "Major, I think something is about to happen around here. Mr. Sawyer seems to have left town and no one knows where he has gone."

"You think there might be an attack on our forces here?"

"Yes sir, otherwise why would he leave at this particular time?"

"Ok, you ride back to the camp and report to Captain Day. Tell him to wait there until he gets orders. I will talk to the Colonel."

"Yes, sir."

Chapter Nineteen

Tom rode to his farm and spent the night there. Bill was not there so he left him a note to stay clear of Linden for a while. He fixed him some food and settled down for the night. He was awaken by a horse nickering and he could tell that it was not his own. He grabbed his hat and his Henry and went out the back door being very quiet. He skirted the barn and came up the path hopefully behind anyone who had ridden up.

Whoever it was, they were not being too quiet. Then he saw them. It was a woman and two half grown children. He stepped out and said in a calm voice. "Good evening, may I help you?"

The children screamed and started to run, but the woman stood her ground. "Mr. Tom, I am Mrs. Kiley from across the ridge over there. We are plum out of food and have been for days, and don't have any money or anything to trade to the store for food. The kids are starving, and we just came over here to see if you could give us some food. We will pay you back whenever we can."

"Why Lena, why haven't you come over here before? There is plenty of food here. I got potatoes under the house in the straw, and plenty of dried beans and peas, and might even have a little bit of that hog I killed before I left. Come inside."

The little family followed Tom inside and he lit a lamp. There was food left on the table that he had prepared when he arrived, and he lit another lamp for the table.

"Sit at the table and I will get you some plates."

Tom got his guests plates and utensils and glasses of water. "Help yourself and eat all you want."

"Thank you Tom. You was always a good man."

Lena put some food in the kid's plate and they started eating before she was through. She looked at Tom and said, "Sorry for their manners, they just so hungry."

"Don't you worry about their manners, let them eat. Your kids are like mine, growing so big."

Tom stoked up the fire in the fireplace, and the one in the cook stove. "Lena, you will spend the night here and go home in the morning."

She smiled and shook her head.

"Where is Ben?"

"I thought you knew, he was killed at Shiloh."

"I am sorry.'

"Lena, my cousin has been staying here for a while. I don't know where he has gotten to but I am sure he will come back here. So be careful of him when he returns. I will write him a note telling him that you are to be given all the food you need for you and the kids, but if you surprise him, he can be rough. So when you approach the house day or night, be sure to yell out your presence. Ok?"

"Okay, I will remember and I will be careful not to surprise him."

"There are a few chickens if the varmints haven't taken them yet. You can take them to your place, and if you keep them penned in for a while, they will accept their new home. Also, there is a big hog here someplace, if you can catch her, you can take her. There is a milk cow, but she will need to be bred before she will have milk. You can also take her. I am not sure if we will return to farm here, but if we decide to leave, I will let you know. In the meantime, please take the food as you need it."

The kids had eaten all they could eat and were getting sleepy. Tom told her where to put the children to bed, and told her that she could have his bed, he would sleep on the floor by the fire. She was so tired, she just fell into the bed without saying another word.

When Lena woke up, she looked around for Tom, but he was not there. And his horse was gone.

She made the kids some food and woke them up. Once they had eaten, she sent her son under the house to collect some Irish potatoes and sweet potatoes. She and her daughter went into the storeroom, and collected some dried goods. Afterwards, she collected a few eggs from the henhouse. They would have to come back for the chickens, and would come back when they needed more food.

Lena was overwhelmed and full of gratitude for Tom and his kindness. He would never know how close to starving she and her kids were. She would have done anything for Tom. Anything. She whispered to the heavens, "God bless Tom McCall."

When she got home she reached inside her pocket to get her handkerchief and a gold coin fell out. She picked it up and looked at it and had to set down. It was a twenty dollar gold piece. "Tom."

Chapter Twenty

Tom rode on to the camp circling back occasionally, to make sure he was not being followed. He reported to Captain Day who was awaiting his return to give him an update of the situation in Linden. He also told him he felt something was about to happen there. "It could be nothing, but I just have one of those feeling, and the fact the rats are deserting the ship reinforces my belief."

"Well, you told Major Shy your concerns and that is all that you can do. We have to stay here to await orders."

There were fewer than twenty men in camp with the rest being in Linden. Tom took the opportunity to let his leg heal. He felt strong enough for another round with the Dr. Boyce, but he did not know where to find Wild Bill. He had decided that in a few weeks he would go back to his farm and if Bill was not there, he would go to the crossroads. He would have to put off his revenge on Mr. Sawyer until he returned. That is, if he ever returned. He at least felt better about Mr. Bing's involvement in the conspiracy.

Chapter Twenty-one

A week after her meeting with Tom and her good fortune, Lena put her two children on her old horse and went to the Crossroads. She needed some things from the store and now she had money to pay for them.

When Lena walked into the store with her two children. She was carrying a double barreled shotgun and an oil can.

Mrs. Singer said, "Lena, how are you? And Dorothy and Eden, how are you? We have not seen you in over a year. Are you ok. Hon, I heard about Dan. I am so sorry."

"This old war has touched everybody I guess. Nothing is the same anymore."

"Yeah, lots of the families have moved out of this area. And of course you heard what happened to your neighbor, Tom and his family."

"Yeah, I just saw Tom about a week ago, we went to his farm. He even gave us some food. He is a real gentleman."

"Yes, he has always been a good man. He hasn't been by here since he got out of prison, guess he is busy."

"I need some things. Can of lard, twenty pounds of cornmeal, box of salt, a can of kerosene, and this candy for the children. How much do I owe you from before?"

"Let me check. Four dollars and sixty five cents."

"Ok, I want to pay that also."

Lena put her hand in her pocket and took out her handkerchief and untied the knot and handed Mrs. Singer a shiny twenty dollar gold piece. There was a skinny young man, with a scraggly little beard that grows when a young man doesn't shave, leaning against the wall in the corner of the store, watching a checker game between Mr. Singer and another man. He had not seemed interested in the goings on with Lena and Mrs. Singer, until he saw Lena untie her handkerchief and take out the gold piece. Then he moved a little closer and took a better look at Lena, but then he settled back into the corner.

"Lord Lena, what did you do, rob a bank?" "Oh, no Tom loaned it to me until I get the money for my husband's death."

Lena leaned in close to Mrs. Singer and whispered, "Tom gave it to me. He put it in my pocket when I wasn't looking."

Lena dabbed the tears from her eyes and wiped her nose on her apron. Mrs. Singer came out from behind the counter and hugged her. "Lena, why don't you stay her for the night? We can have some supper and visit."

"That would be nice, thank you."

Mrs. Singer leaned over Mr. Singer and talked to him a minute, and he got up and went outside and ask his helper to take care of Lena's horse.

When Mr. Singer came back in the store, Mrs. Singer led Lena and the children into the back of the store, and sat them down at the kitchen table. She got the children some cake and milk, and poured Lena a cup of coffee.

The next morning after breakfast, Lena rode back to her home feeling better about her life. Spring was in the air, and she felt like she could go on. She would plant her corn, and her garden, and raise her children.

Three days after Lena returned to her farm she decided it was a good time to go get the chickens and while she was at it, she would look for the hog. As she came up the road leading the horse with Dorothy and Eden she noticed there were fresh horse tracks and figured that Tom was home or maybe his cousin was there. She had her shotgun over her arm and yelled into the little farm house, "Tom, are you there? Tom, its Lena, are you there?"

When she got no answer she yelled, "Tom said we could take his chickens so we came for them. Are you his cousin?"

Feeling a little uneasy, Eden said, "Let's go momma."

Before they could turn to leave, a skinny young man and an older bigger man walked out on the porch.

"Yeah, we're Tom's cousins. Come on in."

"Momma, let's get out of here. I saw that young man in the store down in Crossroads before when we were there."

As Lena turned the horse and started to leave she heard a gunshot, and a bullet whizzed by her head. She stopped and half turned and raised her shotgun and fired both barrels. Lena immediately reloaded. Her shot had caught the bigger man full midsection, and peppered the skinny one. He lay on the porch yelling, "You bitch. You shot me. You crazy bitch. I will kill you and your little brats to."

Lena turned and looked at her children and handed the reign to Eden. "Ride back down the trail and wait for me."

Lena turned and walked up closer to the porch. The little one was still yelling obscenities. The children heard a loud gunshot and turned and rode back to check on their mother. She was standing over the two men who lay there quietly.

After it was over, Lena got week in the knees and sat on the edge of the porch to recover. "Eden you and Dorothy bring up these men's horses. We will have to come back later to get the chickens."

She pulled the horses close to the porch and managed to get both men onboard. She took them into the deep woods to dispose of the bodies. She told Eden and his sister to stay by the house. When she got to a place where she could roll them down a deep gully, she pushed them down from the horses. As an afterthought she decided to search them. She took their guns, ammunition, and knives and hung them on the horses. Then she went through their pockets. Each had a pocket knife and some change, and a bright and shiny twenty dollar gold piece. She could not believe it. She did not know what to do. Who were these men, and what were they doing here? After pushing the bodies down into the gully, she mounted up on one of the horses and led the other one. She went back to Tom's house and went in to leave a note. She did not want to tell what had happened on a note, so she just ask Tom to stop by her house when he came back. Then she rode home with two more horses than she started the day with, and forty dollars richer, and the confidence to be able to take care of herself and her children.

Chapter Twenty-two

Two weeks later Tom rode up to Lena's house and hollered for her.

The kids were the first to come outside and then Lena. "Tom, how are you? Come in, come in."

"How have you been Lena?"

"Thanks Tom, your little gift made all the difference in the world. The kids are fed and I am ready to plant the corn."

"They do look better than the last time I saw you. You left a note that I should come see you. What happened?"

Lena told him the entire story of the two men. When she had finished she held out her hand and showed Tom two shiny twenty dollar gold pieces.

"Where did you get those?"

"From the pockets of the two dead men."

"So it continues."

"What do you mean?"

Tom told Lena about what had been happening to him and who he suspected was behind it. When Tom finishes telling her the story, she held out her hand as to give the gold coins to him.

"No, those belong to you. You probably saved my life."

"Take them, they belong to you."

"No, you will need them to buy seed and for the next winter."

"At least take one of them."

"No, you did the work and you will need all you can get to raise your children. This damn war won't last forever."

"Eden, go take care of Mr. McCall's horse, he will be spending the night here."

"No, I can't stay, I have to go."

"Where do you have to go? How long has it been since you had a decent home cooked meal and a good night's sleep?"

"Ok, you talked me into it."

After supper, when the kids had already gone to bed, he sat and talked to Lena.

"Do you mind if I put my foot up in your chair. My leg is pounding like hell."

Without saying a word, she sat down in front of Tom and gently pulled off his boots. First the good leg and then very gently she pulled off the boot of his injured leg. She got a cushion from the living room and put it in the kitchen chair and places his foot on it. "Does that feel better?"

"Much, thank you."

She washed the dishes and put the food up. She dried her hands on her apron and walked into the other room to check on the children. Coming back she said, "They are asleep."

She moved around to his front and bent down and released his belt careful to not drop his Colts. He did not know what she was doing but he did not protest. She unbuttoned his pants and slipped them down and off his feet. She was surprised to see that the leg of his long john of his bandaged leg had been cut off. She untied the bandage on his leg first smelling it and then throwing it into the kitchen stove fire. She put some salve on the leg and put on a clean dressing. Once she was done, she began a very gently massage his leg watching his face to make sure she was not hurting him. After a few minutes, she stood up and pulled gently on his hand, and led him to her bedroom. She undressed him and turned back the cover for him. Then she undressed and got in bed with him.

Tom woke up the next day to the smell of coffee brewing and bacon cooking. When he got up to dress, his clothes had been washed and were laid out for him.

As he walked into the kitchen he was smiling. "Best night of sleep I had in more than two years."

She smiled and winked, "Good, I am glad you slept so well. I had a great night myself and even got some sleep."

He wanted to reach out for her, but the children were at the table. It had been a long time for both of them and they felt a little embarrassed and ashamed. But these feeling would pass and then they would see it for what it was. They had just taken a break from loneliness.

Chapter Twenty-three

When Tom left Lena, he rode back to his farm being extra careful riding in. When he found that no one was there he left a note for Bill: Leave word with Mr. Singer where you can be located. Tom.

Tom rode to the Crossroads, getting there just after dark. He went to Mr. Singer's store to see if they had seen or heard from Bill. Tom was getting itchy feet to go west and wanted to see if Bill would go with him. He intended to pick up his children and a go, risking the union soldiers and outlaws raiders along the roads.

"Evening Tom. Haven't seen you in a while. What brings you down this way?"

"I am looking for Wild Bill McCall. Have you seen or heard from him."

"He was through here about three or four weeks ago. Said he was going home for a while to see what was happening."

"Yeah, he had some run-in with the local officials so he had to leave the area for a while."

Laughing, Mr. Singer said, "A little run-in with Bill would be like having a big run-in with anyone else."

"Yeah, like having a little run-in with a sow bear with cub. Ain't no such thing."

"Did he say who he had killed?"

Smiling, Tom said, "If I remember correctly the name had a constable in front of it."

Mrs. Singer came in while they were talking and she said, "Tom, your neighbor Lena was in here a week or so ago. Said she saw you."

Then she leaned in close so the other customers could not hear said, "She said you saved her and her kids from starvation. Bless you Tom."

Tom's face turned a little red and he managed to say, "It was just being neighbors. She and her kids got a bad break with losing Dan. I saw her a couple of days ago and they are doing just fine."

He turned a little redder and Mrs. Bing just smiled. "Want a cup of coffee, Tom?"

"Thank you ma'am."

Mrs. Singer came back with the coffee and Tom and Mr. Singer sat down at a back table out of the way. "Tom, there is a lot more traffic on the river and the roads lately. The union is planning something big and it will probably be worse than Shiloh."

"Yeah, I have felt it coming for a while. The north is feeling their oats and hankering to get this war over with. I figure maybe one more year or maybe a year and a half, and it should be over. They have the superior weapons and technology. And they have unlimited numbers of people, and each unit they throw up against us are fresh, and all out units are bout worn out. It's just about over with, but most don't know it."

"Tom be careful with that kind of talk around here. Lots of people might take it the wrong way. But, I am not one of them. I feel the way you do. It is just a matter of time."

As Tom got up to leave he said, "If you see Bill, tell him I was looking for him and please leave a note as to where he might be found."

"Sure will Tom."

Chapter Twenty-four

Tom left the Crossroads and headed to his camp. If he had been able to find Bill, he felt well enough to visit Dr. Boyce again, but he did not want to go alone. People were still trying to kill him.

He arrived at the camp at daybreak and after reporting to Captain Day, he went to sleep.

At around two in the afternoon he was awaken by shouting and lots of noise in camp. He got up and got dressed and walked outside. Captain Day was outside waiting for him.

"The Tennessee Federal Cavalry along with a group from Michigan has overran Linden capturing Colonel Frierson and a lot of recruits. Some of Major Shy unit was captured but most had not been in the city when the Union came in. The Union forces left headed towards the Tennessee River with their spoils, leaving Linden in chaos. They burned down the court house and captured a lot of equipment."

Tom's face turned pale and fell to his knees. He could not breathe. "Any report of civilian casualties?"

"There were casualties, but they didn't know how many or who they were."

Tom looked at Captain Day and Captain Day motioned for him to go. "We will meet you there."

Lizzie was setting on the sidewalk waiting for Matt to come out so they could walk to school. She heard what sounded like thunder and it seemed to be getting closer. Then she heard what sounded like gunshots far away. She stood up and looked down Main Street. She saw the banners and the American Flag first and then she saw the glinting of the sabers in the morning sun and then she saw the riders. They were coming fast and she could not move. They rode past the store and around the courthouse and they just kept coming. So many she could not count them. They were firing their guns and yelling. They were in blue Union uniforms and even she knew they were the enemy. Then the columns broke up and some of the horses were on the side walk and then she was hit by a horse and then another, knocking her down and she started screaming. Matt had been looking for her in the store until he heard her scream. He ran outside and down the walk to where she was lying on the ground. He was cursing the soldiers and as soon as he reached Lizzie, he was shot in the chest by a young Union soldier with a scraggly beard. Lizzie tried to crawl to Matt, but she could not move, she had been hurt badly.

Hearing the screaming over the other noise, Mr. Bing ran down the step and scooped up Lizzie and ran back inside. Then he went back to get Matt. By then, a young officer had ridden up and was scolding the young soldier for shooting civilians. When he saw Mr. Bing, he dismounted to check on Matt. He saw that Matt had been shot in the chest and was dead. He said, "Sorry, how is the little girl?"

"She is in bad shape, probably internal injuries."

"The colonel gave explicit instructions not to harm any civilians. But some of our boys are young. Get inside and keep everyone inside, we will be gone soon."

Mr. Bing started dragging Matt towards the door and then Mrs. Bing came out to help.

The captain turned to the soldier who had shot Matt, "Private Sanksi, did you not hear the colonel's instructions about harming civilians?"

"Yes, Sir, I heard him. But when he came running at us, I just didn't think."

"You will ride at the back of the column when we leave today."

Mr. Bing with the assistance of Mrs. Bing were able to put Matt in his bed. Then they spent their time trying to revive Lizzie.

"Where is Matt? I called for him to help me and he came, but I saw him get shot. Is Matt ok?"

Mrs. Bing lied, "Lizzie darling, Matt is ok. He is in the other room."

When the soldiers rode out of town, Mr. Bing ran and asked Dr. Langdon to come to check on Lizzie. When he examined her, he shook his head and whispered to Mr. Bing, "She has internal injuries. She is bleeding baldly and there is nothing I can do to save her."

Tom's horse was a big strong stallion and he would be tested this day. But Tom knew the limits of horses and he stopped every five miles or so to give him a breather and let him drink. Tom rode into Linden and went directly to the store. The court house was still smoldering. There was a crowd of people there with a group of soldiers. Tom tore through the crowd and saw Major Shy and went up to him.

The major's face told it all. "Who? My son? My daughter? Both?"

Then he ran upstairs into the bedroom and saw in Matt's bed a covered body. He stripped back the cover and saw it was Matt. He fell on his knees and grabbed his son and wept. Then in a second he stood up and ran to Lizzie's room. Mrs. Bing was kneeling at the side of the bed and in the bed lay Lizzie. She was not moving. "Is she dead?"

Looking up at Tom, she said, "She was on the sidewalk. She was not on the street. She was sitting there waiting to go to school and the soldiers rode down the street and circled the court house and they were everywhere and they ran upon the sidewalk. Matt tried to get Lizzie but he could not get her fast enough. They rode her down and shot Matt. Jacob picked up Lizzie brought her inside and then we went back for Matt. Matt tried to help her but it just happened too fast."

Tom moved over to the bed and kneeled down beside Mrs. Bing. There was no visible sign that Lizzie had been hurt. "The doctor say she has internal injuries."

"Where is the doctor?"

Major Shy said, "We had three men wounded and he is with them. He will be back soon."

Then he said in a low voice that only Tom could hear, "Tom she has internal injuries in her abdomen and there is nothing he can do. If he operates, she will just bleed to death."

Tom laid his head down gently on his little Lizzie's hand and wept. "God damn this war and the sons of bitches who started it."

"Matt, are you here? Matt."

Extending his hand and taking hers Tom said, "Lizzie, Pa is here."

"Pa." Tears filled Lizzie's eyes. "Pa. I'm sorry. But I wasn't in the road. I was on the sidewalk and they hit me there."

"I know Little Lizzie. I know it was the bad men who ran you down and not your fault. You don't worry about that now."

"Matt tried to help me but the horses just kept coming and I could not get out the way."

"Sheeee, don't worry now. You just get well."

"Pa, can we go home now. I want to go back to where we were happy."

Tom could not hold his composure and broke down and let out a painful moan that all in the room heard. It was all the pain and hurt filling his soul and it would take his death to purge it.

"God, you can't take my little Lizzie. Take me instead."

The little hand he was holding went limp and he knew she had died. He held it to his lips and kissed it gently and then he stood up.

Major Shy stopped Tom before he left the store and briefed him on what had happened. The tactics the Tennessee Federals had used, how they had scattered the pickets, and how the garrison was not ready including himself.

When Tom walked outside he had already formulated a retribution strategy in his mind. He knew all of that terrain and what was there. He knew exactly what happened and where they came from and where they went. With all the prisoners and equipment they had taken, their columns would be spread out a long ways between Linden and the river and they could not move fast enough to outrun him. He would clear the area all the way to Jackson if need be, but he would find the people who killed his little Lizzie and Matt. Many men would die tonight.

There were about twenty soldiers from his unit mounted and ready to go when he came outside.

Tom looked into the eyes of each man there ready to ride. "Glad to see each of you. Not only are you my brothers in arms, but you are my friends. There is not one of you that I would not trust my life to and I would gladly die for any one of you. But today is special. Today they made it personal. I won't embarrass you by saying that you don't have to go with me. Because I know you are here for me and little Lizzie and Matt. And I will always be grateful to each and every one of you."

Looking at Major Shy he said, "I know that there are many here who want to go but cannot go because of other duties. Thank you for your consideration. But your duties here are as important or more that what we do."

Tom turned and saluted Major Shy and turned once again to the command. "We are going to clean out all the rabble between here and the river, then we are going to clean out the river for ten miles up and down the river, then we are going to ride to the West side of the river and clean out whatever we can there. We will be moving fast. We will take no prisoners. If you have a problem with that, now is the time to speak up. Is there anyone who disagrees with my policy of no prisoners?"

No one spoke up. "If later you change your mind, please let me know."

Tom mounted his big horse and rode out of Linden towards the river without saying another word and Captain Day and the rest followed.

The stolen equipment, horses, and prisoners had slowed the progress of the Federal forces. Tom and his group caught up with the rear of the column about a mile from the river crossing and swept through them killing twelve and freeing eight prisoners. Without slowing down they rode onto the next group and repeated the tactic. Killing eight but there were no prisoners with this group. Even though he didn't know it, he had killed Private Sanksi who was in the first group they had encountered. By this time the column had begun the rush to the river. They had set up defensive positions at the river to defend the crossing. Tom held up his arm and stopped the group. He moved his horse so as to be in the middle where everyone could hear him. "Men, the rest won't be so easy. They will have set up to defend the crossing. Captain Day take half the men and go north to the end of their defenses and I will take the rest and go south. We will hit them on the ends where they are the thinnest and meet in the middle. Let's ride."

The group split with half moving up river and the rest moving down river to circle around to come at the defensive positions from each end. Tom's observations were correct and they completely defeated the defensive positions. The Union cannons were set up to defend the road so they were useless when attacked from the side. The federals were in the process of loading a boat and Tom led his troops onto the boat and killed everyone he saw. He then yelled for the boat crew to come outside. There were four men over fifty and a young boy of around ten who came out on deck. He told his troops and the boat crew to begin unloading the ammo, rations, and weapons off the boat. He rode off the boat and someone yelled that there was a boat about half way across the river. Tom rode over to Sgt Daniels. "James, get your crews on that ship."

James knew exactly what he meant and he started barking orders. "Get these cannons turned and loaded."

The men moved to turn the cannons facing out to the river. The first shot was short. James yelled "Higher!"

The next shot hit the wheelhouse. A second later the third shot hit amidships and started a fire. Then there was a big explosion and the boat disappeared in a flash of fire and smoke. The little group gathered on the banks of the Tennessee River on that night let out a loud yell that could be heard in Washington D.C.

Captain Day yelled, "Lets finish unloading the boat and get out of here."

It was then that Tom noticed that Captain Day was not setting right in his saddle. He rode over to him to see what was wrong. The Captain motioned toward his lower leg. He had been hit by a bullet just at the top of his boot. He looked at Tom and said, "We have to get away from the river before we can stop."

Tom said, "Hold on Captain we will get you out of this."

Tom rode onto the boat they were unloading and yelled, "Get this stuff off the boat, we have to get on the road."

He called to the oldest of the boat crew and said, "Is this your boat?"

"It's my son's boat." And he pointed to the man next to him.

"This your boat?"

"Yes sir."

Tom bent over out of his saddle so he could see the man's face. "You are Mr. Johns, right?"

"Yes sir. And you are Mr. Tom McCall."

"Mr. Johns, do you have someplace you can go with your boat to stay out of sight for a while? Otherwise we will burn your damn boat."

"Yes sir, I do."

"Ok, as soon as this is unloaded, you can be off and take care. I am sure I will see you again."

"James, take this group back to Linden and report to Major Shy. Tell him I am taking Captain Day to a surgeon in Hohenwald. The Captain was hit in his leg and needs a surgeon badly. I will be back to Linden in a couple of days to bury my children."

"Sure Tom, I will take care of it."

Chapter Twenty-five

Tom and Captain Day rode ahead of the troops towards Linden, but turned off to the right at a well warn trail. When they were far enough from the river, they stopped long enough for Tom to put a bandage on Captain Day's let to stop the bleeding. Tom knew the trail well to Hohenwald and it would save them a couple of hours. It was midday when they rode into Hohenwald, and there seemed to be an unusually large number of people on the roads and streets. Tom was a little concerned, but no one seemed to notice two strangers dirty from the trail and well-armed. They didn't even seem to notice that one was in a Confederate uniform. The people were used to seeing strangers coming and going. They rode directly to Dr. Boyce's house and walked in. There were a few people waiting in the outer room and Tom led Captain Day back to the operating room. The big nurse tried to stop him, but then said, "Tom, is your leg acting up again?"

"Hi Martha. No, I have an emergency. My Captain has been shot in the leg and needs some fixing right away."

"Take him right in here hon and I will get the doctor."

In a couple of minutes Dr. Boyce came into the room. "Tom, how is the leg doing?"

"Not me today Doctor, It's my Captain whose been shot."

"Yeah, I know, but I was just asking about how your leg is doing? Help me get the boot off."

Tom took the boot heel and pulled gently until the boot came off. It was full of blood, so he had to be careful not to spill it on the floor. He took the boot outside and empty the blood out and then wash it out with soap and water.

Tom and Martha helped get Captain Day's pants off so the doctor could examine his leg.

"Those damn riffled slugs sure tears a man up. OK, you wait outside you can't help and besides, you need to clean yourself up."

As Tom moved through the waiting room some of the people looked suspiciously at him and some even moved away afraid. Tom led their horses down the street to the hotel. He took their saddle bags and guns and walked in to register.

"Rooms are one dollar a night."

"One room will do and please have your boy take my horses to the stable and tell the smith to have them cleaned and rubbed down and fed."

He handed the man three silver dollars to give to the smith.

"I need hot water for a bathe. Also send up a plate of food. Whatever you serve in the kitchen will be fine."

Tom had his bath and had on clean clothes and felt a lot better, but hungry. When he heard a knock on the door, he figured it was the food, but ever cautious, Tom tucked his pistols in his belt. But it was not the food, it was a local constable and his deputy. They strolled into the room with their hands on their guns.

"What's your name boy?"

"I'm Lonnie Wilt. I am from White Oak Creek. I'm here to see the doctor. I was wounded early in the war and it never did heal and I am back for another operation."

The man that came in with the constable said, "Do you mind if we see that there leg what is hurt?"

"Not at all."

Tom pulled off his pants on the injured leg and unwraps the dressing. The leg was still festered and crusted seeping just a little blood into the bandage from all the hard riding.

The deputy smelled it and then walked back to the door. "He is telling the truth about the leg. It smells like it is dead. Boy, you going to lose that there leg if you don't get it fixed."

"Yes sir. Going to let Dr. Boyce operate on it again tomorrow."

The constable said, "Well I guess you was telling the truth."

Tom said, "Do you mind telling me who you looking for?"

"We looking for a man named Bill McCall. He done kilt a lawman over near Big Ivy."

Tom shook his head and said, "Lot of killing going on these days."

There was a knock on the door. The constable opened the door and it was the food. He stepped aside and said before leaving. "We'll see you later."

Tom didn't feel like eating after the visit by the constable, but he knew he needed to eat to keep his energy up. When he had finished his food, he walked back to the doctor's office. When he walked in, Martha motioned for him to follow her. She led him back to the recovery area. Captain Day was there asleep.

"I will get the doctor to come talk to you."

"Thanks."

"That ball broke the bone, shattering it. I have cleaned it out good so there are no bone or lead fragments in the leg. The problem is that now, the ends of the bone do not meet. I have put two silver screw in his leg to hold the bone in place, so under no circumstances can he put any weight on that leg for over a year. Otherwise it will tear the screws out and he will probably lose the leg below his knee."

"Does he know, doctor?"

"No, he has been asleep all this time. I will tell him when he wakes up. Another thing, he will not be able to ride a horse for a year also. That leg has to grow back enough bone to make it strong enough for the screws to hold. Even after a year, he will still have to be careful and walk with a cane."

"Can you keep him here for a while until I bury my son and daughter? Then I will pick him up in a carriage."

The doctor wanted to ask about his children, but knew if Tom wanted to talk about it, he would tell him. Instead, he said, "That will be fine."

The next day, Tom rode back to Linden. It was a quiet ride so Tom had a lot of time to think about little Lizzie and his big son Matt. He felt that he would never find happiness again. It would be easy for him to blame others, but Tom knew he was ultimately the blame for how things turned out. He could have been a better husband and father. He could have just stayed home. Tom shook his head as if trying to shake the thoughts out of it, but it didn't work. He would never get over losing his wife and children, but if he dwelled on it, it would drive him insane.

Mr. and Mrs. Bing had made the arrangements for Lizzie and Matt to be buried beside their mother. It was a sad rainy day and virtually every citizen and soldier turned out for the funeral. Tom could not be consoled. He openly wept and grunted from the pain when they lowered his children into their grave. Tom spent the evening with Mr. and Mrs. Bing and talked about little Lizzie and Big Matt. How Lizzie was so like her mother when her mother was young. And how Matt was so devoted to her. They went from laughing to crying back to laughing. When Mrs. Bing had gone to bed, Tom ask Mr. Bing to follow him outside.

"Jacob …"

"That is the first time you have called me by my first name."

"Oh, sorry."

"No, it is ok. I hope by now we are friends and the wrongs on my part of the past are forgiven."

"They are forgiven and I would ask you to please forgive me for taking Mattie away from her family. I was selfish and did not realize how much she meant to you and how much you meant to her. All of this has been my fault. But there is nothing I can do but try to go on with life."

"You are being too hard on yourself. This is just life. Every day is lived and we try to do what we have to do to get by. So stop beating yourself up for life. We can neither take the credit nor blame for our lives."

"Thank you Jacob. Thank you for everything."

Tom walked off the porch down to the sidewalk where Lizzie and Matt were killed. He got down on his knees and looked at the moon as if preying. In a minute he arose and walked back to Mr. Bing. "Jacob, I am leaving Tennessee. I am going out west. My Captain was injured and cannot walk or take care of himself. I am going to get a carriage and take him to his home somewhere around Jackson."

"When are you leaving?"

"In a couple of days. He is in the hospital in Hohenwald."

Mr. Bing turned serious and said, "Son, I hear a lot of things in my business. People know I have no leaning either way in this war, and so they tell me things that I normally do not repeat. But, you need to go right away and get Captain Day out of Hohenwald, and tell anyone else you know to stay away for the next week. I can't say more than that. But you need to go right away – early tomorrow will be ok."

"Ok, thank you Jacob. Do you have a buggy I can borrow?"

"Sure. And two great horses that go along with it."

"Ok, I will get up early and be out of Hohenwald before noon."

Tom wanted to ask Jacob more about what was to happen in Hohenwald, but decided against it. He had heard enough and trusted Mr. Bing enough to know he was trying to help.

Chapter Twenty-six

Tom took the main road to Hohenwald and made good time. He was at the doctor's office when Dr. Boyce came down from his living quarters. He was surprised to see Tom back so soon. "What are you doing back so soon?"

"Doctor, I cannot tell you why, but we need to get Captain Day out of here by noon today."

Dr. Boyce knew more than most that war was unpredictable, and that both sides swept through their little town all the time, so he did not ask why. He said, "Did you bring a wagon?"

"I have a buggy."

"That's even better. Ok, I will get him ready. I will give you enough medicine to take care of the pain. But keep the bandages changed and the wound clean."

When Tom and Dr. Boyce entered the room, Captain Day said, "Tom, how are you? What are you doing back so soon?"

"Captain, we have to get you out of here now. I have talked to the doctor, and he has given us medicine for the pain, and to keep the wound clean. But we have to go now."

As they were putting him in the buggy the doctor said, "I have wrapped the leg so it cannot move without something hitting it. So he will be ok to travel, but you have to be careful not to bump the leg."

They were ready to leave when Captain Day said, "Tom stop. Doctor please come here." The doctor came up to Captain Day and Captain Day gave the doctor a little bag. This should cover my bill and maybe the next rebel who can't pay."

Dr. Boyce pored the coins out into his hand. It was all gold. He said, "This is too much. Here take this back."

Captain Day pushes his hand back and said, "Doctor, there is not enough money in the world to pay you back for what you gave me. You gave me back my leg. That is priceless. So you keep this as a down payment on what I owe you."

"Wait here." The doctor turned and went back inside. In a couple of minutes he returned with a chair with wheels and put it in the back of the buggy.

"He will need this later."

They rode back to Linden and checked into the hotel next to the store. Once he had Captain Day settled in, Tom found Major Shy.

"I have been briefed on the operation and everyone says you did a great job leading the raid. That you took charge like an officer and everything went like clockwork. I have put you and the entire company in the report."

"Thank you sir, the men are well seasoned fighters. They could take on Grant's whole damn army."

"How is Captain Day?"

"I just brought Captain Day back from the doctor's office in Hohenwald. He is in the hotel up on main. We had to take him out early because of something I heard about Hohenwald."

"What did you hear?"

"I can't tell you where I got the information, but I heard that the town was going to have visitors beginning tomorrow."

"Ok, I understand I will double the pickets along the road to Hohenwald and shore up or defenses here on both sides of the town."

"There is something else Major. My leg is not going to heal as long as I keep riding around these hills. The doctor has told me that I will lose it if I am not careful. With your permission, I am going to resign from the army and take Captain Day to his home near Jackson. He is in very bad shape. He almost lost his leg and if it had not been for Dr. Boyce, he would have. So I am going to take him home and stay with him as long as he needs me."

"Tom, you have my permission and I will gladly accept your resignation. Your service to the Confederacy has been exemplary and you will receive the paperwork as soon as I get it drawn up."

The next day, Tom rode to the crossroads and Mrs. Singer came over as soon as she saw him. "Tom, Bill was by here yesterday. He said tell you he was going to your place and would wait for you there."

"Great, thank you."

Tom led Mrs. Singer aside and in a low voice told her what happened to Lizzie and Matt. "Oh, no, no, no. Oh My God." Then she broke down crying and Tom held her and they both cried.

As he was leaving, Tom hugged Mrs. Singer and shook hands with Mr. Singer and said goodbye. On his way to his farm he stopped by to see how Lena and her kids were doing. When he approached Tom yelled out, "Lana, are you there?"

The kids came running down the hill towards him and then he saw Lana come out of the barn. He rode up and dismounted. The kids ran up to Tom and hugged him and then Lena hugged him.

Lena got Tom by the hand and said, "Let's go get some lunch."

When they had finished eating and the children had gone outside to play, Tom told Lena about Lizzie and Matt. She could not believe it. She hugged Tom and cried. "You poor man, how can you stand it?"

"I don't know if I will be able to stand it. Right now I have things I must do but later it will hit me hard."

"One of the things I must do is get Captain Day to his family in Jackson. He was wounded during our raid on the sons of bitches that killed my children, and I owe it to him to make sure he is ok."

He handed a piece of paper to Lena and said, "Lena, you are a very strong and determined woman, and I want to do something to help you make a life for you and your children. I am not staying in these parts, I have lost too much. I am deeding you my section of land and everything there to you. You are to take possession right away. Here is the deed and I will file it at the Linden land office."

Lena cried in her hands. "Thank you Tom. I am not crying because you gave me your place. I am crying because you are leaving. We could have made a life together if you stayed."

"I have thought of that also, but the thing in my soul that took me away from here the first time is still there, and it would take me away again. No, I am going out west and start a new life. I hope to build up a big ranch and live to be an old man."

They stood up and Tom kissed her and she hugged him and kissed him back. "Sure you have to go now?"

"Yeah, got miles to ride before I can stop. I will write you and tell you where we settle."

When he rode up the trail to his house, he yelled to make sure Bill knew he was coming. Then he saw him come out onto the porch and waive to him.

"Come on in Tom and have some of your coffee."

"Thank you."

"Mrs. Singer said you wanted to talk to me."

Tom told Bill about what happened to his children and Bill could not say anything. He could see the hurt in Tom's eyes and squeezed his shoulder. They sat there saying nothing for a long time.

"By the way Bill, I ran into a constable up in Hohenwald looking for you. Came into my hotel room wanting to know who I was. I gave him a factious name and finally got rid of him. But he seemed to have a little bloodhound in him. He probably won't stop looking for you. So I have a proposition for you. I'm heading out west. I am going to take my Captain to his home over around Jackson, and stay with him until he is healed enough to take care of himself. And I want to know if you would like to go with us."

Bill smiled and said, "Well, since you put it that way, I will go. Anyway, I have outlived my welcome around these parts."

"We will go to Linden tomorrow and pick up my discharge from the army and get Captain Day and head out. Also, I have to talk to a boatman to get across the river. Just so happens, I have one who owes me a favor. Maybe you could go talk to the boatman while I go to Linden and meet us at the river crossing."

"That sounds good to me."

They rode out of Tom's farm for the last time before sunup. They split up just out of Linden with Bill going to talk to the boatman and Tom going into Linden to get Captain Day.

When Tom went to pick up Captain Day with the buggy he dropped a list off with Mr. Bing to fill of things they would need on the trip. He would pick the supplies up after he picked up Captain Day.

Major Shy was with Captain Day when Tom arrived to pick him up. The Major had the paperwork for Tom discharge. They were presented to Tom in a leather case and Tom stuck them inside his belt. He also had the paperwork for Captain Day. So Captain Day was also a civilian and had changed out of his uniform. Major Shy also gave them passes for the roads controlled by the Confederacy. Tom gave Major Shy the paperwork to transfer his farm to Lena.

They had given Mr. Bing his buggy and horses back when they returned from Hohenwald. So, Captain Day had acquired another one from the livery stable. By the time they had Mr. Day comfortable in the buggy, Mr. Bing was out front with the supplies they had gotten from the store. "How much do we owe you Jacob for the supplies?"

"You don't owe anything."

"Look Jacob, we are in the service of Captain Day who is from a rich family so, how much does Mr. Day owe you?" "Jacob smiled and said thirty-four dollars."

The buggy had a soft ride and Mr. Day was comfortable with his leg propped up. But they would be very careful. Tom tied his horse behind the buggy and he drove.

When they neared the river, Tom saw Bill riding to meet them.

Tom moved the buggy off the road and jumped from the buggy and mounted his horse.

"I will be right back."

As Tom rode up to Bill he asked, "What's the problem?"

"The damn boatman does not trust me. They are scared to death that it is a trap."

"Where are they?"

"Follow me."

They rode down a dirt path to the river to a boat that was tied up. Stepping off his horse, Tom yelled, "Mr. Johns, this here is Tom McCall. I need to talk to you."

They waited a minute and then they saw about six people coming off the boat with guns.

"Come on up so I can see you Tom."

Tom walked up to talk to Mr. Johns as Bill hung back ready.

"Is what your cousin says true, you are leaving for the west and no longer associated with the military?"

"Yes sir, that is true. And we are taking our friend home in a buggy because he is too sick to travel otherwise. So we need your boat just to take us one way across the river. And you will no longer owe a favor."

"Alright let's hurry and get this done while the river is clear. Bring the buggy down here and let's get loaded."

Chapter Twenty-seven

Mr. Day paid the boatman and thanked him for his help. They slowly picked their way along the rough roads and trails, trying not to be surprised by anyone. They spent the night in a hotel in Darden. It was small, but the food was good and the rooms were adequate.

The next day they intended to get up early and try to get to Captain Day's plantation before nightfall. But when Tom checked on Captain Day, he was burning up with fever. "Captain you are burning up, do you just want to rest today and go tomorrow?"

"Hell no, get me up and let's get on the road."

Bill looked at Tom and said, "The Captain don't look it, but he is a tough son of a bitch."

About five miles out of Lexington, they were surprised by four riders, who burst out of the woods on both sides with guns drown and cocked. Tom pulled up the buggy and in a loud voice said, "Easy boy, let's see what's going on."

"Don't move. Nobody reach for anything. I got a hair-trigger and an itchy finger."

No one moved and the man went on, "Gentlemen you are being accosted by the best and meanest gorilla unit in the hills of Tennessee. And if you do what we say, and you are very lucky, you can tell your grandkids about the day you was held up by Captain Champ Ferguson and his band of warriors."

"Sir, I happen to know Champ Ferguson and you are not him."

"I didn't say I was him. I am one of his men. And you need to shut your mouth."

At first Tom thought the thin little man that spoke had no teeth, but then he saw that he had teeth, they were just turned black from chewing tobacco. Just as he started to say something to the spokesman, six more men rode out of the woods. The one in front rode an appaloosa and had on Captain Bars. "What we got here Sergeant? Why you harassing these pilgrims of the South?"

"Sir, they look suspicious and young enough to be in the army, so why ain't they?"

"Well, did you ask them? Never mind, I will do it."

"Gentlemen I am Captain Ferguson and who might you be."

"Sir, I am Tom McCall. The gentlemen in the buggy is Captain Day, Company G, Twentieth, Tennessee."

Before he could go on Bill said, "I am Bill McCall, civilian."

"How you doing Bill? You are surely in better company than the last time I saw you."

"So are you."

They both laughed and the Captain rode over and shook Bill's hand. Captain Ferguson said, "You looking good, no missing parts?"

"Yeah, well I haven't been hung yet, but I am expecting to be any day now."

They laughed again.

"Sergeant, men, this here is Wild Bill McCall, meanest man in Tennessee. He's killed more traitors to the cause than anyone and you don't want him on your trail."

He looked at each man and stopping on Tom said, "This your brother, Bill?"

"No, he's my cousin."

"Tell me what's up with this little group of men."

"Well, it's kind of long and hurtful story so I will just condense it for you. Cousin Tom there got wounded, and is about to lose a leg to gangrene if he don't stop riding and take care of it. He lost his wife, daughter, and his son to the war. All three at the hands of the Tennessee Federals. Did you hear about the raid on the column at the river, that was his revenge? Captain Day got wounded in that raid and is going home to recover. Can't walk on his leg for a year at least and still at any time might lose it."

Captain Ferguson smiled and said, "Damn, if that is the short version, I would hate to hear the long one."

"And how about you Bill?"

"Well, I killed a no good son of a bitch traitor constable over around Summerton a few weeks back and he had a large family. Seems his large family really liked him and took great offense to me killing him."

Captain Ferguson smiled again and said, "Sure you don't want to join me, I will make you rich."

"No sir, not just right now. Seems like the two of us are going to head out west, maybe Texas and get us some cows and horses. You are always welcome to join us when thing get too bad here."

"Maybe someday Wild Bill, maybe someday."

Captain Ferguson kicked his horse and turned and rode off into the woods and his men followed him.

"That is one mean and crazy son of a bitch. We were lucky he knew me and my reputation. He takes no prisoners, Northern or Southern."

"Yeah, thanks Bill. You saved our bacon this time."

"Captain, how are you doing?"

"I am fine, we should be at Oakhaven by sundown. By the way, call me Nat. My name is Nathanial."

They rode steady all day and finally just before sundown they turned down a long lane with giant oak trees on each side. After about a mile, the house came into view. It was dusk and the lights were lit and the setting seemed serene. They could see shadows in the light moving about and as they drew closer, they could hear voices but could not make them out.

Nat said in an excited voice, "Stop. Something is not right. There are too many people there. Turn right and go around to the side of that building over there."

They rode up so the building was between them and the main house.

"Nat, what do you recommend? We don't know who belongs and who don't, so you have to tell us what's going on."

"Put me in my chair and push me closer to the house."

Bill picked Nat up and sat him in the chair as Tom took it from the buggy. They moved closer to the house where they were able to hear men's voices yelling and shouting at someone.

One voice louder than the others said, "Where is the money old man. Don't make us hurt these women folks."

Another voice was heard, "Give up the money and we will let you live. Hurry up you damn rebel."

"They have my father, mother and little sister tied up. We have to help them."

"You just wait right here just in case any come outside after me and Bill gets through."

"Put me on the front porch, please."

They moved Nat to the front porch just outside the door.

Tom drew both pistols and motions for Bill to go to one side and he would go to the other.

"I figure there are about six men to kill in there. Watch the crossfire. Let's go."

They moved quietly to each side of the big room and when Tom started shooting Bill moved into the room. When the shooting started, Nat kicked open the front door with his good leg and shot the man holding the knife to his sister throat. Within five seconds seven men were crumpled up dead or dying. Bill untied Nat's father and he untied his wife. Tom was about to untie the young girl when Nat said, "Leave her tied up, she might just whup us all." And he laughed.

"Nathanial, you are home."

Nat rolled over to his little sister and cut her binds and she hugged him. Then the mother and father saw he was in a wheel chair and slowed their approach.

"Are you alright son?"

His mother was the first to reach him, grabbed him and pulled him to her and they fell onto the floor. Then his dad come over and helped Tom get him back into his chair.

"Mother, Father, Doreen, I would like to introduce Tom and Bill McCall. They are my friends. Tom, Bill, this is my father Jonathan Day; my mother Lillian, and last and least my little sister Doreen."

Tom and Bill shook hands all around. Doreen seemed to be in shock.

"Sorry we messed up your parlor, but we could not take a chance on them surrendering."

"Young man, don't think a thing about it. If it hadn't been for you coming when you did, we would have been killed for sure. These are bad men. They have been in this area for about a week now and they have been raiding all the farms along the river."

"How in the world did they find you tucked back up here against the river?"

"That big one's name is Leon Jackson, he used to work for me about a year ago. One day he and a horse came up missing and we had not heard from him until tonight."

As the family started catching up on Nat's exploits and how he was injured, Tom and Bill began removing the bodies. By the time Mr. Day had come outside pushing Nat, Tom and Bill had the bodies on the horses.

"What shall we do with them?"

"We will have to make sure no one finds them. We do not want them traced back here. Put them around back of the barn in the lean-to and make sure the horses cannot get lose, we will figure out where to put them tomorrow."

They cleaned the parlor of any trace of blood even throwing out a nice carpet in the process. Soon there was no trace of the men who died that night.

"This kind of stuff has been happening all over the country since the war began. There is hardly a farm in the area that has not been ransacked. Ours is tucked in here between the South Fork of the Forked Deer River and Cypress Creek. There is only a narrow stretch of land that leads to Oakhaven and unless you know where you are going, it's easy to get lost."

"Yeah, it is like this all over the state and probably the South. It is kill or be killed. This is no place for the timid."

As they had supper, Nat and his family caught up on the happenings since he joined the army. And Nat told his family about Tom and his loss and the raid where he was wounded. He told how Tom had taken care of him getting him to the finest surgeon who had no doubt saved his life and his leg.

Nat's father looked older than his fifty-two years with his grey hair and skinny build. He looked more like a hands on farmer than a gentry land owner. His mother looked younger than her fifty years. She had taken care to remain young and beautiful. His little sister looked to be about sixteen, somewhere between a little girl and a young woman. She doted on Nat and reminded Tom of his children.

"Father, where are all of our people?"

"Son, they left us one and two at a time until all were gone. The only ones we have left are the Clintons. He and his family live up the creek. We have managed to get by with him and his kids doing most of the work. Of course your father works all day and night almost every day."

"Well, we have to keep this place going and if I didn't work, Will and his kids are just able to do everything."

"How about livestock? Do we have any left?"

"Sure, we have ten head of cattle, about the same number of hogs. We have seven horses and eight mules. And of course we have chickens and ducks. We are better off than most thanks to our isolation. But if anyone ever finds out where we are, then they will wipe us out."

"Tom, Bill, we have extra rooms upstairs for you to stay so whenever you get ready, you can go up."

"Well, ma'am, I thought I might just ride back down the trail a piece tonight and keep a lookout over the next couple of days just to make sure no one followed us in."

Mrs. Day looked at Tom with a combination of surprised and respect. She had not thought of that. And she was sure her husband had not thought of it. Even after what had happened tonight they were not prepared to accept the fact that their lives would never be the same. Their home was in danger and they had to realize it.

"I will get some sleep and spell you in four hours."

"Thank you Bill. I just don't want to get caught sleeping. Anyway, I like being under the stars. Gives me time to think."

Tom mounted up and rode about two miles down the road. He tied his horse to a tree, took his Henry, and walked another two hundred yards. He found a good soft spot under a big tree where he could see the entire road and got comfortable.

Tom was not the kind to be envious of others but if he was so inclined, he would have been envious of the Days. They had the perfect setup. Plenty of water, plenty of bottom land, and the isolation one needs to raise children and live a good life. Nat had ridden with him into hell on the day his children died and he would be in his debt forever. He would stay with Nat as long he was needed. He would protect this little bit of land and these people with his life.

Four hours from the time he had settled himself into position he heard a whippoorwill. The third time he heard it, he answered. When he heard it again, he did not answer. Then he heard it again and answered it. A couple of minutes later Bill quietly walked up to him. "You didn't forget our signal."

"Nope, I was expecting you."

"Everything ok? No bad guys hanging around?"

"All's quiet."

"Good, now go get some sleep."

Tom rode back to the farm and rubbed his horse down and fed and watered him. Once he was finished, he took his bedroll and threw it on some soft hay in the corner of the stall.

"Mr. McCall. Mr. McCall. Mom sent me out to get you for breakfast."

"Ok, thank you. I will cleanup and be right in."

Tom went to the water trough and pumped water over his head and then washed under his arms and then using his old shirt dried himself off. Going to his saddle bags, he took out a clean shirt and put it on. He tucked his Colts into his belt and went to the big house.

The entire family was already seated at the table when he walked in. It was the first time Mrs. Day had taken a good looked at Tom. He was an imposing figure of a man. By now he had regained almost all the weight he had lost in the prison. He was over six foot tall and over two hundred pounds of solid muscle. He had coal black hair that was longer than most men wore. His eyes were green with a light sparkle of brown. He was a man you wanted on your side. Tom caught Mrs. Day's eye and she seemed a little shy.

Tom ate so much he was embarrassed. But he was hungry and the food was the best he had ever eaten. Looking at Mrs. Day he said, "Ma'am, sorry to make a pig of myself, but this is the best food I have ever had. The biscuits are wonderful."

"Why, thank you. Don't get many compliments on my cooking. When our hands ran off, I had to learn how to cook all over again."

Before Tom left the table, Bill came in and sat down. "Any trouble?"

"None. Didn't even see any critters stirring."

They sat and talked until Bill had finished then they went to see about the bodies.

"I have been thinking about what we should do about the bodies. I have concluded that we should probably burn them. There is a place down by the river where we burn garbage. We can take them there."

When they rounded the back side of the barn a man came riding up with a teenage boy behind him. When they saw Mr. Day they slid down and walked up to the group. "Morning Mr. Day.'

"Morning Mr. Day" the teenage boy echoed.

"Morning Will. Morning Bob."

"Will, this is Tom and Bill McCall. They brought Nat back last night. Nat was wounded and is home to stay. He will need a year at least to heal so they will be assisting us until Nat gets well."

Will held out his hand and said, "Glad to meet you. We could certainly use some help."

"Will, we had some troubles last night. Some men rode into the place, tied us up, and threatened to kill us all and they would have if Tom and Bill had not showed up. Now we have to take care of the bodies so no one can trace them back to us. You might not want Bob to be here when we do this."

"You saying that some men came in here last night and tied you up and threatened to kill you. Do you know them?"

"The only one I know was Leon Jackson. He was the leader."

"I remember Leon. He was a mean son of a gun."

Tom said, "Well now, he is a dead son of a gun now."

"Bob, ride home and wait for me. Okay?"

"Okay, Pa."

When the boy had ridden away, Tom and Bill put the bodies in a wagon and Will harnessed a couple of mules and they were ready to go. "We probably going to need some kerosene."

Tom and Bill rode alongside Will and the wagon. A couple of miles down the river, Will stopped the wagon beside a large pit burned black from years of burning garbage and trash. There was a lot of trash already in the pit. The men stacked up all of branches and pieces of wood they could find into a large pile where they placed the bodies. Then they doused them with a five gallon can of kerosene and lit it. They had stripped the bodies of any metal objects that would survive the fire. Anything they did not want to keep, they threw into the river.

Concerned that Mr Clinton might say something to his family or someone else, Tom said, "Will, I know this is all new to you but this killing is going on through the South, especially Tennessee. Right now Tennessee is a living in Hell. You don't know who to trust. So let me make something very clear to you. You cannot tell anyone else about this. Not even your wife or children. If they say something to the wrong person even by accident, then the Federals will burn this whole place to the ground, then you will not be able to raise your family. Do you understand?"

"Yes sir, I understand completely."

Tom's little speech was meant as a subtle warning to Will and he hoped Will would take him as serious as he was.

They made sure all traces of the bodies had burned before they left for the barn.

Chapter Twenty-eight

It was a big farm and Mr. Day had not been able to put it all under cultivation since his hands left. Before they left, he had fifteen field hands and five for the house. His holdings were the typical farm in this area. He had inherited the farm and slaves and he had not wanted either. He had attended Harvard and wanted to be a preacher or divinity college professor. But his father was ill and he felt obligated to return to the farm. He was the only child of five to survive and he felt the age old responsibility to carry on his family's heritage. If the economy had been different, he would have gladly set his slaves free and hired them as workers. But the entire economy had been based on the labor of slaves and to have done anything different would have meant he could not make a living. When he woke up and his last hand had gone, he felt relieved. He thanked his God. But, it was not enough that he should feel relief that it was over, he had to find a way to make amends for all the years his family had made a living off the backs of others. He promised himself and God that if he made it out of this war alive, he would spend his remaining days serving those that he transgressed against. He hoped that his hands would return after the war so he could give the land to them. He had told no one of his plans nor would he until the day came.

Tom had never lived in such opulence. He had always lived on the side of the hill in his little home. He had met wealthy men and had contact with slaves who worked in different jobs in town. But he had never really thought about the aspect of owning someone. He had no hard opinion one way or the other as to who was right or wrong. He could barely read or write so the economics or history of slavery had not crossed his mind. Therefore, he had no idea that Mr. Day had a bad conscious about owning slaves. He only knew that Captain Day had ridden at his side to revenge his children and that obligated him to do what he could for Nat until he was whole again.

If there was one thing Tom knew, it was farming. He was not use to farming on the scale of the Day farm, but the work was the same. Tilling, planting, harvesting, and taking care of the livestock. And it required your full attention each and every day.

The four men and the children of Mr. Clinton were able to plant a decent crop and reap the harvest. But they never let down their guard. If anyone approached their little kingdom, they would deal with it.

Nat healed without complications with the constant attention of his mother and sister.

Occasionally, they would need something from town and would go to Huntersville, which was the nearest town of any size close to their farm. But traveling the road during this time was extremely dangerous. If it wasn't the Federals or Confederates, then it was the outlaws that made traveling dangerous. Plus, they could not leave the farm unprotected. So either Bill or Tom had to accompany Mr. Day when he went to town.

Since Tom was to accompany him, Mr. Day decided to travel the extra miles to Jackson. Also, it was winter time and most of the military units were in camp and not on the roads. Since money was scarce during the war in the South, Mr. Day planned to take three hogs and a young steer to sell. Any kind of meat was valuable during this period and when people came to steal, it was more often for a hog or a cow.

As they loaded the wagon and got ready to go, Mr. Day for the first time seemed to notice that Tom did not have on a heavy coat. "Tom, this is going to be a long cold ride, do you have a heavy coat?"

Tom looking a little embarrassed said, "Well sir, my heavy coat is worn out and I would not want to embarrass you by looking like a beggar."

"Well, on this trip maybe looking like a beggar would not be a bad thing. After all, robbers would not accost a beggar."

Tom smiled and said, "That is true sir."

Tom went inside for a minute and returned with his old coat. "How is this? Do I not look like a beggar?"

"You are right. It is pretty tattered."

"How about you? You don't look like a beggar."

"Well, one of us has to look like they own the pigs and cow."

They all laughed at Mr. Day's comments.

Mr. Day was right about it being a long and cold ride. It was December and the winter had been bad with much snow and freezing temperatures. The roads had been badly rutted and when thawed, very rough. Tom was happy he had ridden his horse otherwise he would have had a problem with his leg riding the wagon.

As they got closer to Jackson they saw more and more makeshift dwellings with smoke coming from roofs. Occasionally small children would be outside playing.

"Who are these people?"

"Mostly they are the families of soldiers whose husbands are serving or have already been killed. Some are farmers who have no place to go. Many landowners in this area have lost their land or been killed and someone else has taken over their property and thrown the farmers off. Many are former slaves who left their homes, and are now on the roads or camped on the outskirts of cities and towns. They have no food or place to live, and are starving or dying of diseases. They do whatever they have to in order to survive, and it is just going to get worse. After the war is over, it will be even more dangerous than it is now. When the soldiers start returning to their homes to find them gone and figuring out that what they were fighting for was lost. The vultures from the north will swarm upon the south taking what is left. It will be worse than the war."

"How the hell did we get in this position anyway? Who the hell started this damn war and why?"

"Well Tom, it's a complicated answer and probably better left to some other time around a table in a warm parlor with a bottle of whiskey."

"Yeah, anyway, it's too damn cold to talk."

When they pulled up to the mercantile store in Jackson, Mr. Day jumped down from the wagon and went inside to talk to the proprietor. In a minute the door opened and Mr. Day came out followed by Mr. Jones. Mr. Jones looked at the steer and then at the hogs and called a man from the back to come take the stock around back where they could be unloaded.

He looked very pleased and said, "Haven't had any meat for about two weeks now and with Christmas coming up, should be able to sell it all on one day."

"We need to do some shopping and then we will settle up on the pricing."

"Well, you just go on inside and shop and my boy will take care of the hogs and steer."

"Tom, you get what you need for yourself and Bill. I owe you more than I could ever pay you for bringing my son back."

"Sir, I am the one in debt to your son. But I do need some clothes for Bill and me but I have the money to pay."

Tom walked back to the where the guns were displayed and as the clerk walked up he said, "Do you have any Henry rifles?"

"Yes sir, we have two left." Looking over his specs at Tom's tattered coat he added, "They are quite expensive."

"I will take them and all the ammunition you have for them."

"They are forty-five dollars each and the ammunition…"

"Tom are you getting what you need?" Then looking at the clerk said, "Give this gentleman whatever he asks for."

"Yes sir, Mr. Day."

"Bring the guns and ammunition up front when you get it."

Each day spent with the Day family reminded Tom just how poor and tattered he and Bill were compared to them. When he was young, he had taken pride in his appearance and even though poor, he did not dress poor. He didn't remember the time he changed. But, with not enough money for food, he had just made due with whatever he had. In that store on that day, he made up his mind not to ever dress like a beggar again. He would even swallow his pride and spend Mr. Day's money. He picked up two pair of pants, two shirts, new underwear, socks, a pair of boots, and new hat for Bill and himself. He also bought each of them a new long leather coat which was heavy enough for the winter and would keep out the rain. He had everything wrapped up and would change when he got back to the farm.

When the clerk put the rifles and ammunition on the counter the proprietor said, "Are you expecting trouble Mr. Day?"

"Sir we have trouble if you had not noticed. The country is at war. There are militias and outlaws roaming the countryside accosting peaceful citizens and we are simply being prepared."

"Yes sir you are right. It is not safe to travel even in the city now without a guard."

"Are you finished shopping Tom?"

"Yes sir. I have taken advantage of your generosity and purchased some stuff for Bill and me."

Holding up a small bag he said, "These are Christmas presents and I will pay for them."

"Good. Then we are ready to go."

Tom and the clerk loaded the wagon with four cans of kerosene, sacks of salt, sugar, and coffee. A few bottles of whiskey. A few bolts of cloth. By the time they had loaded everything, the little wagon was about half full.

They rode back the way they had come, and Tom was even more vigilant than before. He had a bad feeling and was ready for any danger. Then from behind them to the left he heard a woman call out, "Mista Day? Mista Day? Is dat you Mista Day?"

Mr. Day stopped the mules and turned around to see where the voice was coming from. Tom had also turned and moved his horse back a few steps towards the voice. A middle aged black woman was walking towards the wagon. Tom moved his horse to block her way just in case of danger.

"It's ok Tom. I know her."

Mr. Day got down from the wagon and walked towards the woman.

"Mista Day. Lord Jesus, I thought it was you. My boy said he saw you pass earlier today and I didn't believe him. I said what in da world would Mr. Day be coming down our dirty street. But he was right. It is you."

"Miss. Jenna. How are you? What'chu doing here? I thought you went to your sister's house up in Ohio."

"No sir, we didn't even make it out of the county. We was picked up by the Union army and kept with them for three months. They always promising us that they would feed us and take care of us and take us up north. But they hardly had enough food for themselves and they use to take our young girls for themselves. They used our young men in all the bad jobs they didn't want to do. They had our boys picking up the bodies of the dead and burying them."

"What about your husband? Where is he?"

"He done gone. As soon as the Union soldiers picked us up, he lit out. Said he had another family in Maryland."

"Who is here with you?"

"I have my twin boys, and my little girl and Miss. Ransom and her four children."

"How do you live?"

"We tried to find work. Any kind of work, but no one will hire us to do anything. So we send the children out to beg. Sometimes I wish we had not been freed. That we had stayed on your farm. All my children were born on your farm."

"Don't you ever say that again? Don't ever wish to be a slave again. It's better to die a free person than to live as a slave. Haven't you ever heard that before?"

"We are dying now, sir."

Mr. Day looked at Tom and Tom shook his head. Mr. Day said, "Jenna get your children and get Miss. Ransom and her children and get on the wagon. Now. We have to hurry."

Tom helped the women with a few things wrapped up in quilts load the wagon. They placed a couple of pillows and some blankets on the floor to make it more comfortable. The twins looked to be around sixteen but they were small. The little girl looked to be around ten. Miss. Ransom looked to be around thirty. Her four children ranged in ages from twelve to three.

Although being cold and uncomfortable on the ride back to the farm, none of the riders complained. The children would occasionally get down from the wagon to relieve themselves, and Tom and Mr. Day would stop as needed.

Bill rode out to meet them concerned that there were people in the wagon and when he rode up he said, "Where the hell did all these people come from?"

"They just got onto the wagon when we weren't looking."

Bill smiles and shook his cousin's hand. He was glad they were home safe.

Mr. Day drove the wagon directly to the cook's shed. "OK, everyone out. First we have to heat up enough water for baths."

Jenna knew exactly what to do. She started directing the children and Miss. Ransom to collect the wood and water need for bathing.

"Hon, we are going to need clean clothes for all our guests and we are going to need quilts and blankets for them as well. Everything they brought with them will be burned. We cannot afford to spread any diseases."

He had said it out loud so everyone could hear and no one took any offense. Jenna and Miss. Ransom understood how filthy they had become and they were not use to living like that.

Even in the cold of that December night, they all had their bath and got clean clothes to put on. For the first time in months they were clean and had nice clothes. They burned the old clothes along with the quilts and blankets.

And next came the food.

While they were bathing, Mrs. Day, Doreen and Bill had taken food to one of the houses about a hundred yards from the main house. It was called the Cooks house because the kitchen workers lived in it. Bill had built a fire in the stove and the little house was getting warm.

"Jenna, take everyone to the Cook's house. There is food there and places for you to sleep. We will talk tomorrow and make further arrangements for Miss. Ransom and her children."

Jenna took Mr. Day's hand and kissed it and Mr. Day took it away.

"Miss. Jenna, don't do that. You are a free woman, and you never have to kiss a master's hand or ass as long as you live."

When the children heard Mr. Day say ass, they all laughed and got the adults laughing. Mrs. Day put his arm around Jenna's shoulder and led her toward her new home.

"Go feed the children and get some sleep and we will talk tomorrow."

As the children entered the Cook's house they started grabbing the food and eating like they were starving, which they were.

"Wait. Everyone put the food down. First we are going to say a blessing for our good fortune." Everyone stopped eating and put the food down and bowed their heads.

"God, thank you for answering our prayers and sending us salvation. In the depth of despair, when I thought we could not live another day, you sent your servant to save us. You are truly a great and wonderful God. You test us but you never let us fall. You chastise us but you never punish us beyond what we can endure. You send us hunger and illness but you give us food and healing. You are truly a wonderful God and we praise and thank you. And God, everyone says Mr. Lincoln freed us slaves, but it took the words of my former slave master to truly free me today. Thank you Lord. Amen."

"Amen."

Jenna and Miss. Ransom filled the plates of the children and they ate quietly until they were full. For the first time in a very long time they felt secure and not hungry. They slept warm and peacefully that night.

Mr. Day was on the road to redemption with his meager gesture to these two little families. He wasn't quite sure about his next move or where this would take him, but he was ready for it and felt sure about the direction he had turned.

The next morning Mr. Day called a meeting of everyone. They even rolled Nat out to the cook shed.

"Jenna, Miss. Ransom, how was your night. Did everyone get enough food and a good night's sleep?"

"Yes sir. They went to bed with their bellies full for the first time in a long time."

"Good. I know you are crowded in that little house, so today we will move Miss. Ransom and her kids into the house next door."

"Thank you sir."

"Jenna, you know where the clothing storehouse is don't you?"

"Yes sir."

"Take the children and Miss. Ransom over there now and get them some coats and then come back here."

When the two families returned, Mr. Day said, "We have a lot of work to do to make sure we all get though the rest of the winter. We have to kill a couple of hogs and put them in the smokehouse. We have to cut and haul enough wood for all of us. Mr. Clinton will be in charge of cutting and hauling the wood and I will take care of the hog killing. Will, can you get the job done with the help of your son and Jenna's twins?"

"Yes sir. We will get all the wood we need. I know just the place to get it."

"Good, then get the mules hooked up and get on your way."

"Jenna and Miss. Ransom can you make sure Miss. Ransom gets set up in her house and make sure she has all the stuff she and her children will need?"

"Yes sir. We will take care of getting Minnie moved."

"Good, once you are finished with that, come back here to help with rendering the lard and making the soap. We all will eat high on the hog tonight."

Chapter Twenty-nine

On small farms and large farms to the largest plantations, hog killings was a festive occasion. Whether you were killing one hog or twenty it was the same procedure. First you build up the fire and boil the water in a large vat or tub. Once you killed the hog, the first thing you do is douse it in hot water and then scrape away the hair. This was a crucial step if you did not want pig hair in everything. Next, hanging them up for cleaning. The old adage that every bit of the hog with the exception of its squeal was used was true. Even the intestines were cleaned and used as casings for sausage or cooked and eaten on their own as chitlins. One of the most valued uses of the hog was the rendering of the lard. Which involved cutting the thick skin into two inch squares and heating it in a large iron pot over a hot fire. Two miraculous products were produced: Lard, which was used for frying everything and making it taste wonderful; and cracklings, which were crispy and delicious whether eaten as they come out of the pot or cooked into cornbread.

Mr. Day pointed out the two hogs to be killed and Tom dispatched them with a small caliber pistol. They used the mules to drag the hogs around to the processing area. By the time Mr. Day, Tom and Bill had the hogs scraped and hung for the butchering, the women had returned ready to help with the rest.

There is a tradition when killing hogs to take the back strap and fry it up while the work continues and all who participate in the activity gets to eat. It is considered the tastiest part of any animal if cooked right. Mrs. Day had a big iron skillet on the fire and as soon as she started cooking the back strap, everyone got in line to get a piece.

Tom had gotten himself a plate and walked a little ways away from the others to eat. In a minute Jenna's daughter walked over and sat down beside him with her plate. She noticed that Tom was touching his eyes with his sleeve and touching his nose with his hand and she said, "Sir, are you alright? Why are you crying?"

It took a minute for Tom to regain his composure before he said, "I was just thinking about my family. We were all so happy when we killed hogs. There is something about the sounds and smells that made me think of my children."

"Where are your children now?"

"They were killed by the Yankee soldiers."

Then he broke down crying. It was the first time he had cried for his children in a while. The little girl took his big hand in hers and caressed it with her other one without saying a word.

Jenna walked over to where they were sitting and said, "Winnie, I done told you not to bother no body. Sorry Mr. Tom if she bothering you."

"It's ok Jenna, she was not bothering me."

"Mamma, Mr. Tom done lost his children. They was kilt by the Yankees."

"Shush girl. Sorry Mr. Tom she don't know no better."

"It's ok Jenna. Thank you Winnie for your kindness."

When Tom walked back to finish the job of butchering the hogs, Mrs. Day said quietly, "Hon, are you ok?"

"Yes ma'am. Guess all this excitement makes me think of my family."

"Nat told us your story. Hope you don't mind. He pretty much thinks you are the finest man and soldier that he ever met."

"Well, that is kind of him and of you to say, but I am just a dirt farmer."

"Well, I would say that you might have started out as just that, but you are not that now."

She hugged him and said, "Thank you again for bringing our son home."

As Mr. Day, Tom and Bill were working cutting up the hogs, Bill said, "You know that it is only a matter of time before some military unit from one side or the other finds this place and ransacks it."

"I am afraid you are right Bill. It's just by pure dumb luck that we have not been overran by now."

"Yeah, and the people are getting more and more desperate for food."

"How many weapons do you have in the house?"

"We have about a dozen shotguns and a few rifles for hunting."

"We have the seven rifles from the soldiers."

"Well, seems like we have enough weapons but how about ammunition?"

"I have plenty of ammunition for the shotguns and hunting rifles and all the ammunition for the soldier's guns is what they had on them."

"Now who can hold a gun if we need them? Will and his boy do a lot of hunting but I don't think the women or Jenna's boys know anything about guns."

"Bill and I can teach the boys and the women to use guns and they might be of some assistance when the time comes."

"What about the guns you ..."

Mr. Day had started to talk about the Henrys that Tom had purchased at the store, but Tom had put his finger up to his lips indicating that he should be quiet.

Smiling, Bill said, "Ok Tom, what you are hiding?"

"Well, I was going to surprise you with a Christmas present, but I guess now is a good time to tell you. I was able to buy two Henrys at the store in Jackson along with six cases of ammunition. One of them is for you and the other one is for Nat."

"Sorry I messed up your surprise Tom please forgive me? Sorry Bill."

"No problem, Mr. Day. Now I can start practicing with it."

"You will not believe these guns. Sixteen shots without reloading and it is accurate beyond three hundred yards. With three of these, we can put a hole in any line."

During a break, Mrs. Day puts her hand in Mr. Days and said, "Hon, it is good to have the sound of children around here once again. I miss our people, but most of all I missed the children."

"Yeah, me too. Maybe we can get them to stay with us once this is all over."

"No, not Jenna or Miss. Ransom. We have too much to atone for with them so we would tend to give them too much. We are going to have to start all over with people that we have not harmed. We will have enough to remind us of the past."

"You are right. I had not thought of it that way. But it makes perfect sense."

"We will make sure they have the means to go where they want to go and that will be the end of it."

"Yes, you are absolutely right. I am so glad I found you and talked you into marrying me."

"Hey, I thought I found you and had to talk you into marrying me."

Jonathan leaned down and kissed Lillian gently.

It took them all day to butcher the hogs, render the lard, and get the meat stored in the smokehouse. And since they already had everything set up, they took the opportunity to make the lye soap.

By the time Mr. Clinton had returned with the wood, the ladies already had supper prepared and they had a festive time just like one big happy family.

When everyone had gathered under the cook's shed, Mr. Day took the opportunity while they were finishing eating to talk to the whole group.

"Please give me your attention. Children please sit down someplace and be quiet for just a few minutes. You may go on eating but give me your attention."

Once everyone including the children had found a seat and was paying attention to him, Mr. Day said, "It has been a long and hard day and I know you are tired so I won't keep you very much longer. While we have everyone together I want to take this opportunity to say a few things. I am very pleased that we have Jenna and her family and Miss. Ransom and her family here with us. I used to think of myself as an easy master as opposed to being a hard master. But as I look back I see that there is no difference between an easy and hard master. There are no degrees of right or wrong. It is either right or wrong. There are no degrees of being a slave master. The slave is still a slave and the master is still a master. But that it something I will have to get forgiveness from my God. First of all, there are no slaves here. There are only free people here. Free to go and come as they please. Free to walk away at any time. Is that understood?"

Mr. Day paused just to let it set in. Then he continued, "Having said that, you will also be expected to work to earn your way here. The farm is not making any money, therefore we will not have money to pay you for your work. But we will provide you with a place to live, food to eat, and clothing to wear. All that is expected of you is for you to do that work you are able to do. And we have to support each other. We have to take care of each other. Part of taking care of each other is defending this place and what little we have here. Starting tomorrow and each day after that except on Sundays, we will be teaching those of you big enough to hold a gun how to shoot."

There was a murmur in the little crowd and Mr. Day said, "You heard me right. It is just a matter of time before some group of soldiers or outlaws come into our place here and we have to be able to protect ourselves. They will be prepared to kill us and take what we have and we must be prepared to kill them. Do you understand?"

Some were shaking their heads and some in the crowed even answered yes sir. "We will meet here tomorrow morning at eight. Those of you I want to be here are Will, Bob, Jenna and the twins, and Miss. Ransom. Tom and Bill will be teaching you how to handle the guns. How to shoot and how to load. OK, I am done. Anyone else have anything to say.

Jenna stood up and said, "Mr. Day, Mrs. Day, I want to thank you for taking us in and saving our lives. I don't quite know how to feel. I was so happy the day we walked away from this place, to freedom. But I soon found out that we wasn't free to do anything. We couldn't go where we wanted to go or do what we wanted to do. That we had just changed masters. So when I got a chance, I ran away again just to wind up in a shanty full of rats and fleas, wallowing in our own fifth. It's then I thought that I would have been better off staying here in our home. At least maybe my husband would have stayed with me. But that feeling is not complete either. I feel that I will never be free as long as I stay here because this land has too much sweat and blood of the slaves who passed this way. So I want to tell you that as soon as I am able I am going to leave. Until then, me and mine will work hard and defend this place as best we can."

"Thank you Jenna. We understand how you feel and we agree that in order for you to be completely free, you will have to move on from here. When you get ready, we will do what we can to make sure you are safe and have what you need to make it."

The next day, Tom and Bill began the task of teaching the bigger kids and the women to shoot and load the rifles. At first the women were afraid of the guns, and the children were too careless with them. By the end of the week, they gave up and just decided that they would have to do any defending that was done on this farm. Instead of teaching the others how to shoot and load, they turned their attention to setting up defensive positions around the farm. Mr. Day had a lot of bales of cotton that he was saving until the end of the war before selling. Bales of cotton was the absolute best protection against rifle fire, and they took advantage of the large numbers they had on hand. They built bunkers of cotton bales and stocked them with guns and ammunition for easy access during any fight they might have. When they were finished, they had the place covered with bale bunkers from the entrance to the farm and surrounding the big house on all sides. At first attack they, would ring the bell in the cooks shed which would call everyone to the main house.

Tom even tested the system a couple of times and it seemed to work. He was not satisfied but he was confident they had enough firepower with the three Henrys to repel a small unit.

When Christmas came and they had had no problems from marauders they felt blessed and festive. On Christmas day the ladies prepared a huge feast under the cooks shed and even put up a tree. The men had their whiskey and the ladies had their apple cider. And the children had their eggnog. Mrs. Day had made sure that there were presents for all the children. Each of the young boys received a pocket knife and the young girls each received a doll made with love by Mrs. Day. The children received fruit and candy also made by Mrs. Day. Mr. Day gave Bob a colt for him to train as his own.

Mr. Day said, "Bob you are getting to be a young man and you need your own horse."

"Thank you sir." Bob made sure the little colt was not out of his sight the rest of the day.

Tom gave Nat one of the Henrys he had gotten on his trip to Jackson. When Nat took it and read what Tom had carved on the brass he wiped a tear from his eye.

"What does it say son?" Nat read it, "Presented to Captain Nathanial Day on Dec 25, 1863. A Man Among Men, A Hero Among Heroes. From Tom McCall.

Mrs. Day hugged Tom and then hugged Nat.

"Thank you Tom. But now I have a gift for you."

He walked over to a table and took a wrapped package and handed it to Tom. Tom smiled in surprise and took the package. As he unwrapped the package everyone was not sure what it was. They could see that there were pistols, but they were wrapped up on leather harness and they could not make it out. Then Tom opened up the harness and slipping off his big coat, put on the shoulder harness with two matching Remington Model 1858s. Then everyone was able to figure out how it worked.

The harness fit Tom like a glove and he moved around a bit just to get the feel of the two pistols under his arms. It felt a little awkward and he tested it to see if he could draw them and fire. In a minute they felt natural. He was very much satisfied and smiled. He grabbed Nat up and gave him a big bear hug, being careful not to hurt his bad leg. "Thank you Nat. You knew exactly what I wanted."

"These Remington are smaller and will fit under your arms with no problems."

Bill came up and shook the hand of Nat and Tom. As did Mr. Day and Will.

Mr. Day said, "Tom you are the most lethal man I know. With four pistols you could hold off an army by yourself."

Tom smiled, "That is the intent sir."

All was quiet at Oakhaven into the spring and they were able to till the soil ready for planting. Then in the middle of April, Will came to the big house early one morning to report he had seen what looked like the tracks of a few horses along the creek about a mile from his house. He and his kids had gone fishing and happened to run up on the tracks. Mr. Day, Tom and Bill followed Will back to where he had seen the tracks.

"Looks like about five horses came across the creek here and rode north."

"Yes sir. Do you want Bill and me to check it out?"

"Yes, we can't take a chance that people are coming through the creek to attack us."

"Let's ride back and get our gear and while we are at it, we will ride the entire parameter to make sure no one is using this as a staging area."

Nat came in while they were getting ready to go. "Why are you guys packing so much? Do you think you will need that much ammunition? Are you guys leaving for good?"

"No, we will be back. I have learned in the last couple of years that you can never be too prepared."

"Yeah, I guess you are right. Be careful."

"We will be back soon and start the planting."

They packed an extra horse with their bedrolls, small canvas tent, food and cooking utensils, and extra ammo for the Henrys. They intended to keep an eye on the west side of the farm for a few days and wanted to make sure they were prepared for everything.

"If we have any problems here, I will send someone to get you."

"Yes sir."

Tom and Bill rode back to where they found the tracks. They followed them to the river, then followed the river west to a swamp where Cypress Creek and the South Fork of the Forked Deer River meet, then the tracks disappeared. They found a small knoll with a large oak tree where they set up camp and waited.

Chapter Thirty

At midday on the third day after Tom and Bill had gone to check out the western end of the farm, a large force of Union Cavalry rode up to the big house. The leader barked orders and the rider spread out covering the entire area around the barn and houses. Then the leader rode up to the main entrance and yelled, "Jonathan Day, are you here?"

Mr. Day was back in the barn doctoring a sick horse, and hearing the commotion, walked towards the front. "Here Sir. May I help you?"

The leader rode up to Mr. Day and said, "Are you Mr. Jonathan Day late of Harvard University class of forty three?"

"I am sir. And who might you be?"

The leader steps off his horse and holding out his hand said, "Sir I'm the honorable Walter D. Bradsworth, also class of forty three."

"Walter? Could it be?"

They shook hands and then embraced. "I'll say Jon, I would not have recognized you, but I could never forget your gracious home. In fact, I built one exactly like it in Boston."

"Colonel Bradsworth, welcome back to my humble home."

They locked arms and walked back to the front entrance. "I want to introduce you to my wife and son and daughter."

"Just a moment, let me talk to my major."

The colonel turned and walked back to his major who had been waiting. He talked to him briefly and the major waved his hand and about six riders came up to him and he gave instructions.

"Colonel, this is my …"

"Of course she is. Lillian, how have you been? You look lovely as usual." And he kissed her hand.

"Walt, you haven't changed a bit. Always the gallant gentleman."

"This is my daughter Doreen and my son Nathanial."

The Colonel kissed the hand of Doreen and as he shook the hand of Nathanial he noticed the crutches. "War?"

"Yes, sir."

"So many of our young men have been killed and wounded. Too many. I am weary of this fight."

Then he catches himself and said, "Oh well, we must see the finish soon."

Mrs. Day sighed, "Sooner, I prey."

"Please excuse the way we rode in. We have to be ready for anything and I wasn't sure if you were still here. This war has devastated the land and most large farms have been overran by one side or the other. I am happy you are still here and are ok. It has changed little since you brought me here for a visit the summer of forty-two."

"Only we have changed. We have gotten older and wiser. I cannot say I am glad to see you under these circumstances but I understand. Do what you have to do and we will comply. I give you my word of honor that no one here will give you or your men any resistance. We have food that you can take. Please do not kill the big sow, she pregnant. And we will need the two milk cows for milk for the kids."

"We will talk about that later. Right now I need you to show me around the place."

Mr. Day showed him the cooks shed.

"Major, set up the mess here."

"Yes, sir."

As they rode up to the first house, Jenna and her kids came out of the little house.

"Jonathan, do you still have slaves?"

Before Mr. Day could answer, Jenna said, "No, Mr. Day done let us go a long time ago. He picked us up out the squalor of Jackson and brought us here and saved our lives. After you Yankees run us around the country and nearly kilt us."

"Thank you miss."

The Colonel smiled and said, "She seems free alright and well fed. Any more folks you picked up off the street and gave a home?"

"Actually there is another family that I picked up along with Jenna. Miss. Ransom and her four children live in the next house."

"Is that all the people you have here?"

"No sir. There is a white family. The manager of my farm for a long time. Mr. William Clinton. He has a teenage boy and three little girls. We can ride down to see them or have them report to you at the house."

"It's ok, I just have to let my men know so they will leave them along."

Now let's talk about more important stuff. I have to use your house as my headquarters and we will need food and the use of your facilities to quarter my men and horses."

"I understand the needs of war and I understand your position and take no offense."

"Now what were you saying about a pregnant hog and milk cows. Wait just a minute. Major please join us."

A major walked up to the Colonel and saluted. "Major please listen to Mr. Day and take note."

"Please do not kill the big hog, she is pregnant and will have a litter soon. Also, we will need two milk cows for milk for the kids. Also, the old bull is the only bull around so I need him for breeding the cows. The rest of the hogs and cattle you can slaughter for yourselves."

"That is very generous of you, but we will only use your stores as needed."

"Johnathan, do you have bedrooms for me and Major Winston?"

"Yes sir. And we have one more available if you need it."

"No, two will be enough. And we will need a large room to set up our headquarters."

"The large parlor is just the place you are looking for. Just adjust the furniture as you see fit."

That evening Mr. Day had invited the Colonel and Major to have supper with the family.

"Lillian, I hate that we met again after all these years under these circumstances."

"Think nothing about it, Walt. It is wonderful to see you again. And I had rather the Colonel sitting here is you and not a total stranger. At least you understand and know who Jonathan and I are, and how we feel about our fellow men."

"Thank you. We will tread as lightly as possible."

That night after they had gone to their rooms, Mr. Day wrote a note that he would send to Tom and Bill. The next day when he got a chance he gave note, along with a leather bag, to Bob and told him to get it to Tom. But to be careful and not get caught with the note or coming and going to Tom.

When Bob rode home he got his fishing pole and dug some worms and rode towards the river. When he had gone about a half mile two Union soldiers rode up to him. "Where you going boy?"

The suddenness of them coming at him had startled Bob, but he soon gained his composure. "Going town to the river to catch some brim, Sir."

"Brim? What the hell is a brim?"

The other soldier said, "That's a small sun perch. They call them brim down here."

"How you cook'em?"

"Mama fries them whole. We just scale um, cut the heads off, guts um, and fries up. She says that if you leave the fins on, the bones comes out easier."

"How old is your mama? Do you have any older sisters?"

"My mama is pretty old. Nah, I just have three little sisters."

"How about you? You have any brothers or sisters?"

The soldiers were surprised by the question since they were asking for different reasons than the boy."

"Boy you better go on fishing. It's going to be too late pretty soon."

"Ok, see you'll later."

Bob rode north towards the river and then west until he heard a loud whistle. He did not react to the whistle immediately but slowly turned his horse towards the tree. Tom moved slowly down the knoll to meet him. "Don't dismount, just fiddle with the horse's bridle while we talk."

"Mr. Day sent you a note and this here bag. The farm has been overran with Union soldiers but Mr. Day knows the Colonel."

"Ok keep riding down to the river and fish for at least an hour, and take the fish home with you just in case the search you again."

Tom read the note. *Tom, you and Bill need to head west as soon as possible. We have been taken over by Union soldiers. But do not worry about us. The Colonel in charge is an old friend of mine from Harvard and he will make sure we are safe.*

Thank you again for bringing our son home and helping us during the last year.

I have included some silver dollars in with the ammunition bag. This is all I had available at this time. Please contact us when you get settled.

Good luck and May God bless you and Bill.

Signed: Jonathan Day

Tom handed the note to Bill, who read the note said, "He is a good man. They are a good family."

"Let's get out of here before one of the Union pickets sees us."

"Which way Tom?"

"I don't feel right about following the tracks. I don't want to run into a group of raiders, so I think we should cross the river and go northwest."

Chapter Thirty-one

The river was in its banks so it was not very wide but it was deep. As soon as their horses stepped into the river, they were swimming. It was a little swampy on the other side but they soon rode out of the swamp into farmland.

They had no idea where they were, but knew they had to go west. Tom had talked to Mr. Day about his intentions of going west and getting a ranch. Mr. Day told them they would have to cross the Mississippi River and recommended they cross the river just below Dyersburg. He told them there were two ferries there before the war. One at Ashport and the other one at Cotton Wood Point. If they could not get a ferry, they could get a boatman to get them across. But with the war going on, they would have to go there and see what was available. While they were talking, they were looking at Mr. Day's map and if he remembered correctly, Dyersburg was to the northwest of Jackson.

"Bill, we have to get to Dyersburg. So we need to find someone who knows the way."

"The best place to get information is a mercantile store, they always know what's going on."

"Yeah, so let's find a store."

Since they were not familiar with this part of Tennessee, they did not venture far from the main roads. Towards sundown, they rode into the small town of Bells. There were only a few houses and a general store. They tied their horses outside the general store and went inside. There was two men sitting in straight chairs playing checkers. They didn't look up when Tom and Bill entered. There was a middle-aged woman behind the counter who barley looked up.

"Can I help you boys?"

"Yes ma'am. I need some smoking tobacco and some papers. And a bottle of that liniment up there."

"Got a bad lag, do you?"

"Yeah, took a bullet and it won't heal."

"I got some salve here that might help. Drummer brought it in last week. Says the Yankees use it for their wounded."

"If it will help my leg heal, I will try anything."

"Anything else?"

"Dan, you need anything?"

"No, I'm good."

"That's all for today."

"That will be thirty five cents."

"Where you boys from?" One of the checker players had looked up from the board. "Ain't seen you boys around here before."

"We from up around Dyersburg."

"What brings you down this way?" The man who was asking the questions stood up and in so doing showed his little constable badge and his piston on his belt.

"We are heading to Linden. I have a brother there who owns a mercantile store and needs me to help him."

"Not deserters are you?"

"No sir, I have my papers if you like to see them. With this leg, I can't fight no more."

The constable thought for a couple of minutes and the said, "Well, I guess this old war has taken its toll on all of us in one way or the other. Better be careful, the outlaws and the damn Yankees are as thick as ticks on an old dogs balls."

Then he catches himself and looks at the lady behind the counter and said, "Oh, sorry Lattie. In other words you have to be careful going east with the Tennessee Federals and the Union troops. And don't ride down the main road. Better to ride about twenty yards from the road. That way if you see or hear riders you can just go the other way."

"Sir, you sound like you were once a military man."

The other man who was playing checkers said, "He is a military man. He graduated from West Point and fought the Indians out west and even took a commission in the first year of this war."

"Oh, be quiet Grady. My soldiering days are long gone."

"I salute you sir. Thank you for your information and advice."

"You boys didn't say what your names was."

"I'm Lonnie Bing and this is Daniel Hogg."

"You boys could pass for brothers. You sure you are not kin."

"Well, you are right sir. He is my cousin. My father and his mother are brother and sister."

The constable looked pleased that he had been right in his observation.

"You boys have a place to stay tonight?"

"Now Lattie, these boys are too young for you."

"Oh, hush up you old man. I was going to tell them about the widow Wilson next door. She has rooms and she is a good cook."

"Thanks, that sounds good. We need a place to stay and Dan is always hungry."

Tom and Bill tipped their hat to Lattie and Tom said, "Thank you gentlemen and ma'am for your help."

They led their horses next door and by the time they had walked upon the porch a young man with one arm missing came out. "Are you looking for a place to stay?"

"Yes sir."

"Well go right in, I will take care of the horses."

"Let us get our bags."

They went inside to what looked like a normal house just a little bigger than most. There was a woman in the parlor who greeted them, "Good evening gentlemen and welcome. Will you need one or two rooms? I have one room with two beds."

"That sounds good, we will take that one."

"Please sign the book. It will be a two dollars each and the price includes the food for you and your horse."

Tom paid the lady and she showed them their room. "Once you have washed you can come down to supper. We have two other gentlemen staying here and they will join us for supper."

"I don't know about you Tom, but I am getting one of those feeling in the back of my neck like something crawling there."

"Yeah, I started getting it when we was talking to the constable. Something about him didn't seem right. This is the reason I wanted to make sure we took our bags with the ammunitions with us."

Tom washed his face and hands and slicked back his thick black hair. He took his shoulder guns off and left them in the room but tucked his other pistols in his waist. Once Bill had washed up he said, "Ready?"

"Come in gentlemen. Take any open chair."

By instinct Tom took a seat with his back to the wall and Bill sat at the other end closest to the door. They had the table covered.

The other guests seemed to be already there. Tom looked around at the guests. One was an older woman, no threat there. The other two were in their thirties and both wore black suits. Tom could make out that they were both armed under their coats. Tom caught the eye of Bill and made his hand into a gun. Bill shook his head.

Mrs. Wilson came in with food in both hands accompanied by the young man with the arm missing. "We will be bringing the rest right in. In the meantime, you should introduce yourselves."

"The old lady said, "I am Mrs. Trout and I feel lucky to be having supper with all you young men."

"Glad to meet you ma'am. I am Lonnie Bing and my cousin is Daniel Hogg."

"Ma'am, I am John Donner and the gentlemen with me is Sam Davidson."

"Mr. Bing, I noticed you were limping a little when you came in. A war wound I suppose?"

Ignoring the impoliteness of the question Tom answered, "You are right sir. Took a ball that hit the bone."

The mere fact that the man ask the question told a lot about him. First he was a Yankee, given away by his accent, and second that he was probably a military officer, indicated by his tone and confidence.

"Where you'll from?" This time it was the old lady who had ask the question.

"We are from up around Dyersburg, and you madam?"

"I'm from Halls. We are practically neighbors."

"How about you gentlemen where are you'll from?"

"The one that spoke before looked at the other one and said, "We are from Mobile. We are horse traders."

Tom looked at Bill and smiled. He knew the man was playing with them expecting them to say something about his accent. He had taken them for a couple of dumb yokels. But he was playing from a position of strength. That meant he had accomplices. Tom and Bill would have to be careful until they found out who they were.

"I knew a horse trader once. It seems he sold a country family a couple of mules and the next day the mules were not there. They had broken out of their enclosure and ran away. Well, the farmer needed mules to get in his crop in so he went back to the same trader and bought two more mules. Well, would you believe it? The next day those mules was gone. But just in case these mules ran off, the farmer had painted the hoofs red. So he goes back to the same trader and picks out a matching pair of mules and when the trader led them up to the farmer. The farmer takes a rag out of his pocket and wipes the dirt off the mule's hoofs and low and behold, they were painted red. Well, it didn't take long for the word to get around and a crowd gathered. Come to find out, others had purchased mules and horses from the same trader and the next day their purchases had ran off. Well to make a long story short, the horse trader was hanged. On his tomb stone was written: *Here Lies a Now Honest Horse Trader.*"

The old lady laughed out loud. "Now he is an honest horse trader. That is funny. Now he is honest."

Tom smiled. This was the first time he had heard Bill speak more than ten words at a time.

"Sir, I hope your story was not meant to imply that all horse traders were dishonest. One must be careful not to give offense to someone they do not know."

"Sir, if I thought that you were really horse traders I would not have told the story. So you don't have to feign offense just to continue a ruse."

The gentleman who had not spoken all evening now said, "John, these gentlemen are not fooled a bit by our story of being horse traders. Please forgive us for misleading you but if our real purpose for being here was known it might raise the price of land in the area. You see, we are land speculators from Maryland."

The old lady said, "Well I'll be. I thought sure you were horse traders." And then she laughed again.

"Any vacant land over towards Dyersburg?"

"Lots of land all over the country now that people have been run off their farms or lost it to the banks."

"If I was you, I would keeping using the horse trader story. People are even more hostile to land speculators than horse thieves… Oh, sorry. Horse traders."

Mr. Davidson pointing his hand at Bill and said, "Mr. Hogg, right? Do you spell that with one g' or two? Never mind. Sir you seem to be trying to say something all evening. Maybe you would like to go outside and talk."

"Sir I would love to oblige you but right now I am hungry. You know how we hogs like to eat."

"Mrs. Wilson, these pork chops are delicious and your cornbread is as light as the wind. You are a wonderful cook."

"Thank you Mr. Hogg. You are very kind. And I suspect, hungry."

The young man walked in with a pitcher of water and started to pour Mr. Davidson some more water. Mr. Davidson bumped his arm and the young man spilled the water on him. Mr. Davidson stood up and grabbed the pitcher and poured the water on the young man and said, "You did that on purpose. I saw you laughing before at Mr. Hogg story. So you thought you would join in the fun."

Bill stood up and Tom shook his head and mouthed, Not Now. Bill sat back down.

The old lady said, "Sir, I am sure Trent did not mean to spill water on you. He is a good boy. He lost his arm at Shiloh. He had no family or place to go, so Mrs. Wilson took him in."

Seeing his position was indefensible, Mr. Davidson backed down and said, "You are right of course Mrs. Trout and I apologize. Trent, I apologize."

Mrs. Wilson brought in two pies. Leaning over Bill she said, "What will you have? Apple or Pecan."

"Pecan, please."

Continuing with his prodding, Mr. Davidson said, "Might want to give Mr. Hogg one each kind." And he laughed.

"No, one piece is enough, but I would love to have a big glass of cold milk if you have one."

"Trent, some milk for Mr. Hogg."

Tom stood up and said, "Mrs. Trout it's been a pleasure meeting you. Mr. Davidson and Mr. Donner it's been entertaining having supper with you. And good luck in the land speculation business. But if you will wait just a little longer, you can probably just walk in and take the land in the name of the victor."

Turning to Bill, he said, "I will check on the horses before we go to sleep."

Bill nodded and went back to eating his pie.

Tom had just entered the barn and walked up to his horse when he heard someone behind him. He spun around with his hands full Colts but stopped when he saw it was the young man Trent.

"Boy, I just about shot you. Better to make some noise when you come up behind a man. Just let them know you are there and mean no harm."

"Yes sir. Sorry Sir."

"It's ok. You wish to speak to me?"

"Yes sir. I heard the constable talking to those two men inside. They was talking about you and Mr. Hogg being deserters or spies. Anyway, they are going to take you in or kill you. The constable wanted to do it tonight but the two men said wait until tomorrow morning before you left."

"Thank you Trent. Is the constable a unionist?"

"Yes, sir. He was discharged from the army for being too cruel to the southern prisoners. Anyway, that's what Mrs. Wilson said."

"Thank you Trent, now you better go back inside before they miss you."

Tom saddled his and Bill's horses and put the pack on the pack horse and got them ready to travel.

When Tom came back inside, the dinner guests were still setting at the table and Bill and the old lady were talking.

Tom joined them seeing that Bill had a piece of paper and was drawing a crude map. But the conversation they were having did not match the places and roads on the map. Somehow Bill had conveyed to Mrs. Trout that they needed a map of the west. Especially where to cross the Mississippi.

"If I was you, I would bypass Jackson. I read in the paper that the union had taken it over and had set up roadblocks. You will want to go south and cross the river below Parsons."

"Well, that will be out of our way a little, but it is better than getting picked up the Union."

"Or getting killed by the damn raiders."

"Mrs. Wilson, what time do you have breakfast?"

"Starting at six and serving until eight."

"Good. Early but not too early. I hate traveling in the dark."

"You ready to hit the sack Dan?"

"Good evening everyone, see you at breakfast."

Unable to resist one more jab Mr. Davidson said, "Are we having hog again for breakfast?"

Ignoring the rhetorical aspect of the question, Mrs. Wilson said, "Yes sir. Bacon and sausage, redeye gravy, sorghum, and hot fluffy biscuits."

But his dig did not get past Bill who mentally made a mark on his sheet he was keeping on Mr. Davidson or whatever his name was.

When they got into the room, they went over the map and talked about it so it would remain in their memory then they burned it. Tom told Bill what Trent had said and they planned on getting a couple of hours sleep and then quietly getting out of town.

"I know you would love to kill those bastards but we have to be careful."

"Yeah, I know. But if they follow us out of town then they are mine. Especially Mr. Davidson."

"Who do you figure they are?"

"They are definitely Union spies working with the constable to report anything going on in this area. If they follow, we will take care of them and make a statement."

They slept for about three hours. Bill was the first to wake up and he kicked Tom's boot.

"Ok, I'm awake."

They quietly made their way outside and circled around to come at the barn from a different direction.

"I got a feeling that constable is cat smart. He likes to play with the mice he catches. I am sure he has assigned someone to keep an eye on our horses."

"Yeah, I was just thinking the same. Let me go in first and see what I can find."

"Ok, I will be a minute behind you."

Bill carried a big knife which was a combination of butcher knife and crowbar. He slipped it out of his boot and climbed through a window in the barn. He saw dim flicker of a cigarette on the opposite end of the barn from where Tom would be coming in. He waited until the little light got bigger and threw his knife about six inches below it and right in the middle of what he knew would be the man's chest. He heard the knife hit and heard the man fall. There was no other sound. He waited another ten seconds and then climbed the ladder to the hayloft. When he was half way up the ladder he heard someone whisper, "Charley, are you ok. I thought I heard a noise."

"Bill whispered. I'm ok. Do you have a light?"

"Yeah. Coming down."

Bill backed off the ladder and waited. When the man was halfway down, Bill hit him with his pistol and caught his body before it hit the floor. He drug the man to the end of the barn where the other man was. He retrieved his big knife and wiped it off on the man's pants leg.

Bill walked down to the side door and whispered, "Tom."

"Here."

"Come on in."

They made sure their saddles were cinched for hard riding and made sure the pack was tied to the pack horse. They put their bags on their horses and tied them down. Tom took his pistols from his belt and put them in their holsters beside the saddle. They made sure their Henrys were fully loaded with one in the chamber. They were ready to go to war.

They rode slowly and quietly out of town towards the north. Once they had cleared the town Tom said, "That constable is smart enough to set up lookouts on both sides of the town. By going north first, hopefully we will go around them. But once they figure out we have not gone to the east they will come after us."

"Yeah, Mr. Davidson and Mr. Donner will take it personal and they will be the ones who come. What say we set up our own ambush?"

'Yeah, and I hope the constable comes with them. I have started taking a big dislike to him."

"Yeah, and I have noticed that when you take a dislike to someone their life expectancy seems to get shorter."

"Yeah, I get the same feeling about you."

They rode for about three hours slowly picking their way in the dark until they circled back to the main road and then found a place for an ambush. They made sure their pack horse was tied and hobbled so it would be there when they needed it. They found a place to hide with a full view of the roadway. The sun was just starting to come up.

They waited about thirty minutes before they saw two riders coming from the direction of Bells.

"We will let these two pass and wait to see if there are others following."

They did not recognize the two riders. So they could have been anyone just riding on the road, but Tom figured they were the scouts sent ahead to see if they could stir something up.

About ten minutes later a group of four riders coming from the same direction but they were moving a little faster.

"Well lookie here. If it ain't Mr. Davidson. And the constable."

"And Mr. Donner. Don't recognize the other one."

Once the riders had passed, Tom and Bill mounted and with a nod from Tom rode to catch them. Tom was a trained Cavalryman and he was on a trained Cavalry horse. Bill was a civilian, but had probably been in more fights than Tom. As they moved close enough behind the riders that the riders could hear their horses the riders reigned in and turned to see who was behind them. When they turned, Tom and Bill stopped their horses in the middle of the road.

"Are you looking for us gentlemen?"

The constable was the one who answered, "Yes we are. Want to ask you a few questions about a murder."

The man they did not recognize chose that time to lift his double barrel and it was the wrong thing to do. Bill dropped him immediately and the fight was on. The constable was the next to fall and then Mr. Donner. The only one who was not dead was Mr. Davidson who at the first shot took off like a scared rabbit. Bill rode after him followed by Tom. When Bill got close, Mr. Davidson turned and was shot in the head falling backwards off his horse. Tom was the first to notice the two men who had ridden through earlier had turned and was riding back. Tom rode to meet them with Bill trailing. The men dropped at the same time. Dead when they hit the ground.

Tom and Bill caught the horses and put the bodies on them and led them to the place where they had tied their pack horse.

"It these bodies are found we are going to be some hunted men."

"What's new?"

"Yeah, but they will put the dogs on us and they know we are heading west."

"That means we have to get out of Tennessee as soon as possible."

"Well if you would stop making friends in every little town we pass through, we would already be across the Mississippi."

Tom smiled, "Me? You are the one who makes all the friends. I thought you and Mr. Davidson was going to start riding together."

"Looks like we are going to have to make sure these bodies are never found."

They searched the bodies and took all identifying articles. Seems the constable job really paid well. They found over a hundred dollars on him. Mr. Donner was actually Major Schwartz of the Union Army and Mr. Davidson was Captain Lansky also of the Union Army.

Chapter Thirty-two

Bodies were easy to get rid of but the horses would be a problem. If they turned them lose they would just go home, so they had to either shoot them or make sure someone kept them penned up for a while. Horses were expensive and hard to find during the war.

"Let's take them with us and sell them in the next town."

"We will be taking a chance, but let's do it. Anyway we need the money."

They found a deep gully covered by woods and brush and made sure the bodies were all the way to the bottom.

"Not even a rabbit hunter will find them there."

"Now to get rid of the horses."

"We have to move fast to get to Halls by sundown."

They rode as quick as possible without over taxing their horses arriving in Halls around three in the afternoon.

"Let's go directly to the livery stable to get rid of these horses and then get out of here."

"Yeah, but can we at least eat before we go?"

"That sounds good."

An old man was sitting on the porch of the mercantile store and Bill said, "Sir, can you direct us to the livery stables?"

"Directly ahead of you on the right. Talk to Mr. Williams."

"Thank you sir."

"You are welcome young man. Them is some nice horses you got there. Are you looking to sell them?"

"Yes sir, we are."

"Do you mind if I take a look at them?'

"Don't mind at all sir. Are you a horse man?"

"I have bought and sold a few horses in my day."

The old man stood up, pulled up his pants and proceeded to look the horses over. First checking their legs, their neck and then their teeth. As he went from horse, he clicked his tongue with degrees of approval. Finally, he sat back down where he started.

"Gentlemen, you have a combination of the good and bad there. You take that big red there. He looks good, but he is old. On the other hand that little black one is young, but his legs are weak. The other four are ok mounts. Good legs and not too long on the tooth. I will give you sixty-five dollars each for those four and forty-five for the other two."

"Sir you do know your horses. I told Alton about them two when he wanted to buy them. But he thinks he knows more about horses than I do."

"I do know more about horses then you do. It's just that the man who sold these two horses to me had a nice young daughter and she distracted me."

The old man laughed and said, "Them young girls have a way of distracting a young man."

"Tell you what we can do. I will give them four horses to you for eighty-five and the other two for sixty-five. Otherwise I will go down and talk to Mr. Williams."

"Alright, this is my last offer, cash money where you stand. Seventy-five each for the four and fifty each for the other two."

"Is the money in silver or gold?"

"All in silver."

"Sir, you drive a hard bargain, but seem like an honest man."

"It's done."

"Ok, let's go inside and get some paper for a bill of sale."

They followed the old man inside the store and he ask the clerk for some paper to be used for bill of sale.

Tom handed him the bill of sale for the horses and the old gentleman give them four hundred dollars silver dollars.

Tom turning to the clerk said, "Sir, would you happen to have any gold coins?"

"Let me check. I have five twenty dollar gold coins."

"Would you mind changing these silver dollars for your gold coins?"

"I will give you the five coins for one hundred and five dollars. That is the normal change rate even at the bank."

"Ok, I will do it."

As they walked outside, the old man was leading the six horses to the livery stable.

"He will probably sell them for a hundred each to the blacksmith."

"Probably, but he will be happy that he took advantage of us."

"Shall we ask the clerk where we can find a restaurant?"

"What do you say we just ride on down the road? I have a bad feeling about this place. Let's look for another place to eat."

Tom had learned to trust Bills instincts and they mounted and rode on towards their crossing point.

Chapter Thirty-three

They rode north out of Halls keeping to their mapped route. It was sundown when they rode into Fowlkes. They stopped in front of the hotel and Tom went inside. He returned in a couple of minutes with a boy. They took the usual stuff with them and the boy led the horses back to the stables.

An old woman showed them their room and told them that supper would be in thirty minutes.

"You are getting ripe, going to need a bath pretty soon."

Tom laughed and said, "That's funny coming from a man who hasn't been fully submerged in water in over a year."

"Let's just agree that we both could use a bath and some clean clothes."

"Ok tomorrow, we will find a creek and wash up and put on clean clothes."

"Let's just hope there are no fine young ladies at the supper table. They might be offended."

As they walked into the dining room, they looked at each other and smiled. Sure enough there were three young women and an older lady sitting at the table.

"Good evening gentlemen. Just find a seat where you can."

Tom picked his usual seat with his back to the wall leaving Bill stuck between two women.

They filled their plates and ate quietly, a little shy being in the room with so many women. They were used to the conversations of hard men and were afraid to talk too much in fear of saying something that might offend someone.

The young women had no problem talking. In fact they talked incessantly until the older lady with them said, "Ladies, where are your manners. We haven't even met our dinner companions or introduced ourselves."

"I am Miss Waters, and these young ladies are my pupils studying to be teachers. The one there is Miss. Lewis, the next one is Miss. Langford, and last but not least Miss. Appleton. We are traveling to Dyersburg for their first teaching assignment."

"I am Mr. Raymond Billings and this is my brother Ben."

"Are you coming from a college in Memphis?"

"Yes we are."

"Do you know if there are ferries still operating on the Mississippi in this area?"

Pleased that they could be helpful, Miss. Waters said, "The last I heard, there was a ferry at Cottonwood Point."

"That is good information, thank you very much."

"Would any of you happen to know the route out west?"

"Sir, I have book with maps of the way west. Would you like to see it?"

"That would be great. We have a way picked, but if we could find a better one. Plus, we would like to avoid the soldiers and raiders."

When the girls had finishes, one of them went and got her book. They showed Tom and Bill the maps of the route west. Now all they had to do was figure out where they wanted to go.

"If you want to avoid the soldiers and raiders, then you will want to stay south of Missouri and Kansas. I have been reading the papers and that area is a bad place to be."

"We were thinking about the Indian Territories or farther west. I met a man from the Colorado Territory and he said it was a great place to settle. So why don't we plot a course to the Colorado Territory?"

The young ladies were excited about being able to help them draw a map of the known trails to Aurora, which was built during the gold rush in 1859. One of the young ladies was good at drawing and the maps were in great detail including rivers, main roads and trails, and the settlements along the way, including Army posts. Miss. Waters even noted where there was military activity and raiders operating.

By the time they had finished the maps, they were all talking like they had known each other for a long time.

When they were ready to go to bed, they said their goodbyes and wished each other luck.

Tom and Bill rode out early the next morning heading due west where they soon came to the Forked Deer River which they swam. They did not stop to bath as they had planned because the water was muddy. Then they headed northwest towards the crossing on the Obion River.

They approached the ferry carefully making sure there were no troops waiting to cross. Once they saw the course was clear, they rode quickly to the landing. The ferry was on its way back with a wagon pulled by two mules and a dismounted rider holding his horse.

Once the ferry was unloaded they led their horses on and paid the ferryman.

"Where you boys heading?"

"Going to try take the ferry across the Mississippi. Is the one running at Cottonwood Point?"

"Yea, my brother runs it."

"How about troop activity. Any Union troops in the area that we should know about?"

"Gentlemen, I don't know who is in the area. I do not ask questions. I have to carry anyone who shows up at my dock. But when they have a whole bunch of troops to move across these small rivers, they build boat bridges otherwise they would never be able to get all the troops across."

"We understand."

"If I was you though, I might wait until sundown tomorrow before I tried to cross."

"Thank you."

They rode on the main road talking as they rode.

"That guy was trying to tell us something but I am not sure what."

"Well, it sounded like he was telling us that there would be people crossing the ferry sometime before tomorrow at sundown. So they could probably cross anytime and be on the road."

"Yeah, so we need to get off this damn road until tomorrow."

"Let's look at the map."

"The river makes a big turn here. If we tucked ourselves down against the river we would be out of the way. It looks like it all woods back in there."

"Sounds good to me. We can set up camp and maybe even get you a bath."

"I'm only taking one if you take one too."

"Ok, we will both take a bath."

They set up camp tucked back into the deep woods a few hundred yards from the river on a little stream that flowed into the river. They unsaddled their horses and tied and hobbled them so they could move around and eat and drink.

They had some time to kill and they bathed and washed their dirty clothes.

During the night they were awaken by the barking of dogs. The got up and went outside the tent and listened. Their fire was just embers so there was no light except what the moon provided.

"Hunters maybe?"

"Yeah, but they might be hunting us."

"They are getting closer."

In a few minutes a big blood hound came bounding into camp followed by a couple of hound dogs.

Bill whistled a loud whistle.

"Better to let them know we are here than have them stumble upon us and having us killing them."

"Who is over there?"

"We just camping out for the night. We don't mean any trouble."

"Come on in to the camp."

They saw a couple of lights moving in their direction. The dogs had already curled up resting.

By the time they had come into the camp, Bill had built up the fire.

Three men came into camp. The first one in was walking and he had leashes in his hands so they knew he was the dog man. He was small and wiry with a full beard. He had on overalls with no shirt. The other two were riding. As they rode in one of them dismounted and leveled a shotgun in the general direction of Bill and Tom. The man with a shotgun was a big man tall and round with a felt hat. The third man sat the horse like a gentleman. He wore nice pants and shirt. He had a handgun in a western holster.

"Gentlemen do you know whose land you are on?"

"No sir. We on our way west and did not want to be on the road just in case troops or raiders came by. Sorry, we will be glad to move on."

"It's ok, I understand you not wanting to be on the road and you don't seem to be doing any harm."

"You'll coon hunting?"

The dog man snickered and said, "Yeah, we hunting coons. The two legged kind."

"Quiet Bunny."

"I'm W.R. Compton. I own all this land along the Obion so you're on my land. Where you all from?"

"We from a little farm around Linden. We lost everything and are heading out west to see if we can start all over. We taking the ferry tomorrow if possible."

"I am Raymond Billings and this is my brother Ben."

"Did you get the wound in the war?"

"Yes sir. Still hasn't healed. Probably wind up killing me."

"Yeah, I lost my oldest son to the damn Tennessee Federals."

"Then we have something in common sir. I lost my wife and boy and my little girl to them. If it is any consolation, we killed a lot of those bastards."

"I have heated up some coffee gentlemen if you would like to have some."

"Thank you. That sounds good. Bunny, get those damn dogs out of here they smell like skunks."

"We haven't seen anyone since we crossed on the ferry today. How many you looking for?"

"Two young boys and a woman. Aha, it doesn't matter anyway. It's just a matter of time when all of this will be over."

The landowner finished his cup of coffee and stood up and said, "Gentlemen, we will be going. Thank you for your hospitality. Take the time you need and don't worry about it. Just be careful on the main roads. There is rumors of a large group of Union soldiers coming this way from Missouri."

"Thank you sir."

About three in the morning Bill heard a small noise outside the tent and he quietly slipped out the back and slowly moved towards the now sedate fire. He saw a shadow between him and the embers of the fire and he dove at the shadow and wound up with a young boy in his grasp.

"Turn me lose. Mama, Tommie help."

"Hold still, I'm not going to hurt you."

"Leave my boy along. We just hungry."

"Hold it. Stop I have a pistol on you. Stand still."

Tom stoked up the fire so they could see who was in their camp.

"Sit down and be quiet and we will sort this out."

Tom knew the answer to his question before he asked, "Who are you and what are you doing in our camp?"

"We are free people. Mr. Lincoln done set us free. But Mr. Compton don't want us to go. He let everyone else go but us. He ask us to stay and when we refused he put us in the corn shed and we broke the door down and ran away."

"These boys your sons?"

"Yes sir."

The boys were the spitting image of their father.

Bill said, "I can see why he did not want them to leave can't you?"

"Yeah."

Bill fixed them a plate of food and gave it to them. They ate like they were starving.

"How long since you ran away?"

"Three days. Please don't take us back to Mr. Compton."

"Listen to me. Tomorrow a group of Union soldiers will be crossing the river from Missouri. You need to hide by the roadside and wait for them to come by. Then go with them. Hopefully they will take you to someplace where you will be safe."

The woman fell on her knees and grabbed Tom's hand and said, "God bless you."

Then she did the same to Bill. Bill picked her up by the shoulders. He pressed five silver dollars in her hand and said, "Take your sons and go north."

Before they left, Tom put some food in a cloth bag and handed it to them.

"I guess we were not meant to get any rest tonight. We still have all day tomorrow to sleep."

Tom laughed and said, "Now if the damn northern army would just come through our camp it would be complete."

Chapter Thirty-four

In the bottom land of West Tennessee the water dictated your route of travel. Between the Obion River and the Mississippi River there were large dense swamps so if the traveler was smart and knowledgeable they would travel the main road. Unfortunately, Tom and Bill did not know the area and their map they had did not include the swamps so they had a few fits and starts before they figured out that they had to stay on the main road even if was more dangerous. They rode quietly as they moved closer to the river and when they heard someone coming, they rode into the brush. They could tell from the tracks and worn down grass on the edges of the road that a large force had passed along the main road during the day and they hoped that the entire group had ridden by.

They moved down river a bit and approached the ferry slowly listening for any noise. When they heard none, they rode to the ferry. Luckily it was on the east bank and in the process of loading a few wagons and other people on horseback.

Tom paid the boatman and they led their horses forward and stood by them. With Tom holding the horses, Bill walked around and without asking questions was able to acquire a lot of information. A brigade size force had been crossing all day long starting at midnight last night. The Union brought extra boats in to speed up the crossing. They were heading to Nashville. The road west was clear to Tulsa. The South was losing every large battle in the south and east. The Union controlled all the rivers and railroads. It was just a matter of time. The politicians were already looking for people to blame. The south would soon be overran by northerns looking for free land. Free slaves were coming back and killing their former masters. These are just some of the things Bill heard on that little ferry ride.

Later when he told Tom what he had heard he said, "You can chose what you wish to believe or disregard. The way I see it, we are getting out of this place at just the right time. There is something we need to talk about. We are going to need more money than we have on us if we are going to be able to afford to get us a place, no matter where we decide to settle."

"I agree, what are you getting at?"

"There is a lot of money floating around this country and I think we should try to get some of it. Since we have lost everything in this damn war and without sounding like I am making excuses to steal, I feel the people who bled this country owes us and other people some compensation. I am willing to take what I think I am owed and as far as you are concerned, I don't think they have enough money to repay you for what you lost. But we can sure try to get something for your loss. What do you say?"

"I think I understand what you are saying and I totally agree with you. I want more than my pound of flesh. I want punitive damages paid to me and I will decide when it's enough. Beginning today I feel that we should take every opportunity to right this wring. We will play it by ear."

They mounted up and eased their mounts off the ferry and both took a big breath of free air. They had made it out of Tennessee alive and from now on they would live their lives on their own terms. In 1860 Tom and Bill had never came close to killing a man even in the many fights they participated in. But as they left Tennessee they were able to kill without remorse. The war had made them killers and outlaws and they would need something as good as the war was evil to right their course.

As they rode west they found out that the reports of the road being clear all the way to Tulsa was not quite true. They saw many small units of Union Cavalry that they were able to avoid. The biggest problem for Tom and Bill during the waning days of the war was not the Union soldiers but the small groups of raiders, outlaws, deserters, slave hunters, and slaves who were trying to get north, and keep out of the hands of the slave hunters. These were desperate men with nothing else to lose, and they shot first and robbed the bodies.

They found out on their second night on the west side of the Mississippi that camping was a very dangerous activity. They had just set up camp when a group of five men rode in with their guns drawn.

"Put your hand up and stand still."

The man speaking was a small man with a big shotgun lying over his saddle pointed in the direction of Tom. The other four immediately dismounted and started going through the camp.

"Wait."

"Wait for what?"

"Well, I got three men in the woods with their guns pointed at you little man and if you move so much as eyelid, they will blow you out of the saddle. Do you think we are dumb enough to set up a camp in this place without setting out guards?"

"You are lying." The leader had spoken the words, but he didn't seem too sure.

In a loud voice Tom said, "Simon, if this son of a bitch does not lower his shotgun in one second, blow his damn ugly head off."

The other four men had moved to back up their boss and were standing in line. The first one to die was leader falling backward off his horse the shotgun flying through the air. The two on the right and the two on the left died immediately thereafter. All was quiet as they listened for any noise. Once they felt it was safe, they reloaded their pistols and surveyed the carnage.

"Whew, them 44s make a damn mess don't they?"

"Yeah, and a lot of noise and smoke."

"These son of bitches think they can just ride into our camp and hold us up. What the hell were they thinking? How in the hell have they lived this long being so stupid?"

They searched the bodies and the bags on the horses and piled all the stuff on a blanket by the fire.

"Not much there. But at least we have some trading goods. Save our money."

"Hell, as many horses as we come across, we might as well be horse traders."

Tom laughed and said, "Yeah, and gun dealers."

"And knife dealers."

They decided to spend the night in Walnut Ridge if they could find a boarding house. They rode directly to the livery stable to drop off their horses and sell the five they had acquired.

"I can't even think of buying these horses if you can't produce a bill of sale."

Handing the livery man five pieces of paper Tom said, "No problem, here is the bill of sale for each horse and tack. And since we are tired of leading these horses around we are willing to sell them with tack for Seventy dollars each"

"Well now, since you have the bill of sale and you are willing to sell them so I can make a profit, it is a deal."

The man counted out the money and ask, "You boys going to be staying in town tonight?"

"No sir, we pulling out right away. Have to get back to Paragould before it gets too late."

As they rode east Tom said, "Let's ride back east for a mile or so and then circle around this little wide spot. I don't think I am very good at being an outlaw. I am suspicious of everyone."

"Yeah, that livery man was a little too inquisitive. Guess we are just getting paranoid."

"We need some rest. We need to find a place and hold up for a few days."

Once they were headed back west they rode about ten miles from Walnut Ridge and looking at the map found a likely place to stop for the night.

They turned off the main road looking for a place to camp out of sight of the road and happen to come upon an old barn.

"What do you think?"

"Well, it will probably be a magnet for every traveler in these parts, but I am willing to take a chance. Anyway, we tried out in the open and that didn't turn out so well either."

They took care of their horses and then settled down to cooking some supper. Before they bedded down, they put the pack back on the pack horse and saddled their horses just in case they had to move fast in the night. One thing they had learned in the war was to be ready at a minutes notice to ride and if you did not have all the things you needed, you did without.

They set up a two hour watch. Tom took the first watch and when he woke Bill up Bill said, "That didn't seem like two hours."

"It wasn't. I heard riders on the road. Sounded like a lot of them. Maybe twenty."

"I don't hear them now."

"Yeah, they stopped nearby. Probably camping for the night."

"That's bad. If they send out guards, they will surely find this damn barn."

"Yeah, that's what I was thinking. Let's get our stuff and get out of here."

They led their horses further down the path away from the barn until they felt it was far enough away that the pickets would not find them. They tied and hobbled the horses and taking their Henrys they moved back to the barn and waited.

In a few minutes two riders rode up to the barn and then rode through it and then headed back toward the road. In a few minutes they heard a lot of horse's coming towards the barn. They move back instinctually and watched.

They had been wrong about the number of riders but right about the number of horses. The troop of Union soldiers were escorting two large wagons drawn by four horses each. There were eight mounted troops and two on each wagon.

"What do you think?"

"Payroll probably, coming down from St Louis."

"Don't you think there would be more soldiers?"

"Maybe they are following the Brigade that went through here couple of days ago."

"Yeah, that makes sense. Since the activity around here had died down, they probably feel safe sending it down this way and not through Kentucky and Tennessee."

"I don't know. According to Miss. Waters and the newspapers she has been reading, there is still a lot of raiders in Missouri."

"Hell, I don't know. Anyway, there are too many for us to take especially in the dark."

"How about at dusk?"

"Sure, we can do it."

They worked up the plan which involved killing off the pickets which would bring the force guarding the payroll down to eight men.

They settled down to sleep a couple of hours. This time Bill woke Tom up.

"Listen."

"Damn, more riders on the road."

"Yeah and they are coming down this way."

"Damn, more soldiers. There goes our plans."

"Yeah, let's get the hell out of here before Grant's whole damn army gets here. It would have been a problem if those soldiers had shown up during the fight."

"Bill, you have a way of understating the situation."

They moved back to their horses and moved south west and made a big circle to cut the main road well out of the reach of the soldiers.

They stayed in the little settlement of Denton that night and even took a hot bath and ate a good meal and slept in a clean bed. In fact, when the landlady offered to do their laundry, they decided to stay another night.

Wherever they stayed, they always ask about converting their silver dollars to gold coins. They were accumulating a lot of heavy silver. The landlady had two and they gave her forty-two dollars for them. They made sure that each one of them carried the same amount on them just in case they got split up. And of course there was more on the packhorse.

They rode out well fed and refreshed after getting two nights of rest. They would try to make Ash Flat before they stopped again. After that they had to go southwest towards Violet Hill to bypass the South Fork Lake.

They traveled for two more days with no problems. They saw a few people on the road but they were mostly farmers just going to and from town to sale or purchase goods.

Chapter Thirty-five

They crossed the Neosho and the Verdigris Rivers on the small ferries and about a day out of Tulsa they stopped to camp at a small stream. They moved south of the main road about two hundred yards and set up camp. Bill went down to the spring fed creek to get water when there was a shot. Tom immediately grabbed his Henry and ran down to where he last saw Bill. Bill was on the ground with his head squirting blood. Tom looked around for the person who had shot Bill and when he did not see anyone, he turned to trying to treat Bill's wound. He wiped the blood to see how bad the wound was and then wet his neckerchief and tied it around Bills head. He pulled Bill back to where they had camped still looking around for the shooter. He heard someone running towards them and prepared to fire when he saw a woman followed by a young boy.

"My son says he shot someone. Is there some...."

She saw Bill on the ground with his head bloody. "Oh, my God. He did shoot someone."

She fell to her knees beside Bill and started treating him. She pulled back the bandage to see how badly the wound was. She could not tell if the bullet had penetrated the man's head.

"I'm sorry Mama, I didn't mean to shoot him."

"You shot him? Why?"

"I was shooting at a dove in the tree. I didn't mean to hit anyone. I swear."

"Let's get him to the house."

The woman helped Tom put Bill on his horse and they moved slowly following the woman and boy.

They carried Bill in and put him on the bed. She put a towel under his head to catch the blood.

"I don't think the bullet entered the skull. It was just his small squirrel gun."

"Here, I can feel the bullet right under the skin. Can you cut it out?"

"Yea, let me clean my razor first."

When Tom went to the stove to sterilize his straight razor. Bill awoke and sat right up. But he fainted and fell back on the bed.

"Lay still sir, we are trying to take the bullet out."

Bill tried to raise his head up again but decided against it. "Damn, what the hell hit me? A sledge hammer?"

"No, you were shot. Lie still, your friend is going to cut the bullet out. It is right under the skin."

"Wait a minute."

Bill put his hand up to his head and just felt the slick blood. Then he moved hand back about four inches and felt something hard right under the skin.

"You say you are going to cut it out?"

"Yeah, so be still for a minute and then we will let you get up."

The war had made medics of virtually all the soldiers. It was unusual for a man to have spent any time in the war without having to perform some kind of surgery on his fellow soldier. There were not many doctors on the line. And many man would have bled to death if not treated by his friend or comrade. Some were better than others. It required nerves of steel and a sure hand to perform delicate operation such as removing a bullet or sewing up a gaping shrapnel wound. Tom was well qualified when the used his razor to make a small cut and squeeze.

"I have some medicine in my pack I will get. So if you will clean him up, I will be right back."

The young boy had been hanging back afraid that the men would be mad at him and his mother and harm them.

"Can I help, mister?"

"Well, you can take the saddles and pack off the horses and put them in the corral if you want to."

By the time Tom entered the house from getting the medicine, Bill was already setting up.

"I knew that little squirrel gun would not put you down for very long. How you feeling?"

"How do you think I feel? I been shot in the head. How do you think you would feel?"

"Good, he is grumpy. He's ok. Here, rub some of this on first and then before you bandage it up, put some of this on it."

When the woman had finished bandaging the wound she walked over to the kitchen table into the bright sunlight and for the first time Bill had a good look at her.

"I am Bill McCall and that feller over there is my cousin, Tom McCall."

"Glad to meet you both. I am Mary Morningstar McAllister and this is my son Jonas."

Mary was around twenty five with long coal black hair and eyes to match. She was tall and slender and wore a cotton blouse and buckskin skirt with moccasins. The boy was about eleven or twelve with scraggly black hair. He had a cotton shirt that was too big for him and pants with the knees warn out and no shoes. When they spoke they had a distinct Native American accent.

"Are you Cherokee?"

"Yes, how did you know?"

"My grandmother was Cherokee back in Tennessee."

"My family came out of North Carolina in the early days of the long march. It was hard times for my people. As was the custom, my husband bought me from my father when I was sixteen and brought me here to his house. He was many years older than me and we only had one son before he took ill and died."

"Do you own this land?"

"Oh yes, my husband settled this area when he was young man. He came here with his brother and they staked out over a hundred and forty acres. Before he died, we had cattle that he use to take to Tulsa and sell for us to live. But my son was too young to help me, and I could not take care of this place by myself. So what cattle we had are running wild, or have been killed off by the mountain lions or wolves."

Mary got up from the table and walked over to Bill and checked to see if the bleeding had stopped.

"It has stopped bleeding."

She walked back to the cook stove. "I have beans and tortilla if you are hungry."

"That sounds good. We have been living on the road for a long time."

"Do you feel well enough to eat something Bill?"

'Actually, I feel like sleeping."

"No, you cannot sleep. You might not wake up if you sleep after a head wound."

"Ok, then I will just lay here and not sleep."

"Looks like it will be a few days before Bill will be able to travel, so would you mind if we stay here?"

"Yes, you can stay as long as you like. But we don't have much food even for us."

"Don't worry about that, we will make sure we have enough food for all of us."

"Do you have a smoke house?"

"Yeah, but it is not very good. Like everything else around here. My husband was very ill for about five years before he died so the place just ran down."

"Okay, looks like Jonas and I have our work cut out for us. We need to get the smokehouse repaired so we can get some meat in it."

"I would be grateful. But even if you repair the smoke house, we don't have any pigs."

"We will worry about that when the time comes. What is the closest settlement to here where you go to buy things?"

"Catoosa is a small settlement to the north of here. But it is a mean place with lots of outlaws both white and Indian."

"Sounds like every little town in Tennessee except for the Indians. I will ride there tomorrow and see what I can find."

"Jonas, let's go unpack the horses."

Tom took all their food, ammunition, and money into the house. They had dried beans, sacks of flour, sacks of corn mill, salt, sugar, coffee, and lard. They had a half of a smoked ham and two slabs of bacon. When ham and bacon was cured by smoked, it would keep for a long time as long as it did not get wet.

"Momma, look at all the food they have. We can have some meat instead of those rabbits."

"Thank you. Now I can prepare a proper meal for us to eat."

Mary insisted that Bill stay in her bad that night so she could take care of him. Tom made his bunk in the barn loft. The next morning Tom came in for breakfast, Bill was setting at the table drinking coffee.

"You are looking well. How do you feel?"

"Well, my head is sore where you cut the bullet out but other than that, I am fine."

They both smiled.

"I will be going to Catoosa today to get some things. Shouldn't be gone long. But if I don't come back by morning, you will know I met my maker."

"Tom, they ain't no law in these parts so you be careful."

"Mary, how about if I take Jonas with me. Might do him good to get to town."

Tom, Catoosa is a mean place. I would worry too much about him."

"Ok, I understand. But the boy has to be exposed to the world sooner or later."

"Do you have a wagon or any mules or horses?"

"The only wagon I have is that one down against the fence and we don't have anything to pull a wagon. Jonas has an old horse he rides sometimes."

"I'll be back."

Bill watched as Tom rode away. He had a bad feeling but he did not tell Tom.

Chapter Thirty-six

Catoosa was even worse on the surface than Tom imagined. There was only one saloon, a hotel, a mercantile store on one side of the street. Across the street was a barber shop with a hand painted sign that read: HOT BATHS. It addition, there were a few houses scatter around, mostly off the main street. Tom noticed that there was a lot of people coming and going. Even a few in Union uniforms but no one seemed to give them any notice. The U.S. Army had remained in the Territories off and on from the time the Indians were moved to this part of the country. But during the early part of the war the Confederate forces operated in this area. The south made a concerted effort to recruit the Indians to fight with them against the Union and were successful in some cases. The Union also tried and was successful in getting the Indians to join their cause.

As long as the blue coats left him along he would not bother them, and basically they ignored him. He was only one of many hard cases they ran into on a daily basis.

He tied his horse to the hitching rail in front of the saloon and pulled his Henry and laid it over his arm. When he walked in, no one turned or changed their position. No one bothered to notice him and that was just fine with him. It was the first time in a long time that someone had not ask him where he was going or where he was from. He liked being left alone.

The saloon was as run down as the town. The once gilded mirror behind the bar had two bullet holes in it with the expected results. The bar was made from one big tree that had been smoothed and painted black. Table and chairs were all handmade obviously by a local builder and not a furniture maker. The floor had a generous helping of sawdust to soak up the tobacco spit and the horseshit the customers brought in on their boots.

"What will it be?"

"Whiskey."

"That will be a quarter."

Tom laid a silver dollar on the bar and said, "Burn it. Something special going on in town today. Seem to be a lot of people for a weekday."

"Nah, just the war. People coming west to get out of the way of what's coming. And no one ask any questions in the Nation."

"Do you have anything to eat?"

"Well, we do. But if I was you, I would go next door to the hotel. Mrs. Lange serves some good food."

"Thank you."

Tom drank down his forth drink and headed for the door when a man bounded through the swinging doors and let out a rebel yell and said, "Long live Dixie. Who will drink with me to Dixie?"

He was a medium sized man in a grey Confederate uniform with one arm missing.

"Come on you sons of bitches. Have a drink with a one armed man."

When no one moved to have a drink with him he said, "Sons of bitches. I give my right arm for you and you won't drink with me. Screw all of you."

From the back of the saloon someone yelled, "Sit down rebel before someone takes the other arm."

A lot of the patrons did not like what the man in the back said, and moved up to the bar to join the one armed man. Then some of the people in the saloon moved to the back, where the man had yelled from. The rebels had about two to one advantage, and then the undecided including Tom moved to the side of the one armed man. Now it was three to one and it would have taken just one bad move or word to set off a gun battle

The swinging doors burst open and three bluecoats walked in and one in a major uniform walked up to the one armed man.

"Johnnie Reb, are you causing trouble again?"

"I ain't causing any trouble, major. I'm just trying to buy everyone a drink and these damn Yankees don't want to drink to Dixie. How about Major? Will you drink to Dixie or what's left of her?"

"Thank you Reb, I will be happy to drink to Dixie."

The major drink his drink and said, "It would be better if we could get some good Tennessee bourbon around here."

"That's for damn sure."

With the tension relieved in the room, the conversations went back to normal and the men returned to their seats.

Tom held out his left hand to the one armed man and said, my name is Austin McNeil late of the Twentieth Tennessee."

The man took Tom's hand and said, "Doug Harrison of Smithland Kentucky. But out here in the Nation, they call me Reb. Just call me Reb."

"How about me buying you a drink Reb."

Reb smiled and said, "Thank you sir. You are a true southern gentleman."

"Sounds like you been around here for a while. Who are the big operators in this country? Is there still a lot of war activity going on out here?"

"It's mostly hit and run stuff. Quantrill and his gang are still active in the Territory. Just hope you don't run into those bastards. They are in it for the money and just as soon kill a Reb as a Yank. We have free raiders who raid ranches and farms stealing horses and cattle from most supporters of the cause. And then there is General Watie who is a leader of the Cherokee soldiers who raids only military units. He has a wide range. Like Quantrill, you never know where he will show up next. And then you have the rest of us outlaws who have lost our way and don't give a good god damn who dies."

"Have another?"

"Thank you. Now, what are you looking for?"

"I'm looking for a man named Sawyer. George Sawyer. He is responsible for killing my wife and children."

"Was he headed out this way?"

"He ran an iron works back in Tennessee, so I presume he would probably be in the same business out here someplace."

"Sounds like he would settle around a mining community. Not much mining in these parts. You probably should look over in Colorado Territory."

"Mr. Reb, you are a fraud. You are an obviously well-educated and intelligent gentlemen, yet you play the town drunk. The loose cannon. Why is that?"

"Well Mr. McNeil I tell you, sometimes we play a role in the drama that is life in order to hide our real selves and in turn our motives and objectives. I too am looking for someone here in the Territories. Someone who raped and murdered my wife and killed my three year old daughter. He wore the uniform of the South which makes the crime in my mind even more heinous. I was an officer in the United States Army, a graduate of West Point until the war began and then I resigned my commission and joined the First Kentucky Brigade. My name is James Wilcox. I lost my arm at Shiloh. When I was sent home, I found out that my wife had been raped and murdered and my daughter was killed by a man who was in my unit. In fact, he was our neighbor and supposedly a gentleman. My wife was able to identify him before she died."

"What was his name?"

"Lucas Winfred. Last I heard he was on his way to the Territories but I have not been able to even get a smell of him. Of course, he will not be using his real name. Hell, no one here uses his own name. But I will know him when I see him and he will know me."

He reached and took a large knife halfway out of his boot and said, "I have something special planned for him."

"What does he look like?"

"He has red hair and a ruddy face. He has a scar over his right eye which is burned black from a misfire. He is about five foot, ten inches tall. He thinks he is a woman man. That is the reason I always hang around the saloons. Sooner or later he will show up at saloon and I will find him."

"I am headed west and will be on the lookout for him and if I find him, I will let you know. I will leave word with the bartender at the saloon."

"Thank you."

"Good luck."

When Tom left the saloon he stopped by the hotel restaurant then he went to the livery station where he bought an almost brand-new farm wagon and two good mules. His next stop was the mercantile store where he bought food and other supplies to last a month. The owner who had a permanent scowl on her face told him where to find hogs to buy so that was his next stop. As he started to leave the store, he thought of the ragged pants that Jonas was wearing and Mary's faded blouse and buckskin skirt.

"I need some pants and shirts and shoes for a boy about eleven years old. Throw in some socks and underwear. I also need a cotton dress for a woman with black hair about the same size as you. And throw in what women wear underneath." Tom smiled with an embarrassed smile. And even got the lady behind the counter to smile.

The man with the hogs was an old Spanish gentleman names Louis Sabastian Delgado, who insisted that they have some wine before they talked business. They sat down at a large table under a shaded veranda and a young woman brought wine and small bowls of chili and tortillas. Tom was not use to the hot peppers in the chili and drank more wine than he intended. Later he figured the old gentleman knew the more chili he ate, the more wine he would drink and the more he would pay for the hogs.

Tom bought four hogs. Two for butchering and a young sow and a seasoned boar. He also bought two more horses from the gentleman.

But in the end, he had a good time talking history of the southwest with someone who still had land granted to him by the king of Spain. And he was invited back at any time. And when the young woman smiled at him as he was leaving, he made himself a promise that he would be back for a second round with the hot chili.

Tom arrived back at the little house a couple hours before sundown. Bill had been worried and came out to meet him.

"Glad to see you back."

Tom took Bill by the shoulders and looked at his head. "Are you ok?"

"Yeah, I am fine. I had a great nurse."

Mary looked away seeming a little shy.

Looking at Mary, Tom said, "I see what you mean about Catoosa. It is somewhat rundown and full of bad people. But I found what we needed."

Tom handed a package to Jonas and one to Mary and said, "You can open them tonight at supper."

"We have to build a pen for the hogs before we unload them otherwise they will just go home."

"Jonas, you can put our horses in the corral and take their gear off. Just leave the mules hooked up to the wagon for the time being."

Tom and Jonas spent the rest of the afternoon building a holding pen, making sure it was strong and escape proof.

Around sundown, Mary called them to come wash up and eat. She had cooked a full meal for the first time in a long time. Mostly they lived on tortillas, beans, and what they were able to kill. She had been alone with Jonas for too long, avoiding outsiders and very seldom going to the settlement. She was afraid for Jonas and herself. It was a mean and unforgiving country and no woman alone was safe. She had a brother that visited often before the war, but he was part of General Watie's brigade and could only visit when they were operating close to her ranch.

She saw in Bill a strong but gentle man that could protect her and make her a fine husband. She was not worried about love, hoping it would come later. Now she just had to make sure he wanted to stay.

"Mary, you have a beautiful place here."

Looking at Bill she said, "Yeah, with the right man to build it up, it could be a great place to live and raise kids."

"Mary, this food is delicious. And the tortillas you made today are so soft. How do you get them so smooth?"

"Just have to keep grinding the corn until it is smooth. Some people don't grind their corn enough and the tortillas are gritty."

When they finished their supper Tom said, "Ok time to open the packages."

First Jonas opened his and cried when he saw the new clothes. And when she saw her son cry, Mary began to cry. She hugged Jonas. They sat there quiet in each other's arms for a minute and then Mary said, "We have not been able to buy him any new clothes for so long. He has just been wearing what I could find and cut down from his father's clothes."

Jonas hugged Tom's neck and then hugged Bill's neck and said, "Thank you."

"You will have to take a bath before you can put on the new clothes."

"Okay Mama."

"Now you Mary, but be careful. There might be some undergarments you won't want to show."

Mary carefully opened the package and held up a flower print cotton dress. The color was perfect for her black hair. She held it up to her and said, "Tom you are so nice. It is perfect and the other things in the package are perfect also. How did you know what size to buy?"

"You are the same size as the lady at the store."

Mary hugged Bill and Tom and said, "Thank you both. Thank you for coming along when you did."

Bill and Tom walked out on the porch to smoke.

"Good thinking Tom. You are a good man. Thank you for bringing me out of Tennessee."

"Tom, I like this area. It feels right. But the first thing we need to build is a damn house. This mud hut is too far gone to salvage. I walked up on that little knoll to the north today. That would be a great place for a house. You can see the entire area from up there."

Tom smiled at Bill and said, "Sounds like you have given it some thought."

"Tom, I'm tired. I'm tired of riding, starving, and being cold at night when I sleep. But most of all I am tired of the killing and I am tired of being along."

"Well, you got me."

"That ain't what I meant and you know it."

"Yeah, I know what you mean. I agree with you. This place would be a great place for you to settle down. Have you mentioned it to Mary?"

"No, not yet. What do you think? Do you think she would like me?"

"Bill, I think you are exactly what Mary is looking for and needs."

"How about you Tom. Would you consider staying here?"

"I will stay here for a while but then I think I will move on. But I am not in a hurry any more. It seems peaceful enough here."

In a few minutes, Mary joined them on the porch carrying two cups of coffee.

"Thought you might like a cup before we turn in."

"Thank you Mary."

"Thank you."

"Mary, I hope you don't mind but Bill and I have been talking about your place here. We feel that with the proper hand it could be a thriving ranch. Especially now that the war is winding down."

"Good, because I have been talking to Jonas about the very same thing. He likes Bill and not just because he shot him. He really never knew his father as a man and he needs a man to help him grow up. And I have a different perspective on love and marriage than white women. My first husband bought me from my father, but I want to pick my next husband. Bill, I am asking you to stay here with me and Jonas and be my husband and his father if you want to. And Tom you can stay also as long as you want to."

Bill took Mary's hand and said, "That is just about the nicest proposal I ever received. My answer is yes."

Tom shook Bill's hand and hugged Mary.

"How about tomorrow let's get busy building a ranch out of this place?"

Chapter Thirty-seven

The next morning at breakfast they made up a list of what they needed to repair, tear down, and or build. The list read: Corral, barn, and new house. They also made a list of the materials they had on the ranch and what they would need to buy.

Tom and Bill figured out that between them, they had about fifteen hundred dollars, which should be enough to get started. But they agreed that if the opportunity presented itself, they would get some more.

It took them two weeks to cut and hauled the posts and railings and another week to build the corral.

When it came to the barn, they were going to need a lot of lumber cut for specific usage and Tom knew just the person to talk to.

"I will return as soon as I can. Hopefully I will have the materials we need to build the barn. And I will also look for a preacher for you two."

Mr. Delgado welcomed Tom back with a glass of wine and a big cigar. Again they were seated around the big table in the garden. But this time, there were two young men there.

"Mr. McNeil, I would like you to meet my oldest son Raphael and my middle son, Diego. They have just arrived from California. We have a big ranch out there also."

Bill shook hands with the two men and they shared some wine. The two young men shared stories about California and Tom told about his travels and about the war in Tennessee. They spoke their condolences when Tom told them about his family. They drank and ate like old friends.

Tom, did you make it home with the pigs and horses?"

"Yes sir. They are doing fine."

"You know Tom, I knew Mr. McAllister. I remember my father talking about an easterner coming in and staking out a large piece of land to our east. In those days, we were always fighting the Indians and my father welcomed Mr. McAllister as an alley and I felt very bad when he died. When he took his wife, the Indians stopped raiding our lands in this part. So I was grateful to him. If there is anything I can do to help his widow and son, I will be glad to do so."

"My cousin Bill is going to marry Mary and we are building up the ranch. We have built a nice strong corral and we will build a big barn next. And that is the reason I am here. Is there a saw mill around where we can get the lumber to build the barn?"

"Unfortunately, the closest saw mill in in Tulsa. But they should have all you need."

"Well, the problem I have is knowing what to buy. Just how much of each part of the barn do I need to get."

Mr. Delgado smiled and said, "Its ok, the man who runs the saw mill works with an architect who will help you design the barn and then tell you what lumber to buy."

'Sorry to be so dumb, but I grew up poor on the side of a hill in Tennessee and did not get an education."

"It's ok, Tom. I understand. Don't worry about where you began. It is where you wind up that is the measure of a man's life."

"Thank you sir."

"Please let me know if you need wagons and drivers."

"Thank you again. And please let me know if you ever need my assistance. I am a cavalryman and better than average with my guns."

"That is good to know. Especially around here during this period."

Tom rode home and told Bill and Mary what he found out about the lumber for the barn and house.

"I have been talking to Mary about the house. She recommends we build it out of mud and straw on a frame. The walls are thicker for warmth in the winter and coolness in the summer. In the tradition of the Indians and Spanish that live in this area."

"That sounds great. Mr. Delgado's house is beautiful and it is made of mud and straw. You will have to go see it Bill."

"Ok, so we just need the lumber for the barn and a couple of small sheds and the chicken coops and pig barn."

"I will go to Tulsa tomorrow and make a deal for what we need. Might take a day or two, so don't worry."

As Tom rode into Tulsa he stopped the first person he met and ask about the location of the saw mill.

"Sir, the lumber yard is just three blocks down. Talk to Mr. Black. He will help you."

"Thank you sir."

As he rode down main street, he noted where all the business were. When he saw a telegraph office he made a note that he would send a message to Mr. Bing.

"I am looking for Mr. Black."

"You found him."

A big short man with big arms and hands reached out to shake.

"Tom. Glad to meet you."

"I am building a big barn on my place and need some lumber. But the problem is, I don't know how much of each kind that I need. So Mr. Delgado said you might know an architect who might help me."

"Come on inside and let's talk to Mr. James. You and he can work out what and how much you will need based on the size of the building you are building."

Tom and Mr. James decided on the size of the barn and the style. Mr. James was able to sort out the right numbers, sizes, and types of lumber it would take and they presented the order to Mr. Black.

What Tom did not know was that Mr. Black and Mr. James were barely making a living in their profession. Virtually no one was building during this period. Why build something that some raider would burn down the next week. So they were anxious for Tom's business.

"Mr. McNeil, Mr. James and I have talked a bit about your needs and have come up with a proposition. I will sale you the lumber, roof shingles, and nails and deliver it to your place and Mr. James will supervise your build for seven hundred. That order includes enough to build a forty by forty barn with a hay loft, the pig shed, chicken coop, and a covered shed with no sides."

"It's a deal. I will pay you half today and the other half when the job is done."

They shook hands and Tom gave Mr. Black three hundred and fifty dollars.

"We will be there in two days. Can you draw up a map to where you want me to deliver the lumber?"

When Mr. James saw the map he said, "That's the old McAllister place isn't it?"

"Yes it is."

"Did you buy it?"

"My friend married the widow."

"Good, I knew Mr. McAllister. He use to come here before he took ill. I wondered what would happen to Mary."

"Well, we are going to be building a house so we will be back. But, I think Bill and Mary want a mud and straw building."

On his way back through town, he stopped at the telegraph office.

AM IN TULSA. HAVE U HEARD WHERE G. SAWYER SETTLED? SEND REPLY HERE. SGND TOM.

When he was finished with the telegraph office he stopped by the saloon. As he walked in the hairs on the back of his head stood up for no reason that Tom could discern. He hailed the bar tender and ordered a whiskey put a silver dollar down on the bar and when the bar tender came he said, "Burn it."

He drank his second down and then he noticed three men in the back of the bar. The one doing all the talking had red hair and a big red face. He was thinking of an excuse to talk to them when one of the three came up to the bar and ordered a beer.

"Seem like I know that red headed man, you boys from Mississippi?"

"Mister, out here we don't ask those questions and we definitely don't answer them."

"Sorry, just don't meet many people you know out here."

"Anyway, we from Kentucky."

"Thanks. Didn't mean no harm."

When the man went back to the table, Tom saw him lean over and say something to the red headed man. In a minute the red headed man got up and walked up to the bar and ordered a beer.

Now that he had identified the man, he needed an excuse to get him to go to Catoosa so he had to think on his feet.

"Partner says you from Mississippi. What part of Mississippi?"

"Corinth."

"Never heard of it."

"It's just below the Tennessee border."

"What are you doing in this place?"

"Same thing you are and the rest of these people. Running from the war."

"I ain't running from nothing."

"I just meant getting away from the all the killing."

"The reason I ask if you were the old boys from Mississippi, I wanted to see if you might help me out with a little problem. There is fat little bank up in Coffeyville I have had my eye on. But the guy I had with me got hurt. So I need some help."

"How much money we talking about?"

"At least twenty thousand. Coffeyville is a switch over point. They bring the payroll in on a stagecoach then disperse it to the many Union units in the Territories. It will be in the bank overnight. We will hit it early in the morning before the guards show up to get it."

"How you know about it?"

"My cousin works in the telegraph office. He gets all the messages and delivers them."

"Now that we know where, what is to keep us from just doing it ourselves and cutting you out?"

Tom looked at red headed man with his cold green eyes and said, "Because I will kill you if you double-cross me."

"You know where Catoosa is?"

The man shook his head.

"Meet me at the saloon there tomorrow evening at sundown if you want to go. If you are not there, then I will figure you chickened out or double-crossed me."

Tom turned and strode out of the saloon not looking back. Since it was too late to ride all the way back to the ranch, he took a room at the hotel.

The next morning after he had breakfast, Tom rode directly to the saloon in Catoosa and was there only a few minutes when Reb walked in and went to the bar. He ordered a drink and turned to survey the patrons. When he saw Tom, he nodded his head in recognition.

Tom moved to the bar next to Reb.

"I saw Mr. Winfred."

"Where? When?"

"Calm down and I will tell you."

Tom told Reb everything and they made a plan for the next evening.

Tom had asked the bartender about a preacher and as Tom rode out of town, he stopped at the little house next to the church and knocked on the door. A middle-aged woman answered the door. "May I talk to the preacher? My friend wishes to get married and needs a preacher."

"Sure, come in. I will get my husband."

The woman went to the back door and said in a loud voice, "David, you have a guest."

A man's voice said, "Ok hon, be right in."

In less than a minute a tall man in work overalls and dirty boots came in holding out his hand for Tom to shake.

"I am Reverend Prichard, please excuse my appearance. Been working in the garden. Can I help you?"

"My friend is getting married and needs a preacher. Are you available to ride to our ranch or should they come to you?"

"Where are the folks that wish to marry?"

"Do you know where the old McAllister place is?"

"Yes I do. They use to attend church occasionally when Mr. McAllister was alive. In fact, I presided at his burial."

"Who is getting married?"

"My friend Bill and Mary McAllister."

"Mary? That's wonderful. Minnie, Mary McAllister is getting remarried."

"That's great hon, she is such a nice young woman. She deserves to be happy."

"How about it Minnie, shall we take a ride out to marry Mary?"

"I think that would be a lovely ride in the country. When?"

Looking at Tom, Reverend Pritchard said, "When were they looking to get married?"

"As soon as possible. Whenever you are available."

"Today is Tuesday. How about Thursday?"

"That will be fine. Will you be ok traveling along or shall I come escort you?"

"We will be fine. Most of the people in the area know us and we feel quite safe going about by ourselves."

"Alright then, we will be expecting you folks on Thursday."

Tom rode home that evening and arrived at supper time. He told them all about the lumber and the plans for building the barn. When Tom told them how much it costs, Bill whistled but didn't say anything.

Tom said smiling, "If you don't like that news, maybe you will like the next bit of news I have to tell you. I have made arrangements for a preacher to come here on Thursday so you two can get married."

Bill's face turned a little white and Mary started smiling. "Tom, you didn't forget. Did you say Thursday? What will I wear?"

"You can wear your new dress. It is beautiful."

"Aren't you going to say anything Bill? You still have a couple of days of freedom."

Smiling, Bill said, "I guess it just hit me that I was getting married again after all these years. It will take some getting used to. But, it is time."

Mary came around behind Bill and hugged his head in her arms, "Are you sure Bill. Are you sure you want to take on me and Jonas?"

Reaching up and holding her Bill said, "I am sure."

Jonas with a big smile came around and hugged his mother and Bill. They looked like a family already.

After they had finished their supper Tom and Bill walked out on the porch which was their habit to have a smoke.

Tom told him about Reb and his family and what he had planned for the next night. Bill insisted that he would go with Tom and Tom relented. Ok, they would go to town for a drink to celebrate his getting married, and Mary would be satisfied with that excuse.

The next day they all got up earlier than normal, had their breakfast and began tearing down the barn and sheds around the ranch. They salvaged as much of the lumber as possible for future use. The stuff they could not use, they burned. They cleaned the area for the new barn and other buildings so it would be ready when Mr. Black delivered the lumber.

Mary took the arm of Bill and Tom as they walked back to the main house. "Boys, the ranch is starting to look so different. New corral and soon a new barn. I can't wait until we get the new house built. I am so happy. Thank you Bill and thank you Tom."

Bill had already told Mary that they were going into Catoosa that evening to have a drink so when they rode off, she just waived.

On the way in, Tom told Bill of the plan to get Mr. Winfred into a gunfight with Reb.

They walked into the saloon and up to the bar.

"Whiskey."

"Same."

Tom put two dollars on the bar and said, "Burn it."

In about ten minutes, Mr. Winfred and two other men came into the saloon and took a table at the back.

As they walked in, Tom nodded at Mr. Winfred to let him know everything was alright. In a few minutes, he moved back to the table leaving Bill at the bar which was part of the plan.

"Evening gentlemen. Glad you could make it. We are all set. We leave first thing in the morning."

"Set down, have a drink and tell us again about the gold in Coffeyville and just how we plan to get it."

Tom went over the plan in every detail making it sound so easy, the men were already thinking of ways to spend their money.

"Lucas Winfred! You low down rapist murder of women and children. Stand up and face a husband and father."

Everyone had turned to see Reb standing in the back door of the saloon. He was ready for action. But Tom did not turn to see who it was, he moved slightly away from the table and pulled his pistols and pointed them at the two men riding with Winfred. He motioned for them to move ahead of him towards the front door.

Bill was still at his position at the bar and was ready for action.

Everyone soon moved to make room for the fight between Reb and Winfred.

"Mr. Wilcox, you've got the wrong man that wasn't me who killed your…"

"Shut up you son of a bitch and draw."

"I don't want to draw against a one armed man. That …"

"Shut up and draw or you will be shot down like the dog you are."

Winfred went for his gun, but he was a tad slow. When the 44 slug hit him it drove him back against the wall and he slid down slowly leaving a blood smear all the way to the floor.

As soon as Reb shot went off, the two friends of Winfred went for their guns but Tom and Bill were too fast. They crumpled where they were hit.

Bill yelled, "Everyone else stand easy. Nobody moves until we sort this out."

"Reb shot him down in cold blood. We can't let him get away with that. Get a rope."

There was a big boom and a cloud of smoke coming from where Tom was standing. The bullet hit just inches from the ear of the man who had yelled. It was the same man who had tried to pick a fight with Reb before.

"Let me tell you something and this is the last that will be said or done about it. Lucas Winfred raped and murdered Reb's wife and killed his three year old daughter. They were in the same unit and were neighbors. You don't need to know any more about this. Just go about your business. You don't need to know my name. Just know that if anything happens to Reb, I will know where to start looking and I will kill you."

There was no more talk about lynching, and the saloon soon returned to the buzz of customer conversing.

There was no law in the Territories and the Union troops seem to be out of town at the moment, so the only thing they were waiting for was the undertaker.

The bartender came out from behind the bar and said, "Couple you fellers help me drag these bodies outside."

Tom introduced Bill to Reb and they had a drink together.

"Where will you go now, Reb?"

"I don't rightly know. I never made any plans beyond finding and killing that son of a bitch. I guess maybe I will go back to Kentucky. Maybe get a job teaching. Hell even a one armed man can teach."

They had one more for the road and shook hands with Reb and rode back to the ranch. They never saw Reb again.

Chapter Thirty-eight

The first loads of lumber arrived the next day along with Mr. James and two other men they had not met.

Tom introduced Mr. James to everyone and Mr. James introduced the two men with him as W.G. Monroe and Calvin Clay.

Mr. James said, "Please call me Sandy."

Out of hearing distance of the others Sandy said, "Tom, Bill, I asked Mr. Monroe and Mr. Clay to come here in hopes that you would hire them to help us put up this barn. They are both carpenters by trade and work with me all the time. But times are hard and they will work cheap."

The two men looked like brothers. Both had grayish blond hair and looked to be around forty-five. Both looked very strong with big forearms. And they smiled a lot.

Bill and Tom looked at each other and Bill said, "We are going to need help. We don't know a damn thing about building barns."

Tom smiles and broad smile and said, "That is for sure. We gonna need all the help we can get."

Sandy called for Mr. Monroe and Mr. Clay and when they came over Bill said, "Mr. James says you are looking for work. Well we could sure use your help. How does dollar and a half per day sound?"

They looked at each other and reached out their hand to Bill. They shook and Bill reached into his pocket and gave them ten silver dollars each.

"I will pay you the rest when the job is done. Is that ok?"

"Yes sir. Thank you."

"Thank you."

The first thing they built was the shed with no sides. This would be an all-purpose structure to get things out of the sun and rain. This is where Mary would feed them for the duration of the build.

As they finished the shed, the reverend and his wife drove up in their buggy. Mary was the first to notice them and ran down to greet them.

"Mary, how have you been? We were so happy to hear that you were to remarry. Where is the lucky groom?"

"Bill is working on the new barn. Please come to the cook shed and have a seat. The men will break for lunch soon and we will eat something."

As soon as Tom saw that the reverend had arrived he came up to greet them. "Thank you so much for coming. Please excuse our mess and noise. The new barn was scheduled on the same day as the wedding."

"That's ok, I love to build things. Maybe I can pitch in after the wedding."

"You would be very welcome. This is a big job."

Mary motioned for Jonas to come to him. "Jonas, please let everyone know that lunch is being served."

Jonas ran off to tell everyone to come to lunch.

Tom had found Bill and told him to go in and change clothes for his wedding. He also told Mary to change into her new dress.

The food had been set out on makeshift tables and the workers helped themselves. In a few minutes Bill and Mary joined them. Tom stood up and said in a loud voice, "Ladies and gentlemen, may

I have your attention please. You thought you were just going to be raising a barn today, but you are going to be witness to a wedding. Bill and Mary are getting married. "Bill, Mary, are you ready?"

The men started applauding and cheering as Bill and Mary stood up before the reverend. The ceremony was brief with Tom acting as the best man and Jonas giving away the bride. After Bill kissed his bride, everyone came by to congratulate them. In a few minutes, they all went back to work on the barn and even Reverend Pritchard pitched in for a couple of hours before they had to get back to town.

The barn went up unbelievably fast with the expertise of Mr. James, W.G., and Calvin. By the second day, they were all good friends joking with each other and hearing about their families. The three men had not been tempted to go to war. They had families and their business and were a little old for all the rigorous operations. But they felt a little subconscious around the two warriors until Bill told them that he had not served in any organized unit. And of course when they heard Tom's story they wept openly as he did every time he told it. So there was no gilt on the part of the men who did not serve and no animosity towards them by the ones who did. But as with all wars, when it is all over, everyone will claim that played a major and heroic part. If you don't believe it, just ask them. For some reason unknown to themselves or the most learned physiatrist, people embellish their participation in previous wars. And the Civil War was no different. Accordingly, it appears that every man woman and child over the age of ten fought in the war and were accomplished marksman, spy, surgeon, or just plain hero. So, ten years down the road maybe even Mr. Monroe, Clay, and James, and yes even Wild Bill might if you ask them or not ask them, volunteer that they fought with great distinction in the late war of rebellion, and to hell with those damn Yankees.

When all the building were completed, they had a big celebration and the workers even brought their families.

Wiping tears from her eyes Mary said, "Thank you so much Bill, Tom, James, Sandy, W.G., Cal, and of course Jonas. Thank you for my new barn, pig pen and shed, chicken coop, and cooks shed. You all have surprised me with the work going so fast. You are all welcome to visit us anytime. And soon, we hope to have a big hacienda so we can invite you into our home."

Everyone came by and hugged Mary. If anyone one of the group had any prejudice against Mary because of her race, they did not show it.

Tom paid Sandy the rest of what he owed him and Mr. Black and he said, "Before you leave, we would like to talk to you about the house."

"Okay, sure."

Bill handed W.G. and Cal fifteen silver dollars each and said, "Gentlemen you earned every bit of that money. If I ever need anything build or know anyone who might need a carpenter I will let you know."

"Thank you. You have no idea how much you have helped our families. We were literally starving without work."

Tom held out his hand and said, "Things should pick up with the war ending soon."

As they started to leave Tom said, "Do you happen to know a Mr. Delgado. He owns a large ranch just north of here."

The two men looked at each other, then W.G. said, "We have heard of him, but we do not know him or have not met him."

"He runs a big operation. I will tell him about you and see what happens."

"Great, thanks Tom."

When the two men and their families had gone, Bill, Tom, Mary, and Sandy sat down under the cook shed and talked about the house.

"Sure I can design the house, and give you an idea of the materials you will need. And I can frame it for you, but the rest of the job takes specialists. I would recommend you get the local Indians to do that work for you."

"Yeah, I can take care of that part of it. I will work with my people to get it done."

"Have you already picked out the building location?"

"Yeah, on that little knoll over there."

"Shall we walk over and mark it off so I can make some estimations on the materials?"

First they drew the outline of the outer wall. Then they drew the outline of the house. It would be a big house, but not half as big as Mr. Delgado's. But it would have a big courtyard like Mr. Delgado's where they could relax in the shade and have their wine.

Mary was happy and cried.

They told Sandy they would get in touch with him when they had the rest of the plans.

That night at supper Bill said, "We have to talk about money. We have to find a way to get some before we began the house."

"Bill, we used to have some cattle but they are scattered all over the place or maybe stolen by now. But we could see if we can round some up to sell."

"Yeah, if we can get them rounded up before the war ends, we can get a better price."

"Ok, tomorrow we will begin the round up. Early breakfast."

Mary had drawn up a rough map of her land boundaries so they would start by riding the parameter and move steadily inward until they met. But Bill and Tom had already decided that they would round up every cow they found whether it was inside the ranch parameter or not.

Bill took Jonas with him and leaving Tom to ride alone.

The weather in this area can be severe in both winter and summer, but mostly it is mild. So the cattle should have been able to survive if they were not stolen.

On the second day, they started finding cattle. In fact, they started finding a lot of cattle. Having been left to their own instincts for a long time, they did what all animals do. They propagated and they were good at it. With plenty of water and food they were big and healthy. But since they had had no contact with people, they were rank or in layman's language, they were mean.

On a normal managed ranch young bulls are castrated when they are three to six months old. But these cattle had been allowed to run wild and they were hard to handle. Late one evening a rank young bull took a dislike to Jonas and his old horse. The young bull butted the horse knocking the horse off its feet. Luckily Bill was close by and heard Jonas yelling and rode in and picked him up. From then on, Jonas made sure he rode close to Bill. Jonas was learning to be a cowboy and he loved it and he loved Bill.

To their surprise, they rounded up five hundred and thirty three cattle including calves.

The last night of the roundup at the supper table they were trying to figure out where they were going to be able to sell some of them. They wanted to keep all the young cows and at least two of the better bulls. The rest were for sale. They had to find someone to take the cattle quickly.

"Bill, my brother is in General Watie's brigade. Maybe I could get in touch with him to see if they want to buy the cattle. They are always looking for cattle for the troops."

"That is a good idea. How can you contact him?"

"I will ride to my people and get word to him and have him come by."

During all the conversation Tom had been thinking and said, "Bill, Mary, this war is going to end soon. Probably within the next year. When it ends, there is going to be a big demand for cattle up north. Mary, these cattle belong to you, but I recommend you keep all the young cow and just sell the young bulls and old cows. You can probably get five to seven dollars each for them now, but if I am right, when this war ends, you can get twenty to forty dollars for them. If you take some of the money and erect fences and manage your cattle, you will be rich in a few years."

"Mary, I agree with Tom. If we manage this right, we can live well and have what we need to raise our kids."

"Ok, I agree with both of you. Then that is what we will do.

"I will go talk to my people and while I am there I will see if I can find someone to help us work this ranch. And I will find someone who can build our house using the Indian ways with the mud and straw."

The next afternoon Mary and Jonas rode into the small Cherokee village with five head of cattle. The dogs barking let the people know that a stranger had entered the camp. Those who were not outside already soon came out to see what the commotion was all about. As Mary and Jonas rode up to the Chief's House, a small man came out to greet them.

Speaking Cherokee, Mary said, "Father I have brought cattle for butchering."

The old chief directed two young men to put the cattle in the pin next to the creek.

"You are looking well Father. You remember your grandson, Jonas."

"Yes, my daughter and how are you. And you Jonas? You are growing like a weed."

"Come in. Your mother has been ill and cannot come outside."

When she entered the little one room shack she saw a little frail looking woman lying on a bed in the dark corner. Rushing to her side she said, "Mother, what is wrong?"

"I am just old darling. Just old."

"You are not old. I will get a doctor."

"The agency doctor came before. He said I had cancer and that I would die soon."

Mary buried her face in her mother's hands and said, "Oh mother you cannot die. What will we do without you?"

Jonas hugged his mother and they stood quietly for a few minutes.

Her mother fell asleep and she took her father's hand and led him outside.

"Father, I have found a good man and married him. We are building up the ranch and will soon be able to provide jobs for some of our people and food for all. Have you heard from Joseph lately?"

"Yes. He comes here often bringing something that they have stolen from the Union soldiers."

"Next time he comes here would you ask him to come to our place?"

Two of the cows were butchered and the meat given out to all the families. That night at the feast, Mary had a chance to talk to her people about building the house and she found a small family to come work for them. And as soon as they had a big place with lots of cattle, she would hire more of her people and make sure they never wanted for food.

While Mary was gone, Tom and Bill busied themselves around the ranch. There was always more work than could ever get done.

They were taking a lunch break on the little porch when a man came riding in fast.

"Senior Tom?"

"I am Tom."

"Senior, my patron Senior Delgado ask you to come quick. He needs your assistance."

"Bill, I better go see what he needs."

"I will stay here and guard the place."

Tom saddled his horse and made sure he was packing all his pistols and Henry and rode away with the young man.

"Tom, I need your help with something. Normally my vaqueros would be able to handle the problem but I sent most of them as security with my sons to California."

"I understand. I am happy to help you in any way I can."

"A group of raiders have set up operation on my land, and are using it as a place to rob and harass other ranches in this area. I want to run them out."

"I have five riders who can help you. But I don't think they can do it themselves. I will gladly pay you for you trouble."

"I will take care of it. All I ask in payment is that I get to keep what I find on the men and their horses."

"But what if you don't find anything?"

"Then I will just settle for the horses. We will ride out right away."

Tom and the vaqueros rode out to a remote part of the ranch where the boulders made a natural hideout. He left the others to wait for him while he rode in to scout the area.

Tom knew these type of people and felt at ease riding into their camp.

Tom figured there were about ten men in camp at this time. He rode in slowly and at ease. He did not dismount right away. If trouble started, he wanted his horse under him. Stopping next to a group of men setting around a cook fire.

"Got any coffee and bacon for a fellow reb."

"How the hell you know we are rebs? We could be Yankees and then where would you be?"

"Well then I would be killing me some Yankees."

A big burly man with a big black beard said, "Well, we ain't neither one. We what you might call privateers. None denominational. We rob and kill everyone. Including smart asses that happen to ride into our…"

The man died before he was able to finish his sentence. Three others followed him almost immediately. Tom's horse stood steady as the action went on around him. Tom rode towards another group firing and hitting what he was shooting at. He heard two rifle shots and saw two men on his right go down. The vaqueros were helping him. He turned his horse around one way then the other looking for someone standing. There were no others standing. A couple lay dying that he finished off. Then he waived for the others to come in.

"The best way to deal with sons of bitches like these is straight on. They are cowards and can only operate when they have the numbers."

Tom searched the bodies and the saddle bags. He found the normal stuff on the bodies but each had more money than normal. So Tom was not surprised when he found more than four thousand dollars in their saddle bags.

They buried the bodies and rode back to the ranch. The vaqueros excitedly told Mr. Delgado about Tom riding in and killing all the raiders.

Tom did not tell the vaqueros or Mr. Delgado how much money the men had on them.

"Well Tom, looks like you made quite an impression on our vaqueros. I cannot thank you enough for ridding me of that nuisance. Are you sure I cannot pay you more.'

"Thank you, but the horses will come in handy working the ranch. There is one favor I would ask you. We rounded up the cattle on the McAllister ranch and have enough young cows to start a good herd, but we need a different bull. There is a danger that they are too much inbreeding with the ones we have now. Could you maybe let us borrow a couple of bulls from your herd?"

"I will do better than that. I will send a couple over that you can keep. They are some of my best breeding bulls and will improve your herd greatly."

"That is very kind of you sir. Thank you."

When Tom rode up leading ten horses Bill came out to meet him.

"Where in the hell did you get these horses? Did you rob Mr. Delgado?"

Tom laughed and told him what had happened.

"Well, I'll be damned if you ever get out of here without me going with you again. You are having too much fun and I am just staying at home."

"Wait till you go through the saddle bags before you complain too much."

"What did you find?"

"Look for yourself."

Bill started going through the bags and finding the money.

"Whoooooooeeeeeee!"

"Cuz, I am sure glad you are on my side."

Mary and Jonas returned from visiting her people with news that they would be sending someone to help with building the house. Also, her cousin and her husband and two children would be coming to work on the ranch.

"But I have sad news. My mother is dying."

"Is there anything we can do for your mother?"

"No, the agency doctor came to see her. There is no hope."

As was the way of the Cherokee, that was all she said about her mother's impending death. They considered death as part of life.

That night at supper when everyone was finishing their meal, Bill ask Mary to hold out her hands. When she did, he poured a thousand dollars in her hands and lap.

"Bill, where did you get this?"

"Tom just happened to find it and don't ask where. Now we can get the house done."

Mary beamed with happiness and Jonas came over and hugger her.

Chapter Thirty-nine

The next day Tom rode to Tulsa to talk to Mr. Black and Mr. James about the house. On the way he stopped by the telegraph office. There was a message for him:

G. SAWYER ON RANCH SOUTHEAST OF AURORA IN COLORADO TERRITORY.

BING

Tom was not sure if he was happy or sad to know where George Sawyer had settled. But he knew he would have to go there sooner or later. But he was not in a hurry. Anyway the war was not over and there was still trouble in the land.

A week had passed and the frame of the hacienda was ready for the workers who had begun to build the wall first. When finished, it would be a beautiful and functional home for Mary and Bill and their children.

Late in the evening they heard a lot of riders coming down the road towards the ranch house.

Tom and Bill took up fighting positions and then there was a loud whistle. Mary comes outside and yells, "Wait, it's my brother. He is coming to get the cattle."

Tom and Bill slowly moved out from their hiding places, but kept the Henrys at the ready.

The leader, in a Captain's uniform, stopped in front of Mary and dismounted. She introduced him to Bill and then Tom. The Captain gave orders to his men and followed Mary into the house.

"This place is looking better already. Mr. McAllister was a good man, but he was old and sick for many years and could not keep the place up or hire anyone to do it for him. I am happy Mary found a good man."

"Joseph, have you talked to our mother recently?"

"No, I have not talked to her in over a month. Why do you ask?"

"I hate to tell you, but our mother is very ill. She will die soon."

Joseph's only reaction was to say, "I will go right away to see her."

"How many cattle do you have for sale?"

"You can stay the night and rest, eat with us."

"No, we have to go. We are being hounded day and night now. The war is winding down. But it will end last here in the west."

"We have four hundred cattle for you."

"I am authorized to pay you ten dollars a head."

"They are pinned and ready for you."

Joseph got up and counted out four thousand dollars. He shook hands all around and hugged his sister. He picked up Jonas and said something in Cherokee.

"Please come back when you can. And bring your family."

They had turned the young cows out but once Tom had told Bill about the bulls from Mr. Delgado, he decided to sell all the bulls and start with new blood. When he saw the two bulls Mr. Delgado sent over, he was happy he did. They were two big and tough looking bulls and they would definitely improve their herd.

Now they had to set about making sure they had enough hay for the winter. All the farming equipment was old and rusted so they would have buy all new equipment before they could start growing anything. So once again, Tom had to travel to Tulsa to buy new ones.

By the spring of 1865, life had slowed down for Tom and Bill now that they were gentlemen ranchers. They had a very nice hacienda and four Cherokee vaqueros to do the ranch work. There was even less law and order in the Territories with the Union Army thinned out, but Bill and Tom made their own law. Their reputations had spread and no one came at them. The only dangerous raiders in the area were the remnants of Quantrill's unit who now without their leaders, just outlaws.

By July, all the confederate units had surrendered and the war was over and it was time for Tom to find his own peace.

Chapter Forty

Tom rode out leading his pack horse. He would find Mr. Sawyer and do what he had to do and get on with his life.

Aurora was just small mining camp located in the Colorado Territories in the early 1860s. White people started moving in after the Pikes Peak Gold strike in 1859.

Tom would start his search in Aurora. He rode North West through Kansas taking his chances with the memories and the animosity created during the Civil War for southerns. One place you walk into, they might shoot you for being a Yankee and another one they might shoot you for being a Rebel. One had to be slow to pronounce his allegiance but fast with the Colts and Tom was both. He no longer wore any remnants of the Confederate uniform but had not replaced his colts. He had gotten use to the heavy feeling in his hands when he pulled them.

Kansas was sparsely inhabited during those days and he could ride for days without seeing anyone. During the Civil War the Indians had taken the opportunity to settle scores for the land the government had taken from them. They started attacking settlers and any white person they saw on the trail. He had been chased by two small groups since the first day he crossed into Kansas so he was happy when he finally made it to Fort Larned. The soldiers at the fort were to protect the settlers along the Santa Fe Trail from the hostile Indians. Tom spent two days there learning the lay of the land to the west, the hazards of travel going west, and asking anyone if they knew of a Mr. George Sawyer in the Colorado Territories.

For safety he signed on to travel west on the Santa Fe Trail as far as Bent's Fort with a group of six wagons of settlers. The wagon boss' name was John Coffee Hays. He was a no nonsense man now living in California. Sam Houston appointed him to a Texas Ranger Company at the age of nineteen where he was soon promoted to the rank of Captain. He had fought in many battles against the Indians. He also commanded troops during the Mexican American war. He migrated to California with the big move in 1849 and co-founded the city of Oakland. He was a large land owner and this was the second group of settlers he led to his valley. He had needed people to settle in his area to work his many spreads and since he missed the action of the trail, decided to lead the groups himself. No one living or dead was more qualified to be a wagon master.

"Where you from Tom?"

"Sir, I am from Perry County Tennessee."

"Well, it's a small world Tom. I am also from Tennessee. Wilson County. Moved out to Texas in 1836."

"Yes sir, it is."

"Fight in the late war?"

"Yes sir. Twentieth Tennessee Cavalry."

"Is that were you got the leg wound?"

"Yes sir. Didn't ever heal properly."

"Well, I am mighty glad to have you with us for a while."

Tom liked him right away and he liked Tom. He was very happy when Tom ask to join his train as far as Bent's Fort in Colorado. It was a dangerous route and another gun was always welcome.

Six wagons was a good sized train. Small enough to travel fast and relatively easy to protect.

The first day when Mr. Hays met Tom he said, "Tom, I see you have one of those Henrys can I look at it? Looks used. You had it a while?"

"Yeah, seen a lot of use. It takes the place of at least ten people. You might want to pick up a couple from the fort before we head out."

"I will check to see if they have any here."

On the day they lined up to leave Mr. Hays rode up to Tom and said, "Got one. In fact. I got two of them."

"Great, that should even up any fight we happen to get into."

"By the way? How many times have you been on this trail?"

"This is my second and last trip. So I know the way. Where the water can be found and where the trouble might start."

Chapter Forty-one

Mr. Hays rode up and down the line and yelled, "Line um up and move um out."

Tom headed farther west towards Colorado. He tied his pack horse to one of the wagons and rode his horse.

The boss had the days marked out knowing how far they could travel in one day, and how far they had to travel before they found water. He liked to camp on a water source for the animals, and for the convenience of the travelers. This train had been on the road for a few weeks before Tom joined it so, they were used to traveling with each other and camping. These folks had been planning their move for a year to escape the war. They had lost everything except what they had in their wagons.

The first night when they set up camp, Tom was able to meet and talk to some of the people. They were a closed group and did not let people in easily. They were all from the same county in Arkansas and knew each other. They were traveling to California to make a new life.

Tom did not press the issue. He set up his own little camp and waited for the people to warm up to him.

On the third day, Mr. Hays waived for Tom to come up to him and said, "Don't look when I tell you something. We are being shadowed by hostiles on our right and left. We are riding into the Cheyenne territory, and they will wait until they have numbers before they will try anything. The people know what to do when I tell them to circle, so just make sure you know."

Two hours before sundown riders closed in on each side of the train moving at a high speed and yelling. The boss waived and yelled for the leader to follow him. And he motioned for Tom to fall back and bring up the rear. The boss led the train for about a mile until they came to a small banana shaped lake formed from rainwater. It was full of water, about twenty feet wide, and a hundred yards long, and then he circled them into a tight circle. The people knew exactly what to do. They unhooked the horses and moved them inside the circle and they set up defensive positions on each wagon.

The Indians obviously knew the tactics of the wagon trains, and made a wide arc around the wagons. However, the lake prevented them from making a complete circle around the wagons, so they bunched up before they turned back for another run.

Tom and Mr. Hays laid down a barrage of fire with their Henrys as the Indians bunched up on each end of their run. And the fire was devastating.

The Indians had never encountered such fire before, and did not know what to do. The Chief waived the attack off and huddled with his braves.

Chief Black Kettle, the Cheyenne war chief spoke loud, "Our scouts have said that there were only ten men maybe twelve in the group. Yet they fight like there are twenty. Their guns reach out for our warriors more than two fields. We will not waste any more of our lives on these whites."

When the Cheyenne rode off, Mr. Hays gave the order to back off on the wagons and make camp.

That night, Tom was invited to have supper with the leader of the group. The leader's name was James Knight. He had his wife and three children with him. The children were eleven, fourteen, and nineteen. Their farm had been sacked and burned by Union soldiers in 1862 and they had been living in the woods ever since.

As the evening passed, others came by to shake Tom's hand say thank you. They all understood how much he had contributed to their victory. One of the families that came by was James's brother and his wife and wife's sister, who was twenty five. She had lost her husband in the raid when their farm was sacked and destroyed. Her name was Sarah and she was beautiful with long black hair and dark brown eyes.

Tom was surprised he had not noticed her before, and the next day he looked for her on the wagons. He could not find her, until someone spoke to him from the seat of the last wagon. He looked but still did not recognize her. Then she smiled and he recognized her smile.

"No wonder I could not find you, you are dressed like a man."

"Oh, were you looking for me?"

"Yes I was. Today at least."

"Easier to travel dressed this way. It keeps unwanted looks and comments away."

"Would you like to step down and walk a while?"

She handed the reins lines to her sister and Tom helped her step down.

The wagons moved slowly across the prairie, so when people got tired of riding the rough bouncy wagon, they simply got off and walked. And of course the kid were down running around playing.

"Right pleasant walking early in the morning, isn't it?"

"Yeah. Before it gets too danged hot and dusty."

"Yeah, and the heat wakes up the snakes."

"Oooou. Don't mention snakes. I am deathly afraid of snakes."

"Tom, we told you about ourselves last night, but we did not find out anything about you. Where are you from and what are you running from?"

"I'm from Tennessee. I guess you could say I am running after someone instead of running from something."

"You mean to tell me you are running after a woman?"

Tom laughed and said, "No. Nothing like that. I am looking for a bad man."

"Is that the reason you are leaving us in Bent's Fort?"

"Yes. I have had word that he is living just south of a little settlement called Aurora in the Colorado Territories."

"What'll you do after you find this man?"

Tom had thought in his mind a thousand times what he would do when he found Mr. Sawyer, but when Sarah ask him, he did not know how to answer.

"It depends on the man."

"This man must have done something very bad to you or your family for you to be way out here risking your life to find him."

As they walked, Tom told her the entire story. As he talked he got tears in his eyes and Sarah took his hand and held it. When he stopped talking they just continued walking quietly still holding hands.

Then Sarah told Tom about her life. She had married when she was only sixteen to a man ten years older than she. She had two children but lost both of them to illness. They were dirt farmers barely getting by when the war came. They just happened to be in the wrong place at the wrong time. A Union force moving through the country was fired upon by local militia and they retaliated by burning all the homes in their part of the valley and killed or stole all their stock. The Union soldiers even killed their dogs. When her husband tried to fight back, he was killed. She had hidden in the woods in a small cave until her sister and husband came looking for her. They all lived in the woods in caves afraid of being attacked again. They lived off of what they could kill. There were about ten families who lived in the woods. One of the families heard about a man in California looking for settlers, and somehow they were able to contact the man and make arrangements for the six families to go to California.

"You are getting hot and dusty Sarah. Better jump back up in the seat."

"Can we talk again?"

"I insist on it."

Tom tipped his hat to Sarah and her sister and rode up to Mr. Hays.

"Sure is peaceful and quiet out here on the prairie. I'm surprised we haven't ran into any buffalos."

"I never seen a buffalo. I would like to see one."

"Well it's kind of a blessing that we ain't seen any. Where there are buffalos, there are Indians close behind."

John Hays was a modest man. He never bragged about his exploits in the old days but occasionally when appropriate, he would talk about a specific incident just to make a point.

"Tom when I was a young man, I saw herds of buffalo so large a man could walk clear across Texas on their backs without once touching the ground. You can still find large herds, but they are slowly being killed out. And now that the war is over thousands of people will be moving west, and within ten to fifteen years buffalos will be gone. The damn government will figure out that the way to get rid of the Indians is to kill out all the buffalos. So hopefully we will see a big herd on this trip, just so you can tell your grandkids you saw them."

"Mr. Hays, you sound like you have respect and sympathy for the Indians."

"Tom I have fought Indians all my adult life, and I have a lot of respect for them. But sympathy? Nah. Empathy more than sympathy. Most are able to live their life and die with honor, and that is all that you can ask for whether you are white or red."

"Tom what are you going to do once you've found who you are looking for?"

"How did you know I was looking for someone?"

"I would be looking for someone if what happened to you happened to me."

"I am looking for Mr. George Sawyer. He was a profiteer during the war selling to both sides. He ran an iron works just out of Linden. His son killed himself and he blamed me and set out to kill me and mine. I want him to answer for it."

'What will you do after you find him? I mean, where will you go?"

"I don't know. I have a cousin who has a place just out of Tulsa in the Territories. He wants me to come back and help him build up a big herd."

"The reason I ask, I have lots of holdings in California and I could use a good man like you. So if you ever need a place to go, come find me in Oakland. Everyone knows me there, and they can point you in my direction."

"Thank you Mr. Hays. I appreciate the offer and will take it very seriously."

They rode silently for a while and then Mr. Hays said, "Tom, we are getting low on meat. I have been seeing a few deer in these draws. Maybe about an hour before we camp you could ride down into one and see if you can scare up a deer or two."

"Be glad to. Give me something to do."

As he rode along, Tom was looking for places where deer might be holding up. The next long draw he saw, he got Mr. Hays' attention and motioned that he was off hunting. Tom rode quietly down the little valley to the end where there was a small pond. He did not see any deer so he decided to dismount and wait for a while. Right at sundown, he finally got a shot on a small buck. Not enough meat, but it would have to do for the night. He gutted the deer and threw it over his horse and rode to camp.

The men made fast work of the skinning and distributed the meat among the wagons.

"Surprising there is not more game along the trail. Are there that many Indians in this area?"

"Nah, deer tend to migrate. So you never know where you will find them. We just keep our eyes open and we will run into them from time to time. What we need is a couple of buffalos. Hopefully we will find some soon."

Next morning before daylight, Tom rode back to the waterhole where he killed the deer the night before. As he moved quietly, he heard noise that sounded like a big animal grunting. He took his Henry and tied his horse to a sturdy tree and moved towards the sound. Although he had never heard a buffalo wallowing before, he suspected that was what he now heard. As he raised up to look over the little mound, he saw a huge black animal wallowing from one side to the other, in a hole it had warn into the hill.

"Well I'll be damn. My first buffalo. I didn't know they were that big."

The buffalo did not look to be in a hurry so Tom waited until it was light enough to see where he was shooting.

Not knowing anything about buffalos, he did not realize that there was nothing on the American continent with the exception of the grizzly bear, meaner or more cantankerous than a full grown buffalo bull. They travel along except the mating season because when they travel together, they are always fighting.

The buffalo had finished his wallowing and went to the pond for a drink. That is when Tom decided to take his shot. Since he had not hunted buffalo he did not know where to place his bullet. The Henry had plenty of stopping power, and many of the buffalo hunters that came to the plains later brought Henrys and used them with great success. But unfortunately Tom's first shot missed the vital organs and the buffalo just got mad. Tom was surprised when the beast did not fall and even more surprised to see the beast coming right at him. He fired another shot that hit the buffalo high. Still did not slow him down. He had been backing up and when he felt the reign of his horse, he mounted up and rode towards camp with the buffalo chasing him. When he rode into camp he dismounted and yelled, "Buffalo coming in."

He knelt and fired again this time finding the heart and the buffalo skidded to a stop about twenty feet from him.

By the time he fired his last shot, Mr. Hays had his Henry ready to shoot. But the rest of the people had no idea what was going on. They just came out to see a buffalo standing or walking in the distance.

Mr. Hays walked over and touched the buffalo's eye to make sure it was dead.

"Cutting it mighty close weren't you Tom?"

"Well, I didn't want to skin it by myself and haul it back here, so I just figured I'd bring in back on the hoof."

They both laughed.

Mr. Hays patted Tom on the back, "Good work. This will do us for a couple of weeks."

"Are all buffalos that damn mean?"

"Well, the lone bulls are mean. Most of the rest are pretty docile. Kind of like cattle."

By now everyone including the kids came out to see the buffalo. The men set up a tripod to hang it up so it would be easier to butcher. They spent the day butchering the buffalo and smoking it so it would not spoil until it was eaten.

That night they had a party. The families brought out their musical instruments and played and danced. The music made Tom feel homesick for the first time since he left Tennessee. He danced with Martha and the oldest daughter of Mr. Knight and a couple of more women of the train.

At last they all had accepted him, and felt friendly enough to laugh at the way he came riding in yelling buffalo, being chased.

They were good people. They would make wherever they settled better. But they still had a long ways to go.

Chapter Forty-two

The next afternoon they came upon a track of prairie that had been worn down to the dirt. Hardly a blade of grass was still standing. It was about three hundred yards wide and as far as they could see both ways.

"Buffalo. Big herd. Came through here about five or six hours ago."

"Which way were they headed?"

"North east. The way you can tell is to look at a specific hoof print."

"Yeah, I see now."

"The important thing is I don't see any unshod horse prints."

The next morning Mr. Hays pointed to the storm clouds to the west and said, "Going to be a bad storm. Hopefully it will go around us."

"Yeah, getting caught out here on the prairie in a thunderstorm must be hell."

"Nothing to do but ride it out. The worst thing is losing stock and having to spend days looking for them."

About noon, the whole train was talking about the impending storm. They started making sure their wagons were ready for the wind and rain. They tied extra ropes on the stock and tied the ropes to the wagons as instructed by Mr. Hays.

The wind started around three with the rain coming about ten minutes later. Mr. Hays was looking for a place to camp not too high and not too low. Finally he saw a wall of a small cliff off to the south and waved them to follow him. By the time they reached the wall the full force of the storm hit. Mr. Hays positioned the wagons up next to the wall so that most of the wind blew over them. Now the only problem was the rain and hanging onto the stock during the lightning and thunder.

Mr. Hays and Tom went from wagon to wagon making sure everyone was buttoned down tight and had a good ropes on their stock.

Tom's heavy rain coat he got in Tennessee had come in handy many times but especially tonight. There would be no sleeping tonight unless he slept standing up. The ground was too wet even if he put up his little tent.

It was a fast moving story and their preparation served them well. They fared better than most in such storms due directly to their leader.

The water from the rain had soaked in quickly to the dry prairie, so traveling the next day did not prove to be a problem. They traveled for the next three days with no incidents. But on the fourth day just after they got on the trail Mr. Hays waved Tom up to him.

"Tom it is not unusual to see broken down wagons on this trail but something about that one looks different. Looks like it is loaded with something. Would you mind riding up there and checking it out?"

"Not at all."

The closer Tom got to the black object the clearer it got. It was a wagon and it was loaded with what looked like... Then it hit him and he said, "Buffalo skins."

He knew that buffalo hunters were good marksman from long distances, so he rode in on the wagon very slowly, looking all around him for any sign of anyone. Then he started smelling it and it was rank. He saw that one of the wheels had broken, and was unrepairable without the proper tools.

Tom rode in a wide circle around the wagon looking for fresh tracks. He found four relatively fresh and distinct tracks west from the wagon. Then he rode back to Mr. Hays.

"Wagon with buffalo hides. Wheel broken beyond repair. Four horses maybe more heading west."

"Good job Tom. Probably four men. We have to be careful not to run into them."

Mr. Hays moved the wagons to the north of the buffalo skinner's wagon so they would be upwind.

Two night later after camp had been set up and the cook fires were burning high, someone from outside the parameter yelled, "Hello in the camp. Can we come in?"

Mr. Hays and Tom both armed themselves with their Henrys.

"Come on in with your hands clear."

Mr. Hays whispered to Tom, "When they come in, take a walk around to check for more."

Tom shook his head.

Two men walked into camp armed only with their handguns which immediately made Mr. Hays more suspicious. They were filthy and smelled like death.

"We was on the trail and saw your fire. Been running a little low of food. Thought you hospitable folks might offer us some food and coffee."

"Sure, you are welcome. Have a seat and someone will get you some food and coffee."

"How far you'll going on this trail?"

"Stopping in Santa Fe and waiting for a bigger train to come by."

"I thought when I come in there was a big feller standing here. Where did he get off too?"

"You must have been mistaken, we are all here."

"Yeah, maybe I was. My brother there says these here wagon trains on this here trail always carry a lot of money. You know just to buy stuff you need along the way. Is that true? Do you'll carry a lot of money?"

When he said money they both drew their sidearm. There were two rifle shots so close as to be one and the two men fell back and lay still on the ground.

Mr. Hays had his rifle pointed in their direction but did not have time to fire. In a minute Tom walked into the camp carrying three rifles. His Henry and two Sharps.

"Where are the other two? I didn't hear any shots."

Tom touched his knife handle.

"Is that all of them?"

"Yeah.

Tom handed Mr. Hays one of the Sharps. Holding up the other one ask, "May I have this one?"

"You can have them both. You earned them."

"Thank you, but I just need one."

"The Henrys are faster, but the Sharps shoot farther."

"Gentlemen, let's get the bodies out of here and get them buried."

With all the men of the train helping it did not take long to put all four under the ground.

When they had finished burying the bodies Mr. Knight asked, "What shall we do with the belongings and the horses and tack?"

"Take what you want and leave the rest. The horses might come in handy further on down the trail."

The men took what they wanted of the belongings and tied the horses to their wagons.

Chapter Forty-three

The trail became a routine. Tom was able to kill a big elk a few day on and they had a party again. It rained occasionally, but there were no more really bad storms that hit them.

Tom made it a habit of walking with Sarah early in the morning, if he was not busy hunting or something else. They became good friends and sought out each other, whenever they had a chance.

One evening when they set up camp early, he invited her to take a walk. He swung his Henry over his arm, and led his horse up stream of the little creek where they were camped. Once they found a log over the creek, Tom tied the horse and they sat on the log talking.

"Sarah, I know it's probably has not been long enough for us to have gotten over our spouse, but I am falling in love with you. When you are not around I am always looking for you, and when I am out away from camp, I miss you. I think about you all the time. The way you smell and the way you smile. I don't have anything yet. Not even a shack to live in or any way to make a living for us both, but someday I will have something. And when that time comes, would you consider marrying me?

"Short answer. Yes."

He leaned over and kissed her on the lips for the first time. She kissed him back and they embraced. When he felt himself tense up, he moved back.

"We better go back to the camp before we do something we shouldn't."

She kissed him and said, "Tom we are more than grown up we are widowers needing someone to love and be loved."

He did not pull away this time.

Feeling a little guilty and thinking they had been gone from camp too long, they hurried back sure that everyone's eyes were on them.

"Tom, by sundown tomorrow we will reach Bent's Fort. Are you dead set on leaving us and going to find Mr. Sawyer? You are more than welcome to come along with us."

"Part of me wants to go along with you, but I don't like leaving things undone."

"Well, you are always welcome to come to Oakland. And I know Sarah will be waiting for you."

"Was it that obvious?"

Mr. Hays smiled and put his arm around Tom's shoulder in a fatherly way and said, "Tom, we all knew even before you did."

"She is just what I need to settle me down. If everything works out up north, I will ride fast and try to find you on the trail. But I don't want Sarah to know. She would just worry too much if I did not show up."

"Ok. We will be looking for you. When you leave us, we will be turning due south to Santa Fe. And then turn west on the Gila Trail. We started too late to take the northern route. Winter will be here soon."

Tom and Sarah spent the next two days as close as they could get. And even after they arrived at Bent's Fort he did not leave right away, but waited until they left.

Chapter Forty-four

As the wagon train left Bent's Fort, Tom rode out with them a couple of miles. He rode up and shook hands with Mr. Hayes and then rode back to Sarah's wagon and kissed her goodbye and rode away.

It would take him a few days to get used to being along, but he knew he had to get his mind back on business. He was riding in an unforgiving land. He rode parallel to the Arkansas River to Pueblo where he crossed it. The next large settlement Tom came to was Colorado City, which was the Capital of Colorado Territory.

Using the name of Callaway Sanders, Tom checked into a hotel. He needed a bath but before he took a hot bath, he needed to buy some new clothes. The trail had taken a toll on the ones he had. First he took his packs from his horses and had the young man at the hotel take them to his room. Then he had him take his horses to the livery stable.

He found the mercantile store and went in. The store was busy and he looked around. It had been a while since he had been inside a building. It seemed strange. But he liked the smell of the store. He picked up four pair of pants and four shirts, a bundle of socks and four pair of underwear. He was trying on boots when the clerk came over to assist him.

"May I help you find some boots sir?"

"Yeah, been wearing these for a while now and they are beginning to wear out and leak."

"So you rode for the south in the war?"

"How would you know that? Can you tell by my accent or my boots?"

"No sir. By your spurs. They are the type used by the Confederate cavalry."

"You sure know a lot about spurs."

"Yes sir. We have some very nice Mexican spurs that you might like. What color boot are you looking for?"

"Dark tan or brown."

The clerk went into the back room and brought two boxes. He opened the first and said try these on. Is this a color you would buy?"

Tom tried them on and they were too small. But he liked the color.

The clerk saw that they were too small and opened the other box. The boots were the same color and were a perfect fit.

"Perfect. This is a new style of boot called the cowboy cut from Texas and here is a pair of spurs that will fit these boots."

"I will take all of this with me. Please wrap it up."

"How about a new hat sir? We have some new ones. Come, let me show you."

Tom liked his old hat and didn't think he needed a new one, but it would not hurt to look.

"Try this one. It is made by Mr. John Stetson up in Central City. It is for men who spend a lot of time outdoors."

Tom tried it on and looked at himself in the mirror and said, "I like it. I will take it."

When Tom walked into the saloon that evening he was the best dressed man in the place. And with his pistols tucked into his wide belt and his Henry over his arm he was an imposing figure.

In addition to bringing in settlers, the gold strike also brought shady gamblers, land speculators, and outlaws. And they all entered the saloon at one time or the other.

Tom was used to fighting mounted and with plenty of room, so when he entered the saloon, he felt a pinned in. He was a little nervous and the noise and crowd did not help.

He found a small opening in the crowd around the bar and moved in to ask the bartender for a whisky. When the bartender gave him the drink he said, "One dollar sir."

Thinking that a dollar was too much Tom looked at the bartender and said, "How much?"

"One dollar."

Tom paid the bartender and turned to walk to a corner where he could put his back to the wall, so he could survey the crowd. But the man standing in front of him with his back to him without turning around said in a drunken slur, "Who the hell you pushing. You think you own this damn bar."

Then he turned around with a mean scowl on his face. But when he saw how big Tom was and the guns he was toting, his expression softened.

Tom said, "Well sir, at a dollar a drink. I damn well made a down payment on it."

The man smiled and said, "Well I never thought of it that way. But that means I should own the damn thing by now all the money I have spent here."

Tom walked over to the wall and put his back on it. He surveyed the crowd but wasn't quite sure why. Maybe he though Mr. George Sawyer just might show up here. But even if he was in the crowd, he would not know it since he never saw him.

He studied the layout of the saloon and focused on the faces. The gambling tables were busy as were the wheels. The girls were selling whiskey and whatever else they had to offer. An older lady come up to him and said, "I'm Miss. Lucille I am in charge of the girls. Would you like to meet one of our young ladies? You look like a healthy young cowboy."

"I'm just having a drink now and waiting for someone. Maybe later."

"Who you waiting for? Maybe I know him."

"Maybe you do. Do you know a man named George Sawyer?"

"Well there is a fellow named Sawyer has a business in Denver."

"What kind of business?"

"He provides buffalo meat for the Army and he sends the hides back east."

"How do you know about him?"

"I used to work in Denver before I came down here. Some of his hunters used to come into the saloon smelling of death and decay. Do you think that might be the man you are looking for?"

"It just might be him."

Tom counted out ten silver dollars and handed it to her and said, "Thank you."

As she walked away she said, "Why, thank you big spender."

Early the next morning Tom rode north towards Denver. He had a lead as to where he could find Mr. Sawyer, and he did not want to waste any time. As he rode he formulated a plan. Since he had never met Mr. Sawyer, he assumed that Mr. Sawyer did not know what he looked like. So he would play it close and check out the lay of the land before he did anything.

When he rode into Denver he was careful not to have people notice him. He wanted everyone to think he was just another man looking to strike it rich.

First place he stopped was the hotel to get a room and some food. After he took his bags to his room he walked into the little restaurant on the first floor of the hotel. A middle aged woman told him to sit anyplace. He took a seat at table in the back of the room where he could see everyone.

"What will you have sir."

"Steak and potatoes and beans. I'll just have water to drink."

Tom did not want to ask about Mr. Sawyer, just in case word got back to him that someone looking for him. He knew that sooner or later Mr. Sawyer, the business man, would show himself.

He had just received his food when two rough looking men came in and sat down in the front of the restaurant. They were dirty and Tom could smell them even from where he was sitting.

There was an old woman and a man setting at the table next to them. As the waitress passed by their table, the woman whispered something to the waitress. The waitress went directly to the table with the two men.

"Gentlemen, you know we don't serve buffalo hunters in here unless you clean up first. Now you will have to leave. I am getting complaints."

These were rough men used to hunting and killing, but they just simply got up and left without a word.

The waitress came by and said, "These hunters that work for Mr. Sawyer smell so bad when they come in, they run my other customers away. I guess I will have to talk to Mr. Sawyer again when he comes in."

"Yes ma'am, they did smell right bad."

"Bad? Bad ain't the word for it. They smelled like death."

"Is Mr. Sawyer one of your prominent citizens around here?"

"Yeah, he has the mercantile store, or at least his wife and daughter does, and he owns a lot of land east of here. Has a big southern style home. Some say he is stuck up, but he always been friendly to me."

When he finished his meal, he walked down the street to the mercantile store. He wanted to meet Mr. Sawyer's family.

There were four people in the store when Tom walked in, and he just strolled around looking at everything. Without being obvious, he studied the middle-aged woman, who was probably Mrs. Sawyer, and the young woman, who looked to be around twenty. The young woman was not very pretty but neatly dressed and poised.

Mrs. Sawyer came up and said, "Yes sir, what can I help you with?"

"I need a couple of boxes of .44 rim fire for my Henry rifle."

"Yes sir. That's a big gun. Are you a buffalo hunter too?"

"No ma'am. I am a trail boss for wagon trains. Headed east to pick up a group of settlers."

She handed him the ammunition and he paid her.

"The reason I ask you if you were a buffalo hunter was because my husband runs a buffalo meat and hide business, and I thought you might be here to work for him."

"No ma'am. But on my last trip west I did run upon a very large herd of buffalos down on the Kansas border."

"He would probably be interested in that kind of news. Does your wife say anything when you go on one of these trips across the country?"

Tom was caught a little off guard by the question since it came right of the blue so he said, "I am not married. Actually I don't have any family left at all."

"Sorry, I didn't mean to bring up a sad subject."

"It's ok. You had no way of knowing."

"How long are you staying in town mister...?"

"Calloway Sanders. Just a few days."

"Are you busy tonight? Maybe you would like to come to our home for supper. You can meet and talk to my husband."

"Well, I don't want to impose."

"Not at all."

"Annie, come here. This is Mr. Calloway Sanders. He is a trail boss for wagon trains heading west. I have invited him to supper."

Holding out her hand she said, "How do you do Mr. Sanders?"

"Nice to meet you miss."

"Please call me Ann."

"Call me Cal."

"Mr. Sanders if you will come back here at six, you can follow us home."

"Thank you ma'am. I will be here at six."

Chapter Forty-five

Tom took a bath and put on his new clothes, new boots with the fancy Mexican spurs, and his new Stetson hat and rode his horse to the store at six ready to go.

In a minute a very nice carriage pulled up and the livery man got out. He held the horses until Mrs. Sawyer and her daughter came out of the store and got into the carriage.

"Glad to see you are on time Mr. Sanders."

"I am always on time to get a good meal. I tire of my own cooking on the trail."

"Well, we have a great cook. She is from Germany. Lots of people came into this area during the initial gold rush but very few of them found any gold. So they have to take any job they can get to support their families."

"Where are you from Mr. Sanders?"

"Originally from Missouri. Now I live in California. I have a large spread there and need families to settle the area."

"We are from Tennessee. My husband was a businessman there but with the war going bad, we thought we would go west. His brother came here first in 59' to stake out some land. So we followed and staked out our own land. This is a fast growing area and we decided to open a mercantile store. It was the best move we made.

Then my husband got a contract with the army to supply meat for the soldiers, and then he started buying and selling hides and now he can't keep up with the orders."

"You just have the one daughter?"

"We had a son but he was killed in the war."

Ignoring the lie, Tom said, "I am sorry. All of us lost loved ones in the war."

"Did you lose someone in the war?"

"My wife and two children."

"Sorry. I am glad it is over. Maybe the killing will stop."

When they reached the house a young man came out of the barn and took the buggy and Tom's horse.

The house was a large antebellum mansion. Mr. Sawyer had brought the south with him to Colorado.

The inside was as fancy as the outside. They had a butler, and two or three maids and of course a cook. The butler took Tom's hat and led him to the parlor.

"Drink sir?"

"Whiskey please."

"Please have a seat and when the ladies have freshened up, we will have supper."

"Thank you sir."

When Tom finished his drink, he poured another one. He was bracing himself to meet the man who had been the cause of all his problems. But he was not ready for the person who walked in. Mr. Sawyer was a small bald man with spectacles and a suit two sized too large. He was not friendly when he held out his hand.

"You must be Mr. Sanders? I am George Sawyer. My wife said she had met you and was inviting you to supper."

"Pleased to meet you sir. Sorry to impose on your hospitality, but, I so seldom get a good meal."

"She said you were a trail boss or something of the other leading a group of settlers."

Tom smiled and said, "Well, I have a large place in California and I need settlers to come work for me and settle the area."

"Oh, well that makes sense. I could use a family or two to work for me. The only thing keeping me from building up my businesses is lack of good laborers."

"Sirs, supper is served."

"Come on Mr. Sanders. Bring your drink."

The women were already seated and Mrs. Sawyer motioned for Tom to take the chair beside her daughter. There was another person at the table that Tom had not met. He was young with medium build a big mustache and a soft handshake. Mr. Sawyer introduced him as Mr. Sunday.

"Mr. Sunday works for me in my meat and hide business."

"Speaking of hides, on my last trip I ran across a herd so large it reached from horizon to horizon. The grass was trampled for three hundred yards wide. They were headed northeast."

"There are millions to be made in the hide business and I am getting in on the front of it. The only problem is that I can't get enough hunters. Soon I might have to start paying two and a half dollars per hide."

"George, do we have to talk about those smelly buffalo hides all evening?"

"I am sorry darling. Just a habit I guess."

"Mr. Sanders, you look familiar to me. Have you ever been to Tennessee?"

The question caught Tom off guard and he felt himself flush a little. But he recovered and said, "Closest I ever came to Tennessee is going down the Mississippi River on a steamboat. Afraid I didn't see much. I was busy losing all my money to a riverboat gambler. That was the first and last time I ever gambled."

Mr. Sunday laughed a little too loud and a little too long at Tom's misfortune and he took a stern look from Mr. Sawyer. But the rebuke seemed to fall on a blind person.

"I once took a riverboat from St Louis to New Orleans with my parents. That was before they lost all their money and land in the war."

Continuing the boat ride theme, Miss. Sawyer said, "Someday I would like to take a boat all the way to France. I studied French in my school."

Glancing at Miss. Sawyer, Mr. Sunday said, "Maybe you can go to France on your honeymoon."

"First I will have to find a husband. So let's not get the cart before the horse."

"That is what I meant. Maybe after you are married, your husband will take you to France on your honeymoon."

All this time Miss. Sawyer had been watching Tom, and Mr. Sunday had noticed it and seemed a little jealous, which caused him to talk too much and say silly things.

Taking back the conversation, Mr. Sawyer said, "What is all this talk about getting married and honeymoons? There is no hurry. You are barley twenty. Still plenty of time."

"Father, you make it all sound so solemn."

Asking the question she wanted to ask all evening, Miss. Sawyer said, "How about you Mr. Sanders? Are you married?"

"I was married. But my wife died along with my two children."

"The war?"

"Yes."

"Sorry. I lost a son. I will never get over it or forgive the bastard that caused his death. I still have people searching for the son of a bitch. Oh, sorry darling."

"Is he still in Tennessee?"

"Not sure. But he is a mean son of a bitch. He has killed everyone I sent after him. But I will not stop trying to find him until he is dead. I have contacted the Pinkerton Agency and they are now working on finding him."

"Well if anyone can find him, it will be the Pinkerton's. They are the best."

"I am not familiar with them. But it sounds like you are serious about finding this guy."

"I am. I will not give up until I die. He took my only son."

As he spoke, Mr. Sawyer got more excited and red faced.

"Father please don't get so worked up. It is not good for your health. Remember what your doctor said."

Tom had found out what he wanted to know and after one more drink in the parlor, he said his goodnights and rode back to town.

Mr. Sawyer was not going to forget or forgive. And now he had turned it over to a national detective agency which had come to prominence during the war by protecting the president. Now they had agents everywhere. For some reason he could not kill Mr. Sawyer in cold blood now that he had met his wife and daughter. Or, maybe it was because he was in love with Sarah. He had to disappear and California seemed like a good place to start.

Chapter Forty-six

Tom rode south the next morning before daylight. He had to get as far away as fast as he could, and he was missing Sarah and a little worried about her.

The next morning Mr. Sawyer went to work early. He had thought the man who came to his house looked familiar, and he could not shake the feeling that he had seen him before. When he got to his office, he started looking through some folders he had. When he found one that read News Paper Clippings he opened it and thumbed through the photos and articles. Then he found the one he was looking for. It was an article about a Confederate Prisoner in Ohio who had been granted parole because his wife had been murdered on a train while she was going to visit him.

"This is it."

Unfolding the article there was a photograph of the man. "Got you, you son of a bitch."

Mr. Sawyer walked outside and hailed the first buffalo hunter he saw. "Mr. Schultz, I have a job for you and your boys. See this here man? I want him killed today. I will give you eighty dollars now and two hundred more when the job is done. Here is a picture of him. He will be riding a big horse wearing a big hat. Be careful he is very dangerous. He has killed everyone I have sent after him.

He will probably headed south so that is the first place you should check."

"Yes, sir. We will find him and kill him. Do you want to see the body?"

"No. Just dispose of it so no one finds it."

Mr. Schultz said, "Let's go boys, we have a job to do. Easy money."

"Pa, can we each get a gold piece now. That will leave you two."

"Yeah, Pa can we hold one of those gold coins now. We won't spend them."

"Alright, but no matter what, do not try to spend them. Otherwise Mr. Sawyer will get mad and not pay us the rest."

"Let's ride. He has at least two hours on us so we have to go fast as we can."

Tom was anxious to get back to Sarah, but he also knew how to take care of his horse. He never suspected that Mr. Sawyer would figure out who he was or that he would have a picture of him.

The hunters were riding their horses too hard, but they only saw the gold and did not care about their horses. They even had the horses pulling the wagon running.

When they topped a little knoll they saw a rider up ahead.

"Is that him Pa?"

"Can't tell yet. Let's get closer."

"Pa I can hit him from here."

"Let's move closer."

They kept riding for another five minutes.

"There is little hill over to the right Pa. That would be a good place to shoot form. Just like hunting buffalos."

"You think you can make that shot?"

"I can make it Pa."

"Ok, go over there and set up."

"Jake, I bet you a dollar you can't shoot him right in the heart."

"I'll take that bet."

It was a long shot, but they had been hunting buffalos for a while now and Jake was a good shot. He lay prone and adjusted his sight and held about a foot above Tom's left side. He took the shot and Tom fell to the ground.

"Let's get down there Pa."

"Don't be in such an all-fire hurry. Let's move in slowly and make sure he is dead. Mr. Sawyer said he had already killed the others he sent after him."

Tom lay on the ground with his shoulder pounding and burning like a hot poker had been rammed through it. The bullet had hit him in the muscle part of his shoulder but with enough impact to knock him out of the saddle. Not knowing who or why someone shot him, he lay still as dead. His horse walked a few feet from his hand and stood still. As he fell, he instinctively moved his right hand to his pistol so he would be ready when someone approached.

Tom lay there playing dead for what seemed like an eternity, but in actuality it was only a few minutes. It was extremely hot and the ants were crawling over him and biting him. The flies were flying about his head and face. He was miserable and wished it would end. His horse stood in the same place waiting for him to get up. He would occasionally paw anxiously wanting to go somewhere. Tom made a shush noise to let the horse know he was still alive and awake. They were both thirsty and ready to move.

The horse shook his bridle and took a step towards Tom and nickered, and Tom could tell he had smelled or saw another horse. In a couple of minutes Tom heard more than one horse approaching. He smelled the wagon before he heard it creaking. It smelled like death. The riders were quiet and Tom heard them dismount and walk up to where he was laying.

He felt a rifle barrel push into his shoulder and it took all of his strength not to move. But he knew they would be cautious and make sure he was dead before they let their guard down. Tom's whole left side was covered in blood so from where the man stood, he could not tell where he had hit Tom. When Tom did not move they had assumed that he was dead.

"See Coonie, I told you I could make that shot. Had to be over two hundred yards. Right in the heart."

"Jake, you was just plain lucky?

"Lucky my ass. I am just a damn good shooter. Pa can tell you. He knows how good I am."

"Mr. Sawyer's going to be happy. We going to get two hundred more dollars."

"Listen to me, you boys talk too much. Ain't nobody supposed to know about this so don't go running your mouths about it. And we can't go spreading this money around either."

But Pa, ain't we going to get drunk and get us some women over in Aurora?"

"We'll get drunk and get some women, but we have to be careful. If Mr. Sawyer find out we talking about our deal he will kill us."

Now Tom knew what it was all about. There were three of them and they were hired by Mr. George Sawyer to kill him. But how in the hell had Mr. Sawyer figured out who he was? Did he recognize him? Did someone identify him? There were too many unanswered questions.

"Alright, get his stuff and throw him on the wagon and let's get out of here."

As the one with the rifle turned him over, Tom shot him in the chest and he flew backward. Tom rolled to the side and shot the next one in the neck and he went down holding his throat. Next Tom shot the old man in the left side before he could get to his shotgun. They all lay where they were hit and the only one not dead was the one Tom shot in the throat. He had his hand over the wound, but blood was still gushing from it. It was just a matter of time before he bled out.

Tom leaned over him and said, "Who sent you to kill me?"

"Help me and I will tell you."

"Tell me and I will get you to a doctor."

"Mr. George Sawyer sent us. He showed us a picture of you. Paid us to kill you."

That was last words he uttered. He went completely limp and died.

Tom's shoulder started to hurt after the adrenalin had dissipated and he fell to his knees.

Tom caught his horse and got a bottle of whiskey from his saddlebag and poured it onto his shoulder and it hurt even worse. The pain took Tom to his knees again, where he stayed for a few minutes. Tom stuck his bandana into the wound as best as I could to help stop the bleeding. He would need to see a doctor as soon as possible.

Once Tom took a good look at the men and their wagon, he realized they were buffalo hunters.

"So Mr. Sawyer had found out who he was and had hired some of his buffalo hunters to murder me."

The one who shot Tom had a big Sharps rifle great for killing buffalos or man. Tom picked it up and dusted it off. Its owner had taken good care of it. When Tom searched him he found a couple of silver dollars and one brand new twenty dollar gold piece. He had a bandolier with about ten shells for the Sharps. Tom took the money and the shells. The next one only had a handgun and it was rusty and in bad condition. When Tom searched his pockets he found another twenty dollar gold piece. The old man just had the shotgun which was rusty and wired together and probably more dangerous to the shooter than the person being shot at. Tom found some lose change and two twenty dollar gold pieces.

"Son of a bitch always pays his hired killers in gold coins."

When Tom rode out of Denver he had intended to leave Mr. Sawyer and his family along. But now his bitterness had returned and he intended to end it once and for all.

While he was searching the bodies, Tom had thought of a way to kill Mr. Sawyer and make it seem like the buffalo hunters had done it in a robbery attempt.

Tom loaded the bodies into the wagon and drove to where he knew there was a place to ambush Mr. Sawyer. He hobbled his horses about a mile away from the place, and left the body of the youngest hunter with it. He tied the horses to the wagon and stopped just out of sight of the road to Mr. Sawyer's house and then he waited. Two hours had passed when he saw Mr. Sawyer riding down the road.

Tom took careful aim with the Sharps and shot Mr. Sawyer in the middle of his chest. Mr. Sawyer fell back off his horse and lay still. Tom pulled the wagon onto the road and positioned it so it seemed like it was blocking the road. He took Mr. Sawyer's hand gun and shot it five times. Then he positioned the bodies of the hunters in positions where it would appear they had died there by being shot by Mr. Sawyer. He positioned the one horses so it would appear that when the man was shot, he hung onto the reigns. He then riffled through Mr. Sawyer's pockets making sure they were turned inside out to make it seem like a robbery. He took all the money and dropped a few silver coins on the ground to make it seem the one person who got away was in a hurry. Then he mounted the hunter's horse and rode fast away towards the east. When he circled around to his horse he put all the money in the dead man's pockets then he put the dead hunter on his own horse. He put the Sharps on the horse and then he hit the horse so it would run away. When they found the last of the hunters with the money, everyone would believe the hunters had murdered and robbed Mr. Sawyer.

Chapter Forty-seven

Once he had killed Mr. Sawyer, Tom rode south avoiding everyone. He lived on the trail bypassing any settlements until he reached Santa Fe. He needed to see a doctor, but he could not take the chance so he doctored himself as best he could. He had used the medicine he had gotten before and it worked to keep the infection down.

Once he reached Santa Fe he saw a doctor who cleaned and bandaged the wound. Next, he bought what provisions he would need. He ask about the little wagon train bossed by Mr. Hays. The sales clerk remembered when they passed through. Tom figured they were about five or six our days ahead of him. He also ask about where he could find a newspaper with news of Denver. The clerk told him to check with the local newspaper office. When Tom went to the newspaper office he did not ask about a Denver paper, he just ask to look through the papers. He read about what was going on back east and in the south. About the third paper he looked at, he found what he was looking for: PROMINENT BUSINESSMAN ROBBED AND MURDERED BY BUFFALO HUNTERS. Mr. George Sawyer's body was found on the road from Denver to his house by his employee, Mr. Sunday. Mr. Sawyer was robbed and murdered, but he was able to kill two of his assailants, whose bodies were found approximate to Mr. Sawyers. The third man who managed to get away with the money was later found dead. Remarkably, Mr. Sawyer had managed to kill all three men. All the money taken from Mr. Sawyer had been recovered...

It had worked out just like Tom wanted. But Tom was still worried about the Pinkerton Agency. Would the agency stop looking for him now that their customer was dead? He would still have to be careful, and not use his real name.

Tom headed south to pick up the Gila trail traveling steady, but careful to look over his shoulder occasionally. This was a well-traveled route, but it was still dangerous. He set up camp late, and moved out early each morning. He was just hoping he would not pass the little train while they were resting on a side trek.

On the fifth day he saw a lot of dust about a mile ahead. It seemed to Tom to be too much dust for a wagon train. He kicked his horse and started moving at a gallop. When he got closer he heard gunshots, and figured the wagon train was in trouble. He kicked his horse into a dead run and was soon on a knoll overlooking the scene. The wagons had circled but did not unhook the horses.

Tom stopped and took a small pack from his pack horse to use it to steady his rifle. First he shot the Sharps until he ran out of ammo and then he emptied his Henry. He had unseated at least fifteen Indians. After reloading his Henry he put it in its holster. He mounted and with both hands full of his Colts rode towards the train. This was his element and he was very proficient. He unseated at least seven more on his way in. He found a small opening and jumped his horse over it into the circle. He dismounted and without a word, started shooting again. He handed his empty Henry to Sarah and give her a little nod and smile and kept firing. He was a good shot with the pistols but he was a deadly shot with his Henry. In less than a minute, Sarah handed his Henry back to him fully loaded and he unseated ten more. By this time the raiders were rethinking their advantage. They had not expected such firepower from such a small group.

They pulled back to where they felt was out of range of the white man's rifles to talk.

The Apache War Chief Victorio began, "These people are led by a great warrior and they have guns that they do not have to load. There will be many wives and children in our village tonight already..."

While there was a break in the action and all the people of the wagon train were reloading and checking on the wounded, Tom approached Mr. Hays and while they were shaking hands asked, "Do you have your Sharps and ammunition. Get it for me."

When Mr. Hays handed the Sharps to Tom he said, "What do you intend to do?

"Going to shoot the chief and then see what happens."

"They are a very long ways away."

"Yeah, but it won't hurt to try."

Tom rested the Sharps over a wagon wheel to steady the big gun. He moved the back sight and adjusted it for wind and elevation. When he felt he was on target, he took a deep breath and let it out slowly. At the end of the breath he squeezed the trigger. He immediately reloaded.

The entire wagon train had their eyes on the Indian Chief.

After what seemed like a minute they saw the Chief fall back off his horse.

Everyone cheered and started patting Tom on the bank.

War Chief Victorio was not able to finish his words before the bullet hit him. He fell backwards from his horse like he had been hit by a sledge hammer. Then the Indians heard the shot. His sub chiefs all crowded around him.

Chief Victorio managed to say, "The whites have strong medicine with their guns. Take me home to die."

The wagon train watched as the Indians put their chief on a horse with another rider to hold him on the horse. They rode away slowly.

"Glad to see you Tom and just in time."

"Glad I hurried on to catch you."

Sarah came to Tom looking a little shy. He took her in his arms and kissed her.

Mr. Hays bellowed, "We still have three hours of daylight before we camp, so let's go."

When the wagons were lined up again Mr. Hays rode up and down the line and said loudly, "Wagons move out. Let's go people, we don't have all year."

The little wagon train moved slowly into the setting sun, with Tom and Sarah walking along side holding hands.

POSTFACE

On the trail to Oakland, Tom finally told Mr. Hays the entire story of the circumstances surrounding his travel to Denver. Turns out that Mr. Hays was a personal friend of Mr. Pinkerton. In fact, he had done some work for the Agency. He contacted Mr. Pinkerton and made sure Tom's name and image was removed from all the Agency's files. Tom and Sarah were married at the next town and they purchased a wagon so they could travel together. They made it to Oakland and Tom worked for Mr. Hays for three years. One of Mr. Hays' businesses was transporting goods from back east to California. So it was natural when Tom went to him with a proposition that he had been thinking about for a while. One of the things missing in the newly opened west was good drinking whiskey. And Tom remembered that Mr. Daniels's family had made the very best. He proposed that Mr. Hays loan him money to start a whiskey distribution company. He would contact Mr. Daniels to make arrangements for the whiskey and then ship it on Mr. Hay's wagons. Knowing a good business deal when he heard it, Mr. Hays jumped at the chance. Tom became the largest whiskey distributor in California and then the surrounding states. In ten years he was a multimillionaire. But his most cherished possessions were his four children. Two boys and two girls. One of his sons attended Harvard because Tom remembered how honorable and graceful Mr. Day was, and the other one graduated from West Point. His daughters attended the newly founded Stanford University.

Bill turned Mary's ranch into one of the largest ranches in Oklahoma. With the money he made from the sale of their cattle, they bought the surrounding land until their holdings was more than five thousand acres. They only hired Cherokee people to work their cattle. Mary's brother became the ranch manager and moved his and Mary's entire family onto the ranch. They lived well from the cattle sales. Bill and Mary had five more children in addition to Jonas. Bill and Mr. Delgado ran that part of Oklahoma and things were quiet. Then in 1901 oil was discovered on their land and they became even wealthier. Whereas they were rich in property before, when the oil boom hit, they were cash wealthy. Bill and Mary were old by this time, but they had taught the children well and they used the money to better the community. They built schools for the Cherokee as well as the white community. They help people establish businesses which would make the whole area better.

Oakhaven survived the war intact. After the war when the carpet baggers came looking for land they could steal, the Day family was ready. In fact, they were able to purchase the land surrounding their holding until they had doubled the size of Oakhaven. Nat had completely recovered except for his noted limp. But he wore two new colts in his waistband and one tucked under each arm. He would talk or he would fight, depending on who was standing before him. Mr. Day never hired a black man to work in his fields again. But he did open an orphanage on his land for black children and hired bright young black women as teachers and older women as caretakers of the children. Every child that graduated from the orphanage school could attend collage paid for by a trust fund established by Mr. Day. The trust fund along with the

279

orphanage was completely administered by black people. It stayed in use long after the death of Mr. and Mrs. Day. It finally closed in 1920 for lack of children, which was the absolute best reason. Mr. Day tried very hard to reach the point where he was even with the bad and good of his life before he died. If he gets points for having his heart in the right place then he made it.

Tom's neighbor Lena met a young man at the crossroads on his way home from the war and invited him out for supper. He stayed. They married the next Sunday and they managed to make a living on their little farm and raise ten children.

Mr. and Mrs. Bing had made a small fortune in the war and decided to move back to Michigan where they originally came from. Tom never heard from them again.

Tom's beloved Tennessee was the last to leave the Union and the first to return. But being the first to return did not immunize her from the turmoil but pushed her towards it. It was almost as violent after the war as it was when it was ongoing. And there were entire communities where the people had been either killed or displaced. Many soldier returning found strangers living in their homes and they had to keep on fighting. Lawlessness was rampant and mixed with the dynamics of two races trying to figure out how to live together with no slaves or masters, then there was a blueprint for chaos. And chaos ensued. Pauli's Exclusion Principle applied in Tennessee – there were two masses trying to occupy the same space – two peoples – two philosophies – two worlds. It would take decades for things to settle down. Guilt beget hate. Hate beget guilt. Hate beget hate.

The story continues.

www.ingramcontent.com/pod-product-compliance
Lightning Source LLC
Chambersburg PA
CBHW020243180626
46810CB00006B/2331